WHEN *the* HEAVENS FALL

WHEN *the* HEAVENS FALL

A WINSLOW BREED NOVEL

GILBERT MORRIS

HOWARD BOOKS
A DIVISION OF SIMON & SCHUSTER, INC.

NEW YORK NASHVILLE LONDON TORONTO SYDNEY

Published by Howard Books, a division of Simon & Schuster, Inc.
1230 Avenue of the Americas, New York, NY 10020

In association with the literary agency of Greg Johnson

Library of Congress Cataloging-in-Publication Data

Morris, Gilbert.
When the heavens fall: a Winslow breed novel / Gilbert Morris.
p. cm.
Sequel to: Honor in the dust.
1. Elizabeth I, Queen of England, 1533–1603—Fiction. 2. England—Court and courtiers—Fiction. 3. Great Britain—History—Tudors, 1485–1603—Fiction. I. Title.
PS3563.O8742W437 2010
813'.54—dc22 2009052651

ISBN 978-1-4165-8747-7 (pbk)
ISBN 978-1-4391-7082-3 (ebook)

10 9 8 7 6 5 4 3 2 1

Manufactured in the United States of America

Edited by David Lambert and Lisa Bergren
Interior design by Jaime Putorti

To Mary Moye

Many thanks for your encouragement and for your friendship!

Johnnie and I could not do without you!

PART ONE

The Bad Seed

1

"Now, you just behave yourself, Master Brandon Winslow, and keep your bloomin' 'ands where they belong!"

"Why, Becky, they belong right *here*."

Becky Elwald slapped his hand and tried to frown, but she was unsuccessful. "You're a saucy one, you are! Tryin' to destroy a young woman's virtue, that's wot!"

Brandon whispered, "You're a lovely girl, Becky. And you're the one who agreed to meet me at such a late hour. Surely you knew what to expect." Perhaps she needed a few more minutes of sweet talk and then he'd win her heart as well as her willing kisses. At the age of sixteen, Becky had a figure that would tempt a saint.

Becky abruptly shoved Brandon back and shook her head. "You said you'd read me poetry. I thought you had love on your mind, not lovin'. Get out of this barn! If my pa catches you, he'll skin you alive."

"He couldn't catch me if he tried. Come on, sweetheart, give us another kiss." He caught her wrist and pulled it up to his lips for a soft, tender kiss.

She stilled, and Brandon sensed her relinquishing the fight. "You ain't but fourteen," she whispered, "too young for this sort of thing."

"I'm old enough. And you are too delectable to ignore."

Becky's lips parted as he leaned down, and he knew he had won her. She wasn't the first girl who had caught his eye, and as the future Brandon Lord Winslow, master of Stoneybrook, he certainly had his pick among the young women of the shire. But her hesitation and reluctance had piqued his interest—that and the challenge of avoiding her stern father. It was rather like plucking a ripe pear from the tree of a curmudgeonly orchard owner. Finding her alone, away from her father's squinting gaze, it had become a delightful game.

Brandon ignored Becky's feeble protests and continued his quest. He had given little thought to girls until this year, preferring to spend his time in hunting, learning the ways of knights, and mastering the weapons that his father provided for him. But now he wanted to know what the mystery of women was all about. He lowered her to the straw and smiled as he felt her surrender beneath him. He ran his hand—

"What be you a-doin', girl? And you, boy, you got no right to be here!" James Elwald burst into the barn, his eyes blazing with anger, a staff in his hand.

"Brandon just came to—to visit, Pa!"

"You think I'm blind? Get you in the house while I deal with this rascal!"

Brandon rose and moved swiftly toward the barn door, but Elwald raised his staff and brought it down, striking him hard on the shoulder. He raised it again, rage in his eyes, but Brandon was strong for his age and very quick. He caught the staff as it came down and yanked it from Elwald's hand. Without a second's hesitation he swung the staff, and the blow struck the older man in the head.

Elwald crumpled to the ground. Becky—who hadn't made it to the door—let out a scream. "You killed 'im, Brandon!"

Brandon's heart skipped a beat. He well knew what would happen to him if Elwald were dead. All his father's influence could not help him if he'd killed a man. He leaned over and put his hand on Elwald's chest.

He looked up at Becky with a reckless grin. "Why, he's all right, Becky. He'll have a headache, but he's too mean to die."

Becky was trembling, and her eyes were enormous. "'E's a vengeful man, Brandon. You'd better get out of 'ere!"

Brandon laughed, came forward, took her in his arms, and kissed her. "I'll be back. We'll finish what we started."

But there was real fear in Becky's eyes as she pushed him away again. "Stay away from 'ere if you know wot's good for you! You don't know my pa."

Brandon laughed, then turned and left the barn. Outside the door, a huge yellow dog rose to greet him. Brandon put a hand on his head. "Well, how about that, Eric?" he said. "If the old man hadn't come in, I would have had Becky. What do you think of that?"

Eric barked, then reared up to put his paws on Brandon's chest. He was covered with scars from fights with other dogs and even a few with wild pigs and their saber-like tusks.

"Ah, well, there'll come a day! Let's get back before Father finds out I'm missing."

Brandon broke into a loping run, and the dog came after him at a gallop. He was not even breathing hard when the shadow of Stoneybrook Castle rose before him twenty minutes later. A huge silver moon threw argent beams on the frozen earth, and a ghostly hunting owl sailed overhead as he and his dog passed through the gate. There was no one stirring at this time of the night, and Brandon loved the silence that held the castle as if in a spell. He'd taken more than one thrashing from his father for sneaking out on midnight forays, but he knew he would do it again. It was not that he did not love his father, but a wild longing took him at times, driving him to find an adventure to break the monotony of daily life. He could bear a beating but not the boredom.

He whispered, "Come on, Eric. Let's go to bed."

Brandon moved along the stone floor to a winding stair, making no more noise than one of the tiny mice that shared the castle with the Winslows. Stoneybrook was an ancient castle; the walls were almost as strong now in 1546 as the year it took form. It was not as large as many others built during earlier days, but it was home to the Winslows and something to be proud of.

Moving quietly, Brandon made his way up the stairs and entered the room on the third floor that had been his place for as long as he could remember. Without bothering to undress, he threw himself on the bed, and the big dog whined and plopped down beside him. Brandon hugged Eric for warmth but was too excited for sleep. He relived the sweet kisses he'd stolen from Becky and already was purposing in his mind how he would find her alone again—in a place where they wouldn't be interrupted.

"Get out of that bed!" Stuart Winslow grabbed his son's hair and pulled him up and out of his slumber.

Instinctively Brandon launched a blow; and his fist hit Stuart in the chest.

Stuart shook him, furious now that the boy would not wake. "Why, you dare to strike your own father, do you?"

Brandon groggily said, "I'm sorry, sir. I didn't mean to hit you. You scared me."

"You were never scared of anything in your life, Brandon! I wish to heaven you were!" Stuart Winslow studied his son. *Will he ever grow up?* "Get dressed!" he commanded. He stared at his son a long moment, then said angrily, "What kind of blood has come down to you, Brandon? Some northman raider, if not worse." He was irritated at how long it was taking for the boy to dress. "Come. Quickly."

"Where are we going?"

"To face your sins," Stuart said over his shoulder. He left the room, closely followed by his son and the big dog. He took the stairs two at a time. Reaching the ground floor, he found his wife, Heather, waiting for them. She was forty-one but could have passed for ten years younger. She was a woman of quiet spirit, but now there was fear in her eyes. No doubt she saw the anger in his own. They'd had a good marriage and still loved each other deeply, but Brandon had become a problem that neither one of them could solve.

"Will you be able to make it right with Elwald?" she asked, following them toward the great hall.

"I doubt it." He stared at Brandon and asked harshly, "Didn't you know James Elwald would come for you, boy?"

Brandon looked surprised, caught but not overly concerned. Stuart took a firmer hold of his son's arm, knowing what he was thinking. "I've gotten you out of trouble many times, but you'll pay up this time!"

As soon as the three entered the great hall, Stuart saw two female servants who were replacing the stale rushes on the floor with new ones. He didn't miss the sly grins they didn't bother to conceal. *They know well what Brandon is like. Has he been sniffing around them, too?*

Up ahead, in the middle of the great hall, Stuart's brother, Quentin Winslow, waited for them. He was thirty-three. With the same blue eyes and auburn hair, he bore a striking resemblance to Stuart and Brandon.

"A little trouble, Brother?" He fell into step with them.

"A little? This whelp tried lifting the skirts of Elwald's daughter!"

Quentin had been a rough enough young man himself in his youth, but he had found God and was now preaching the gospel. He said nothing, but there was grief in his eyes as he looked at his nephew. "I'm sorry to hear that, Stuart."

"Not as sorry as he'll be!" Stuart snapped. Grasping Brandon's arm again, he hauled him toward the two men who were waiting for them at the end of the hall. "Here's the boy, sheriff."

Albert Fortner, the local sheriff, was a rather small man but well built. He had a smooth face and a pair of watchful gray eyes. "Sorry to disturb you over this problem, Lord Winslow."

"A problem? You call it a *problem*?" James Elwald shouted. His face was flushed with anger. He gestured at Brandon. "That's him! He tried to rape my girl Becky, and when I tried to help her, he tried to kill me. Arrest him, sheriff!"

"Be quiet, Elwald. I'll handle this," the sheriff said. He kept his voice soft and said, "As you just heard, Elwald wishes to press charges against your son for certain advances upon his daughter and for attacking him as well."

"Don't you deny it, either!" Elwald shouted. "You've ruined young girls in this county before!"

Stuart turned to stare at Brandon, his face set in a hard expression. "Did you try to rape that girl, boy?"

"No. I was just stealing a kiss." Brandon stared with impudence at Elwald. "And I'm not the first to have done it."

The sheriff had to hold James Elwald back. "Did you hit this man with a staff?" he asked.

"Yes, I did. I'd do it again, too," Brandon said defiantly. "He hit me first!"

Stuart stared at his son and could feel his wife watching him. He knew she wanted him to protect Brandon, but there was only so much he could do or wanted to do this time.

"Elwald, the boy's guilty. I'll let you decide what to do with him. You've always been a good man. I've been proud of you and your work, and if you want to charge him, I won't fight you in court, and there'll be no hard feelings on my part. But I see no reason for the court or the sheriff to be in the middle of this. If you want to settle this matter between the two of us, I'll see you get fair play."

James Elwald's face softened as he thought over his master's words. He had worked for the Winslows for several years and most certainly didn't want to endanger his position. But a man had to stand up for his daughter. Winslow understood that.

"The boy deserves punishment, but I'd get no pleasure, sir, in seeing him in jail. You always treat a man fair. I think we can settle this between us man to man, father to father."

"Good," Stuart said with a nod. "Shall we discuss this in the next room?"

"Well, that's best, I think," Sheriff Fortner said. "I wish you good day."

Stuart led Fortner and Elwald out of the great hall, leaving Brandon alone with his mother and his uncle.

"You've disappointed your father, and me too, Son," Heather said.

"Why, Mother, it was nothing. I was just playing."

"I think it was more than that."

"Your mother's right, Brandon," Quentin said. "I think you've gone too far."

Brandon could rise to any challenge, but he obviously did not want to hurt his mother. He dropped his head, unable to respond.

The three waited until the two men came back.

Stuart said, "Brandon, apologize to Elwald."

"No, sir, I won't do it. He hit me first."

Stuart stared at his son and shook his head. "But, Son, can't you see your own wrong? What about Becky? What about—" He paced away and ran a hand through his hair in frustration before turning back. "All right then. It will have to be the hard way. I'm going to thrash you, and you're going to work for Elwald for one month. If you take one step toward his daughter or show any insolence to Elwald or cause him any other difficulty, I've ordered him to tell me. I'll thrash you again, and your thirty days will start again at day one. Now, come and take your beating."

James Elwald watched the two go and then turned to face Lady Heather and Quentin. "I'm sorry it came to this. But I got to look out for my daughter. She's got a wild streak in her, I'm afraid."

Heather whispered, "And so has my son." It hurt her to think of Stuart whipping Brandon. He had not done so for some time now but had tried kindness and other methods, all to no avail.

When Stuart and Brandon came back, Brandon's face, Heather saw, was pale as paste, and he moved like an old man.

Stuart's face was set. "Take him, Elwald. Bring him back in thirty days—not before."

Quentin understood that Stuart and Heather needed no company at this time. "Send for me if you need me," he said.

After Quentin left, Stuart turned to Heather. "Do you hate me for whipping him?"

"No, I love you, Husband, as I always have. We've tried everything else. Maybe this will change him," she said sadly.

Stuart chewed his lower lip, a nervous habit he had when he was disturbed. Finally he put his arm around Heather and led her away. As they moved out of the great hall, he said, "I thought having a son would be the joy of my life—as he once was—but he's a grief to us now."

Heather stopped, turned, and took his hands in hers. "I gave our son to God on the day he was born. We'll believe that God will bring him out of this. Brandon *will* find God! The good Lord will not let his gifts fall to the ground."

2

Stuart glanced up from his book to stare at his wife, waiting at the window. Heather stood beside the tall arch looking out through the wavy glass. He knew she looked not to the green hills but to the empty road, awaiting Brandon's return. It had been a long month without their son.

Stuart looked about their room. He had spared no expense in making it as attractive as possible. He had even had a fireplace built to drive away the cold and lessen his wife's homesickness for the cozy cottage they'd shared when newly married.

Heather straightened and leaned closer to the window. "Stuart, look! Elwald is bringing Brandon home."

Stuart put the book down and came over to her at once. Together they watched the two figures approach in a horse-drawn wagon—tiny in the distance. "I hope he's all right. It was a hard thing for him."

"I'm sure it was a good thing in the end," Heather replied. "Come," she said with excitement. "Let's go down and welcome him home."

They descended to the first level then hurried out the massive door. As they stepped outside, Brandon leaped from the wagon. His mother ran to him. She threw her arms around him and hugged him fiercely. "I'm so glad you're home, Son."

"It's good to be here, Mother." The words were almost without emotion, but he added, "I've missed you."

Stuart had waited, giving Heather time to greet him, now he stepped forward and said, "Welcome home, Son. I hope things go better from here on."

"Thank you." The words were spare, and there was a bitter expression on his face, which troubled his father.

Stuart turned and walked over to where Elwald was waiting. "Thank you for bringing him home, Elwald."

"No trouble, sir. No trouble at all."

"Did he give you any problems?"

"Well, not really, sir. He done all the work I put him to, and he done it well. It's only that . . ."

"Elwald? It's only what?"

Elwald looked him in the eye. "Something's off with the boy now. It's like he's all froze up or something." He turned away, as if sorry he'd said anything at all.

"Did he make another advance to your daughter? Did you have to beat him?"

"Not a bit of it, sir." He shook his head. "Didn't look at my girl, not even once." He shrugged. "Probably just wanted to get the thirty days done and get home."

Stuart followed his gaze to Brandon and Heather, who were waiting at the entrance, quietly talking. "Yes, probably," he agreed. But he knew that neither he nor Elwald believed it. "Well, I'm glad you had no trouble with him. I hope you won't hold it against him."

Turning, Stuart walked over to where Brandon was standing beside his mother. "Let's go inside. I'll tell the cook to fix a special meal. We're celebrating."

"Celebrating what?" Brandon asked, fixing his eyes on his father.

"Why, to have you home, of course," Heather said quickly. "Come along. You and I will talk to the cook."

❧

The Winslows ate early, and Quentin joined them. It didn't take long for Quentin to see that the boy was punishing his parents with his silence, doing nothing more than answering direct questions with the slimmest of answers. Stuart focused on his brother, obviously trying to fill the silence. He talked to Quentin about his upcoming preaching and the new members attending the church, and as usual, they ended up debating fine theological points.

The meal finally was over, and Heather ushered Brandon away to show him a new book that she had just purchased.

Stuart watched them go, then turned and said heavily, "I don't know, Quentin. He's not himself. It's as though he's changed into another person."

"It's been a hard lesson for the boy, but he'll get over it."

"I hope so." He hesitated, and then gave in to the words rotating in his mind. "He hates me."

"No, he doesn't. He's fourteen years old, and he's trying to find his way. Don't you remember the agony of being fourteen? I certainly do! You're not a child, and you're not a man. You're not anything. You don't know if you'll ever be anything. Brandon's had a pretty rough shock. He's always been willful, but this is the first time it's ever really caught up with him." Quietly he added, "He's not that different from you."

"I was fairly wild myself, I suppose. Maybe all boys are, but I got over it."

"It took a fair amount to bring you around, as I remember it. Before Heather, before Tyndale, really you had only yourself in mind. Is he any different?"

"Perhaps not. But I must try to break through the wall he's built around himself."

"That's a good idea, Stuart. I'm sure he'll come around. Let me have a talk with him. Sometimes a lad will close the door to his parents but will talk to someone not so close."

In a little while, Heather returned to them and reached out a hand to her husband. He took it, and they shared a look of silent commiseration.

Quentin excused himself and went at once to Brandon's room. He knocked, calling his name softly. When he heard a rather surly reply, he stepped inside and moved to where Brandon stood staring out the tall narrow window.

"What is it, Uncle? Have you come to preach me a sermon?"

"No, my sermons are too good to waste on a wild young fellow like yourself."

Brandon turned and laughed. "You're exactly right about that. I'm not worth the trouble."

"None of us are worth the trouble we give God."

Brandon stared at Quentin for a moment, then shook his head. "You're a preacher. I'm the sinner here."

"And do you think preachers are sinless?" Quentin did not raise his voice but smiled slightly, adding, "You've not committed any sin that I haven't myself."

"Have you ever committed fornication?"

"Yes, more than once."

Brandon was taken off guard, for he had obviously not expected such a reply. "I don't believe you."

"I won't give you any of the details, but when I was just two years older than you, I lost my innocence to a young woman named Sally Maddox." Quentin felt Brandon's eyes on him and said, "That wasn't the only time I sinned with a woman, and that wasn't the worst sin I've ever committed."

"What was the worst?" Brandon demanded.

"I'll tell that only to God," Quentin answered. "The terrible sins, Nephew, are not those of the flesh but those of the spirit."

"Of what do you speak?"

"Sins of the flesh such as fornication, murder, theft—all of them grieve our Lord, but even worse is when you violate a sacred trust with God—such as breaking a vow to God or another person. Truth is the foundation for any man."

Brandon took the words in and seemed to be lost in them. "I can't believe you were ever false to anyone, Uncle."

"But I was—to my own parents. I was far more wicked than you, and the sorrow of my life is that I gave them grief. I won't tell you the details, but I will tell you this: not a single day has gone by since I wronged them that I haven't grieved over it."

Brandon waited for his uncle to continue, but Quentin put his arm over Brandon's shoulders. "Good night, Nephew," he whispered. He left at once. Instinctively he knew that Brandon was staring after him, his mind a cauldron of confusion.

Stuart got into the big bed beside Heather, and she put an arm across his chest and drew him close. "I'm so glad Brandon's home."

"So am I. He doesn't seem happy, though."

"I think he's ashamed of what he did."

"Well, I hope that's it."

"What else could it be?"

"It could be that he's unwilling to forgive me. When a boy is fourteen and on the brink of manhood, it's hard to take a whipping like that. It embarrassed him and humiliated him. And then I sent him off for his thirty days of service."

"He'll come around." Heather put her hand on his cheek and turned his face toward her. She kissed him and whispered, "I know he will."

He ran his hand over her hair. He was quiet for a time, then said, "I think I'll go and visit Princess Mary. I promised Queen Catherine before she died that I'd do so. She's gone now, but a promise must be kept."

Heather paused, wondering if it was wise to expose another

generation to the temptations of the king's court, but then said, "Stuart, take Brandon with you."

He thought it over a moment. "You think he'd go?"

"I think he will. He'll be bored at Stoneybrook, now his hands are idle. And it would be good for the two of you. You can spend time with him and stay over in London. Do some of the things that a young man would like to do."

"All right. I'll do it." He pulled her toward him and whispered huskily, "You're a good wife, Heather. I love you more tonight than I did when we first married."

Heather felt a fullness in her throat. She wanted so much to tell him how much she loved him, but every word seemed weak and futile. How could she make him understand how empty her world was when he was not with her? How could she tell him that his very presence made her feel warmer, her heart lighter? She squeezed him and nestled a bit closer. "I love you so much, Stuart, and you mustn't grieve over Brandon. He's going to be alright. I am certain of it. You concentrate on having a good time, and if he seems sullen, simply ignore it. He's got good Winslow blood in him. He's lost his way, but he'll find it again."

Stuart had tried to have some sort of conversation on the way to Whitehall Palace, but Brandon said very little on their journey to London. He had tried to keep the conversation going and had remained as outwardly cheerful as he could, but still there was a barrier between him and his son that he could not get past.

Hours later, when they were not far from the palace, Stuart said quietly, "I hope you get over your hatred for me, Son. I know your punishment hurt your pride, and I'm sorry it came to that."

"I don't hate you, Father," Brandon said rather stiffly. He said, "I simply don't—" He looked away, as if embarrassed.

Stuart checked his horse and reached for Brandon's arm. Reluctantly Brandon came to a stop. "Out with it. Say it."

"I don't fit in."

"Fit in with what?"

"I'm not like you or Grandfather or even Uncle Quentin. You're all good men and I'm not."

"Why, Son, none of us are perfect. I'd hate you to know some of the things that I've done and some of the thoughts I've had. But we all grow and change. Brandon, you can become the man that you choose to be."

Brandon raised his head, and his eyes met Stuart's. There was pain in them, and he said, "That's the trouble, I guess. I have no desire to be noble."

Stuart was stunned into silence. "We'll speak of this later."

They rode the remaining mile in silence, entered the drive leading to Whitehall, then dismounted, tied their horses to a railing and walked up to the gate. A guard took their names and left to seek permission for their entry. Stuart and Brandon walked over to a stone bench in a corner and took a seat.

Brandon asked in a whisper, "Do you really think the Princess Mary will see us?"

Being here, at the palace, seemed to shake Brandon out of his introspection. Stuart was glad to seize the opportunity to talk of any subject with his son. "I was the Princess Mary's playmate, in effect, when she was a child. Of course, I was older than she, but I would play with her. Her mother, Queen Catherine, encouraged me to come often. I've known Princess Mary a long time." He paused, then said quietly, "I feel sorry for her, Brandon."

The statement visibly shocked Brandon. "You feel sorry for her? She's a princess."

"King Henry was never kind to his children. He doesn't care about them really. All he wanted was a son, and then when he finally got Prince Edward, he wasn't the kind of son that King Henry wanted."

"He doesn't love Prince Edward?"

Stuart shifted in his seat. He didn't want to be telling any secrets, but it felt good to be in conversation with his son, and the subject obviously intrigued the boy. "King Henry has never loved anyone—except himself." Stuart saw that this shocked Brandon again, and he added, "The king wanted someone just like himself, and Prince Edward will never be that."

Brandon shifted in his seat. "Why not?"

"The king was a strong young man, able to defeat any man in his kingdom with sword or lance. He was larger than most men, a sportsman. Prince Edward's nine now and could not be more different from his father—"

Stuart was pleased to see another servant with whom he was familiar return with the first. "It's good to see you again, my lord. It's been a long time."

"It's good to see you too, Hanson. You're looking well."

"Getting older, sir. Princess Mary will be glad to see you. You were always her favorite. Simply let me announce you."

They waited, and Hanson soon returned. "Come along. Princess Mary is waiting for you."

They followed the tall servant down the hall and entered a large room, where a woman rose and came to greet them. She was dressed in a deep-purple gown with a stiff pointed stomacher. She came forward, smiling at Stuart, and said, "Why, it's about time, Lord Winslow. You have forsaken us."

Stuart bowed and kissed her hand. "Clearly it was not my intention to do so, Princess. I beg your forgiveness. I've missed you greatly."

Princess Mary was thirty-one years old. She had been an attractive child and by all reports had kept her looks for a while after she grew to maturity—but there was something missing from her now. Stuart could not put his finger on it, but he knew that Mary was unhappy. Perhaps she always had been. Quickly he said, "I would like you to meet my son, Brandon. Brandon, the Princess Mary."

"My, what a tall fellow you are!" Mary moved to face him and extended her hand. Brandon took it and followed his father's example.

"It is my honor to meet you, Princess. My father has told me so much about you."

"Not everything, I hope. I was beastly to him at times."

"I can't remember anything like that," Stuart said. "I remember we had some fine times playing with your dolls."

"Yes, indeed!" Mary smiled, and her eyes lit up. "I remember those tea parties. I had all my dolls named, and you could never remember them."

"I'm afraid you're right—that was never my forte—but I enjoyed my visits." He shifted from one foot to the other and lowered his voice. "I miss your mother."

"No more than I." Sorrow clouded Mary's face. She looked down for a moment and said, "Every day, Stuart, I miss her, think of her."

At that moment a young girl came into the room, and Mary turned and said, "Oh, Elizabeth, come here. Stuart Winslow has come. Do you remember him from his last visit?"

The young Princess Elizabeth was quite striking. She had a fair complexion, cinnamon-red hair, beautiful skin, and bright, intelligent eyes. She came over to them at once. "I remember you, sir, although it has been some time. And I can see that this is your son. He's very like you."

"Yes, Princess Elizabeth. This is my son, Brandon Winslow."

Mary studied him and then asked, chin up, "And are you a good boy, Brandon?"

"No, Princess. I'm afraid not."

Both Mary and Elizabeth laughed at this. Stuart frowned. "And why are you not good?" Elizabeth demanded.

"Because I was shaped in iniquity and in sin did my mother conceive me."

Mary and Elizabeth both stared at him. They recognized the quotation as being from the Bible, but Mary found his answer amusing. "Well, I must confess I am quite shocked," Mary said. "I always considered your father a good man and believed his son to be the same."

Elizabeth was delighted. "I'm so interested in sinners! Sister, you visit with his father, and I will take Master Brandon's confession. Come along, Master Brandon."

Brandon smiled, and his father could see he liked the young woman. "Princess Elizabeth, you're neither priest nor old enough. I fear my iniquities would quite shock you."

Heart palpitating, Stuart said, "Now, that's quite enough, Brandon—"

"And how old are you, Brandon?" the princess asked, ignoring Stuart.

"Fourteen."

"Why, I am only one year younger, but everyone knows that women are more mature than men. So, come, let me hear your confession."

Mary laughed and sat down. "Be careful of her, Brandon. She's wild as a hawk."

Stuart and Mary watched them leave, and they could hear Elizabeth's voice even after the door closed. Stuart frowned in the direction of the closed door. "Do you think they'll be all right unsupervised?"

"Cease your fretting, Father Winslow. The children will be fine—and shadowed by Hanson, no doubt." She pointed to the chair across from her, clearly wanting him to take his ease.

Stuart breathed a sigh of relief and sat down. "She is quite a girl, isn't she? The last time I came to visit she was only about four or five, and yet clearly she remembers me."

"She's actually quite brilliant. She's learning Latin and

Greek so quickly that I keep needing to find more learned tutors. Now please sit down and tell me about your family."

Stuart sat down and gave her a brief summary of his life. When he ended, she said, "Oh, how I've missed you, Stuart! It's so good to hear about you and Stoneybrook. It sounds as if you are in exactly the place you wish to be."

Stuart shifted in his seat. "You know it wasn't my decision, Princess, to discontinue our visits."

Her smile faded. "Oh, I am aware of it. My father forbade visits. He kept me closed off from all the world."

"I tried several times to see you, but I was never admitted. It was only recently that I learned that you were again able to receive visitors."

Mary rose and strode to the fireplace, clearly agitated. "My father separated my mother and me. We loved each other dearly, and he wouldn't even let me see her for years. I hated him for that."

Stuart did not know what to say. "How is the king?" he asked finally.

"Dying."

"Well, I'm sorry to hear that."

"I should be, Stuart, but how can I love a man who dismisses his true wife and executes two others? And now . . ." She shook her head, as if willing herself out of a dream. "Catherine Parr is a good woman. There is no romance to their marriage of course. He only wanted to marry her so that someone would nurse him through his illnesses. But Catherine is good to all of us. We love her very much. Even little Edward is fond of her."

"And Edward will be king."

"In name, but there will be a Protector for him, given his age."

"What's the boy like, Princess?"

"He's . . . very strange, very religious. He delights in sermons and talking with learned preachers and theologians."

"Well, I suppose that's not all bad," Stuart said, thinking of his own years as a boy and his meetings with Tyndale.

"It doesn't seem good to me. Not in a nine-year-old. And he's quite frail. Frankly, I don't think he'll live to rule."

Stuart blinked in surprise. "Then you would be next in line."

Mary shook her head. "You know how it is in England. There are many who would prevent me from taking the throne because I'm Catholic."

"Well, come, now. Sit, as you bade me to do. Suppose for a moment that there was no opposition. If you were queen, what would you do?"

A glow came to Mary's eyes, and she took a seat, but her back was straight, and she rubbed her hands in excitement. There was a strength in her, Stuart saw, though it was not obvious at first glance. There had to be strength within her in order for her to endure all Henry's neglect and ill-treatment. She stared into his face and said, "I'd bring England back to the true faith. No more beheadings, no more fear. I would love my people. I think, Stuart, they long to return to the old faith, but my father made that impossible."

"I could never keep up with your father's religious views."

"I don't think he has a firm grasp on them himself, but I would bring my people out of heresy and back into the true church, the Catholic Church."

There was a light of fanaticism in Mary's eyes. Stuart shifted, suddenly uncomfortable in his chair. He had thought it through, and like the great majority of Englishmen, he had no desire to see England turned back into a Catholic nation. But he made himself sit still, listening, as Mary began to tell him about her plans if indeed she was ever crowned queen.

❧

Elizabeth had been picking Brandon apart with questions, prying into his mind. It did not take long for him to decide that she was a very clever girl, coming at him bluntly if he refused to respond.

She asked him about his studies, and he said, "I'm not much of a student. I would rather ride and hunt and fence—you know, pursue the things of men, not scholars and children."

"You're very handsome," she said, sliding her hand through the crook of his arm as they walked. She cast an impish look at Hanson, the servant, who followed them by ten paces, but seemed unafraid of interruption.

Brandon blinked then laughed. "You shouldn't say such things, Princess. But if I may say it, you are very beautiful."

"Really?"

"Oh, yes."

"Have you had any love affairs?"

Brandon could not find an answer, and her intense glance made him flush at the neck.

"Why, you can blush! That *is* rare. You may amount to something." She leaned closer and whispered, "Tell me, Brandon Winslow, would you like to kiss me?"

Brandon was shocked. "You're the Princess Elizabeth! It wouldn't be—suitable."

"I know who I am. But you strike me as a boy unafraid of serious conquests." She moved on—the question about kissing her clearly only one of many she had in her mind—asking about the girls he knew, and Brandon found himself pinned into a shadowed corner when she demanded to know the details of who it was that he had loved.

"I cannot speak of that, Princess. No gentleman kisses and tells." He glanced over her shoulder, frowning when he could not see Hanson beyond them in the hall.

"Really?" Elizabeth surged forward and kissed him on the lips, surprising him. He stared at her hard. The last time he'd kissed a girl—

"Now, will you tell your father you kissed me?"

"Of course not!" Brandon sputtered, moving past her and into the hall. He saw Hanson, still ten paces away, talking to two other servants, obviously distracted.

Elizabeth tapped her chin and nodded. "Well, then *I* will tell him. I'll tell him you tried to steal my virginity."

"No! Don't tell him that, Princess!"

Elizabeth noted his fear. "Forgive me. I forget myself at times. Would your father be very hard on you?"

Brandon leaned against the wall and closed his eyes. In a moment, he found himself telling her the story of his banishment and beating.

"Do you hate your father for beating you?"

"It was humiliating."

"But if you had a young daughter," Elizabeth said, "and a young man tried to have his way with her against her will, what would you do to him?"

"I would thrash him," he said begrudgingly, kicking the toe of his boot into the stone floor as if he might chip off a bit of it.

"I'm sure you would. My sister thinks your father is the kindest and the most trustworthy man in England. She's seen enough of the other sort! Listen to me, Brandon Winslow. I've learned to know a little something about men too." Anger swept across Elizabeth's face. She shook her head and said, "You should thank God every day that you have a kind father who loves you."

Brandon listened, thinking of how the king had killed this girl's mother, and he nodded. "I'm certain you're right, Princess."

"You must forgive your father. Will you do that?"

"Yes, I will."

Elizabeth hugged him and touched him on the cheek. "There's a good fellow! Come, now, I'll show you my father's falcons, and you can confess more of your sins."

Brandon could not help but laugh. "You're not what I expected in a princess. Will you ever be queen?"

"No, Edward will be king, and if he dies, my sister Mary will be queen. But I would dearly love to wear the crown someday."

"Well, I think you'd make a fine queen."

Elizabeth reached out and pulled his hair. "You have beautiful hair," she said. "Auburn. It's almost the same color as mine. You know, if I were queen, I'd surround myself with handsome young men like you—and all of them would fall in love with me."

"I'm certain they would."

"Well, you can appeal to my vanity while we look at the hawks. Wasn't your father once the king's falconer? Come along, now."

❧

The day after they returned from the visit with Mary and Elizabeth, Stuart noticed that Brandon had cast off his sullen behavior and was showing interest in the work of the estate—and even better, showing some affection for his parents. Better yet, during their fencing lesson Brandon seemed to absorb both instruction and praise.

"You'll be too good for me soon," Stuart said. "We'll have to get an expert."

"I don't think so." Brandon said, sitting down beside his father. Stuart was pleased to see that the boy was panting as hard as he. Brandon wiped the perspiration from his brow and said, "Will we go back to see Princess Mary—and Elizabeth?"

"Would you like to?"

"Yes, I would. I like Elizabeth very much."

Stuart paused. "What about Mary?"

"Elizabeth says her sister thinks you're one of the few men she knows that she would trust."

"Well, I should hope that she could trust me. I have a great affection for Princess Mary." He patted his son on the back. "We'll go back soon for another visit."

The two had put up their swords and started for the stables to take a ride when Brandon said, "Look, there comes Uncle Quentin."

Quentin came riding up at a gallop and pulled the horse to a quick stop beside them. The animal was lathered and heaving for breath.

Stuart said, "What is it? What's wrong?"

"The king is dead," Quentin said as he dismounted. He stared hard at Stuart. "King Henry died yesterday."

"Then Edward will be king," Stuart whispered.

"Yes. God save the king. May he be a better man than his father."

The three of them headed immediately for the castle.

Brandon fell into step beside his father. "Does this mean we can't make our visit?" he asked quietly.

"After the funeral and after we've given the family time to mourn, we'll go see them often. They'll have need of a friendly ear."

"I feel sorry for them, Father. They're bound to be sad, despite everything, aren't they?"

"Yes, I feel sorry for them too. They've had a terrible life, and little good can come in their direction, the way things stand."

"Do you think King Edward will be cruel to them as their father was?"

"He's but a boy! And I've heard he's very fond of his sisters. Maybe you'll get to meet him next time we visit."

Stuart put his arm around his son. He squeezed the boy and said, "I feel that muscle growing in that sword arm. You're going to be a fine soldier one day, my son."

3

"You're up to some mischief, Stuart Winslow. I can tell from that look on your face." Heather let her embroidery work fall to her lap and waited expectantly for Stuart to confess what was on his mind.

Stuart grinned broadly. "I don't know why you should say that. You're always suspicious of me, Wife."

"That's because you're always guilty. What is it now? What have you done?"

"Well, I must confess I have committed a horrible sin."

"I can't believe that. What horrible sin?"

"I forgot your birthday last week. That's the most horrible thing I can think of that a man can do to his wife."

Heather looked down at the embroidery, touched it with her fingertip, and then glanced up. "I was disappointed," she said. "Brandon never seems to remember. But it's the first time you've forgotten."

"Well, I've come to make it up to you. I'm going to give you a big kiss just to show you what a good man I am." He came over, leaned over, and kissed Heather on the cheek. He held her close for moment, and then he said, "I hope you're not disappointed by my simple belated gesture."

Heather could never be angry with this husband of hers for

long. It had occurred to her that women with bad husbands never knew what they were missing in this world. She smiled, reached up, and put her hand on Stuart's cheek. "I'm never disappointed in you."

"Well, that's good to hear. But just to show you that I'm an even better man than you think, I didn't forget your birthday. It was just that I couldn't get the present put together in time, but I have now." He walked quickly to the door, stepped outside, and then came back with a mound of white fur in his hands.

"What in the world!" Heather exclaimed. She stood up at once and reached out to touch the silky fur on the garment that Stuart was holding out to her. "It's so beautiful!" she whispered. "What is it?"

"It's ermine. I hate to tell you what I had to pay for these furs, but even the Princess Mary doesn't have anything any better than this. Here, put it on."

Holding her breath, Heather allowed him to hold the gown. She slipped her arms into it and then hugged it close. "It's so smooth," she whispered. "It's beautiful, Stuart!" She blinked against sudden tears. She never cried during hard times, but kindness always brought tears of gratitude, especially when it involved Stuart. She put her arms around his neck and kissed him. "That's the finest present any woman ever had from a husband."

"Well, I shall expect a proper reward. We'll talk about the nature of that reward tonight."

Heather stepped back and laughed. "I know all about your rewards. They're always the same." She turned around, still stroking the silky ermine fur. "I wish we had a mirror big enough for me to see all myself in." The only mirror that she had, of course, was a small one, no more than ten inches square of polished metal. "Some day they'll make a mirror big enough for a woman to see all of herself."

"I've engaged a painter to do your portrait. He can do it in that ermine if you like."

"What about you?"

"Oh, I'll just wear my old clothes, as I always do—if I get into the painting at all. No doubt the painter will only have eyes for my beautiful wife."

She came to him again and kissed him. "You're the best husband a woman ever had."

"I think you're right about that." He grinned and pulled her close. "We've had a good marriage, Sweetheart. I'm thankful for that. Never once have I considered getting rid of you and getting another woman."

"Well, I should think not, the way I've spoiled you!"

She took off the coat reluctantly and said, "I must go to London now to show off what my husband's given me."

"Any time you like."

For a moment a shadow crossed Heather's face. "We'll have to take Brandon with us."

At the mention of their son, Stuart lost the sense of happiness that had filled him. "I wish he were more like my father."

"And I wish he were more like you."

Indeed, the two of them had seen little change for the better in Brandon. After a brief respite, he returned to his wayward behavior. He was sixteen now and constantly in trouble. More than once he had been caught poaching, when he had acres of Stoneybrook forest at his disposal. Stuart and Heather had given him everything he needed and had tried to show love beyond what most parents showed. But Brandon seemed to be a bent twig. He was the terror of young girls—at least, of the mothers of young girls.

Over and over Stuart and Heather discussed Brandon's present and future, but they could not find the answer to the puzzle before them.

Heather said, "I still think that God will use him, Stuart. On the day he was born I gave him to God."

"You always say that, and I always believe you."

The two sat down and spoke for a while about other estate matters. Finally Heather brought up the question that was not far from the minds of most people in England. "What will happen when King Edward dies?"

"He may live for a long time."

"The rumors are that he can't live beyond a year or two. What will happen then?"

"It will be up to King Edward. He can name his successor. I expect it will be Princess Mary. That'll be a sad day for England."

"I thought you liked Princess Mary."

"I do like her. But . . ." He stood up abruptly and turned to the window, eyes wide and far away.

Heather stared at him. "But what, Stuart?"

Stuart looked over to her. "Her mother was a devout Catholic, and Mary has taken her religious direction from Queen Catherine. It's no secret that if she ever ruled England, she would make a Catholic country out of it."

"Can she do that?"

"Queens and kings have a lot of power. She could make it . . . unpleasant for Protestants."

Heather frowned. He was holding something back. "What do you mean by unpleasant?"

"Think back, Heather," he said, pacing now in his agitation. "King Henry had people executed who didn't fall into his line of proper religious thought. Remember what happened to Sir Thomas More? He was a Catholic and a favorite of Henry, but he died because he wouldn't give in to Henry."

"And William," she whispered, remembering Tyndale. "Henry didn't execute him, but he was responsible for his death."

Stuart shook his head, his face a mask of dread. "I'm afraid Mary will crush everyone who's not a Catholic."

"God will take care of us."

With a laugh Stuart came over and leaned down and kissed

her. "I love your faith, Heather Winslow. You put me to shame. You're a good reminder to me that I should not fret over things that are beyond my control." His eyes moved back to the window, and Heather followed his gaze. Brandon was pacing on the small knoll.

"Your daily fencing?" Heather asked drily.

"Indeed." He kissed the tip of her nose. "We'll go to London and show off that beautiful robe of yours next week, perhaps."

Stuart left the castle and went out to the stable that housed the horses and most of the weapons. He found Brandon waiting for him. "Sorry to be late, Son."

Brandon grunted in response.

"I gave your mother that ermine robe I showed you."

Brandon lifted his chin and eyebrows with mild interest but immediately moved toward the swords. He looked older than his years, six feet tall now, not completely filled out but lean and muscular. The sun caught his auburn hair, and his eyes were as blue as the cornflowers that covered the hills of England at certain seasons. *I wish he were as good as he looks,* Stuart thought. "Ready for a bout?" he said.

"Yes, sir."

They took up swords and at once fell into position. Stuart grinned in anticipation of the challenge ahead. His own father had seen to it that he was a good swordsman, but he had never been great. Brandon, flourishing under the instruction of a former soldier Stuart had hired, had clearly inherited his grandfather's prowess. Stuart knew Brandon routinely eased up, just to keep him engaged. But once in a while, he could still surprise him.

The two circled each other, and soon the bright morning rang with the clash of the blades. Stuart tried to break through Brandon's guard, but the young man simply could not be pinned down. Around and around they went, the swords flashing in the sun, and finally Stuart knew that Brandon could have ended the bout at any time. He stepped back, lowered his blade, and shook his head. "You're too good for me, Son."

"Oh, I don't think so, Father."

"Yes, you are. You're better than most soldiers. That's what Debois says, and he's seen the best of them."

"You've taught me as much as he has. Maybe I'll follow in Grandfather's footsteps and be a soldier some day."

"I hope not. It's not a good life, Son."

"I want more than this, Father. To see different lands, a soldier's adventure would be good for me."

"A soldier's adventure often leads him to death. Or dismemberment. It's a hard life, Brandon, not nearly the glory you've made it out to be." They had had this argument many times before, and he saw how frustrated the boy was. "We'll find something for you to do, Son. It's high time you took more responsibility here at Stoneybrook as the future master. Don't you think you might like to take over when I'm gone?"

"No, sir. I just don't care about things like that." Stuart let the silence rise between them. If not Brandon, who would take over Stoneybrook?

Brandon toyed with his blade and said, "When are we going back to London?"

"I'm going to take your mother there. I think we'll call upon Princess Mary," he added casually. "I'm hoping to—"

"Could I go too, sir?"

"Your mother and I would like that."

"Let's be off immediately!"

Stuart laughed. Other than fencing, it was the first real sense of interest Stuart had seen in the young man, and his excitement softened the tension between them. "Perhaps the day after tomorrow. The master of Stoneybrook can't just up and leave."

"I might be able to wait that long," Brandon said, ignoring his admonishment. "I'll go for a long ride now to keep my mind off of it."

"Be careful. Lightning's got a lively way of throwing riders and then stepping on them."

"He can't do that to me!"

Stuart watched him go and shook his head. He was so gifted—fine-looking, strong, and quick. *I must find a way to shape him into a good man.*

Stuart and Brandon left Heather with their hostess in London—a longtime friend—while they went to Richmond Palace to seek an interview with the Princess Mary. It had been more than two years since they had made their last visit, and Stuart was filled with a strange sense of foreboding.

Brandon said now as they walked up the palace steps, "Do you think we might see the Princess Elizabeth?"

"That depends on her. She's pretty headstrong, I understand."

"I liked her," Brandon said.

"Well, I think everybody likes Elizabeth," he said crossly. Did the boy think they could have access to any one of the royal house any time they pleased? He sighed. "She's very much like her father in some ways."

Brandon looked with surprise at his father. "Like King Henry?" he whispered. "But he was a wicked fellow! Everybody says so."

"Well, it's safe enough to say that now, but he would have had your head chopped off if you had said it while he was alive."

"Not really, sir!"

"Yes, really. He had men executed for nothing at times. The things I saw—"

Brandon narrowed his eyes. "As the king's birdkeeper? You were a servant, yes? Not a part of the court."

Stuart grimaced. He did not want to enter this conversation, not here, not now. Heather and he had worked hard at concealing the stories of his youth, not wishing to lead Brandon further astray.

"Father?" Brandon peered at him, intent on knowing more. "How well did you know the king?"

"He came to Stoneybrook once with all his minions," Stuart hedged. "Father had to keep them all in feastings and wine for weeks. It nearly broke him. But you should've seen the fine dances that went on. Henry was magnificent. Later . . ." his voice dropped and he stared at the ground. He shook his head.

"And you think Elizabeth might follow in the ways of her father?" Brandon pressed. "Is that it?"

"No, I meant she has many of his gifts. He was a great dancer and a scholar of sorts, and Elizabeth has all that."

They reached the top of the stairs and were greeted by two armed soldiers. "Yes, sir?"

"I am Stuart Winslow, master of Stoneybrook, an old friend of the princess. This is my son, Brandon Winslow. Will the Princess Mary admit us?"

"Sir, if you will wait here, I will go and inquire."

The wait was short.

"The Princess will see you, sir." The guard turned, and they followed him. Brandon's eyes moved quickly, trying to absorb every detail. It was more ostentatious than he remembered, as if flaunting the wealth of the royal family. When they got to the end of a long hallway, the guard knocked and, hearing a voice, he opened the door.

"Please proceed."

Stuart stepped through the doorway and Brandon followed him. They found Mary seated at a table. Beside her was a boy. Instantly they recognized Edward, king of England. Stuart hesitated for a moment, then approached and bowed deeply. "Your Majesties." Thankfully Brandon followed suit.

"This is the gentleman I've told you about, Brother," Mary said, casually looking in their direction. Her face was sallow, and she had gained weight. "This is Master Stuart Winslow, and this, I believe, is his son. I've forgotten his name—it's been so long since Master Winslow has bothered to come and call upon us."

"It is Brandon Winslow, Princess," Stuart said smoothly, ignoring her jibe.

"Oh, yes, I remember now." She turned to the king and said, "Two of your loyal subjects."

Edward had a thin, aesthetic face and a studious look. His voice was reedy, and he looked as frail as he was said to be. "Your Majesty, it's a privilege to see you," Stuart said with a deep, slow nod. "I hope God sends you good health."

Edward studied them, his eyes quick with intelligence. He said, "We've been playing chess. I've beaten Mary every time. Do you play chess, Master Winslow?"

"On occasion, Majesty."

"Good. Sit down and play."

Mary vacated her seat for Stuart and went to Brandon. "Master Brandon, it would be very boring for you to watch a chess match. I'll send you with a servant to call upon Princess Elizabeth. She's out preparing for a ride. If you'll go out to the stables, I'm sure she'd be glad of the company."

"Thank you, Princess," Brandon said quickly.

After he was gone, Mary smiled at Stuart, who was gazing in concern after the young man. "A likely-looking lad," she said. "Very much like you."

"We Winslow men all look alike." Surely Brandon knew not to make any untoward advances on a princess—

"And how is your dear wife?"

"Very well, thank you."

Edward said eagerly, "Come, now, pay attention to the game, not my sister." Two guards behind him took a step closer. Stuart eyed them, but not for too long.

"I warn you," Mary said, "the king is an excellent chess player. He's also a fine scholar."

"Well, I'd better beat him at chess, because no one ever called me a scholar." Stuart looked across the chessboard at the tiny king and felt a sense of doom. *This boy can't live for long. He looks as though he's dying already.* He remembered well the ways of the court: no one was to beat a king of England. The key was to make the battle look as difficult as possible before giving in.

❧

Brandon was led to the stables. When he got there, he saw Princess Elizabeth at once. She was wearing a riding outfit, and her reddish hair caught the sun as it peeked out from under her hood. He advanced slowly.

She turned to meet him. "And who is this?" she exclaimed. "I remember! You're the young fellow who said that you were born in iniquity and conceived in sin." She laughed with delight. "Are you a better young man now than you were then? How old are you now?"

"Sixteen, Princess, and no, I'm afraid I'm no better."

"Well, you look better." She came up to him. "What a tall fellow you are!" She smiled, and her eyes twinkled with pleasure. "I'm glad to see you again. Did you ride here?"

"Yes, I did."

"Let me have a horse brought out. We'll see what kind of a horseman you are."

Twenty minutes later the two were riding across the green that surrounded Richmond Palace. Brandon found it easy to keep up with the princess although she obviously had the better animal. His own steed was a stallion, and he delighted in its strength and speed, but finally called out, "Princess, you need to show more care. Your horse might stumble."

Elizabeth turned and laughed at him. "One cannot spend one's life worrying about things that probably won't happen," she called back.

They continued to ride for an hour. When they arrived back at the castle, the horses' mouths were white with foam.

"Come," Elizabeth said, "help me down."

At once he went over to her and put his hand up. She put her hand in his, and he clearly saw she had no need of help in dismounting. She was not a beautiful young woman, but there was so much animation, so much life in her face that to Stuart she was undeniably attractive.

"Come along. I want to introduce you to some of the ladies of the court. Don't tell them you're sixteen. Tell them you're eighteen. You look it anyway. Perhaps you'll make a conquest."

Brandon grinned. "Lead on, Princess."

He fell into step beside her, and she looked up at him. "Tell me about some of your love affairs of late, Brandon. I grow so weary of those in the court. I remember that the last time you came you were in trouble over some milkmaid or such. Are you still charming the young girls in your neighborhood?"

"I don't know how to answer that, Princess."

"You don't have to. A young man as fine-looking as you can have his pick. Come along. We'll see what the ladies of the court think of you."

❧

The ladies of the court, all older than Brandon, were much impressed by him. Elizabeth seemed delighted as she introduced him. She told him, "Go on, then, Brandon. Tell the ladies about your conquests in the land of Stoneybrook."

Brandon blinked with surprise, and his face reddened. "Well, I'll gladly oblige your request, Princess, and tell about mine if you will first tell about yours."

The women were silent, shocked by Brandon's boldness, but then Elizabeth suddenly laughed, clearly delighted by his audacity. She had a fine laugh, coming from deep in her chest. "I would not dare leave you alone with the ladies. I'm afraid you would corrupt them all."

"Not so, Princess! I'm perfectly safe."

"When a man starts saying how safe he is, ladies, it's time to keep watch on your virtue," Elizabeth said, winking at the young women. "Come, now. Tell them about the most beautiful girl you ever loved. I command you!"

Brandon lost his embarrassment and began to make up wild, improbable tales of romantic escapades. A half-hour later, Elizabeth finally said, "That's all for you."

"Oh, don't take him away," said a young woman with sparkling black eyes and a very fetching figure. "Let us have him for a while."

"No, Annette, I'm afraid you would corrupt him." The young ladies all laughed. Elizabeth left the room, followed closely by Brandon. "Come, I'll show you some of the books I've been working on."

She led him to a vast study, walls lined with books. There was a huge fireplace and a small, forlorn fire burning inside it. He followed her silently as she went from book to book, telling him about each of them, until she asked over her shoulder, "Are you a scholar, Brandon?"

"Not at all, Princess. I want to be a soldier. Soldiers don't need to be scholars."

"Why would you want to be a soldier?"

"It would be exciting."

"Are you so very tired of your life that you're willing to risk it?"

"Well, to be truthful, I am a little weary."

"Come. Tell me about yourself and life at Stoneybrook."

Despite Brandon's best efforts to lead her away from such a line of thought, Elizabeth soon deduced that he was a trial to his parents.

"Your father seems like such an amiable man, and I trust your mother is a fine lady."

"They are both the best people I've ever known."

"What a wonderful thing for a son to say!" Elizabeth exclaimed. She lowered her head, and for a moment it seemed that she would speak of her own family. As every Englishman knew, her mother was Anne Boleyn. Henry had branded her an adulteress and had her executed when Elizabeth was but a child. A pained expression touched Elizabeth's face, and she said, "I'm glad you have good parents."

"Well, enough about parents," Brandon said uneasily. "What about you, Princess? You could be queen."

"Oh, no. If my brother were to die, Mary, who is older, will be queen."

"Do you think she'd be a good queen?"

Elizabeth laughed. "You don't know much about royalty and palaces and the court, do you, Brandon? No, I will never answer that question." She passed her hand across her face and said, "I'll tell you, though. If I ever do become queen, I'll bring you as an ornament to my court."

"I'd rather be a soldier, Princess."

"We don't always get what we want, Brandon." There seemed to be more in Elizabeth's words than she had thought to reveal, for she said, "Come. I'll show you the hawks. We've got a new peregrine. Rumor has it that your father began our fine flock."

❧

"Well, the king is a very scholarly young man, Princess," Stuart said. The door had closed behind Edward, who had retired after winning two chess games in a row. "He's an avid reader, I take it?"

"Oh, yes, and very interested in religion. We've had quite engaging conversations, though I am much older."

Stuart shot a quick glance at Mary. He was saddened that she had aged so much since he had last seen her. She was silent for a time, and then dissatisfaction scored her face. "I've had a hard life, Stuart."

"Indeed you have, Princess."

"I've never said so publicly, but my father treated my mother abominably."

"I would agree with you. Indeed I would."

"Yes, you were always kind to my mother. She thought a great deal of you." The heavy lines of Mary's face lightened, and she smiled, which made her look somewhat younger. Still there was a look of ill health about her. "I remember her saying that it would be good if I married you, but, of course, according to your own testimony, you have the best wife in the world."

"Indeed, I do, Princess. She's a lovely woman." He smiled and said, "Moreover, she's a saint to put up with a fellow like me for all of these years."

"Are you a good Catholic, Stuart?" The question came bluntly and sharply.

"Why, I try to serve God as best I can."

The answer did not seem to satisfy Mary. She frowned and said, "I remember well that you consorted with the Protestant smugglers. It was only my father's good grace that saved you and yours or your heads would've been on the block, no?"

Stuart looked her in the eye. "He spared us, yes."

Mary lifted her chin. "God has chosen me, Stuart, to bring our people back to the true faith."

Stuart faltered. "God has his ways," he said at last, "of seeing his desires to completion."

Mary seemed pleased with his response, extended her hand, and he kissed it. "I have treasured your friendship. I don't have many friends. Come again soon."

"Indeed I will. I promise."

Stuart left and found Brandon waiting for him outside. "Did you find the Princess Elizabeth?"

"Oh, yes, we had a ride, and she took me to meet the ladies of the court."

"Were they beautiful ladies?"

"Some of them were."

"Well, did they find you amiable?"

Brandon laughed. "Yes, they did, but I think they would find a swinekeeper amiable. They're all absorbed in romantic thoughts."

"Well, my advice—not that you're apt to heed it of late—is to stay as far away from them as you can. Come along."

They mounted their horses and started back to the manor where they were staying with friends. Thoughts of his younger days and the misdirection of his path consumed Stuart. If he didn't act soon, Brandon would end up in similar trouble—with the village girls or the law or, judging by the princess's interest in him, as part of the king's court. One of these days, he was even liable to fancy himself enough a man that he'd run off to join some man's military cause. None of those were tolerable outcomes. Not for a son of Stuart Winslow.

He cleared his throat. "I've made a decision, Brandon, concerning you."

"Yes, sir? What is it?"

"I've decided that you will to go to Oxford."

"Oxford! I—I don't want to go to university."

"It'll be the best thing for you. I know you want to be a soldier, but that's not a good trade. Not a profession suitable for the future master of Stoneybrook." *Especially with the unrest bound to come when Mary becomes queen.*

Brandon said quietly, "Father, you're trying to make something of me that I'm not."

"I'm trying to make a man of you."

"Well, I'm not the kind of man you desire me to be! I'm totally unfit for either the church or the law or even for the business of running Stoneybrook—and you know that I'd be a fine soldier!"

Stuart declined to argue, and the two were silent as they rode back to the manor along the river. When they dismounted at the stables, Stuart said heavily, "You'll go to Oxford, Brandon. Your mother, Quentin, and I have prayed much about this—and we feel it's best for you."

"I'll hate it!"

Stuart had known it would be like this, but he could find no other course. "You'll do your best, Son, as befits a young man with the name of Winslow. Who knows? You may like it after you get there."

"No, sir, I will not!" Brandon said, and every line of his body proclaimed rebellion.

4

Even after all these years I hate London! It would suit me if I never had to set foot in it again."

Stuart Winslow glanced at his father as they walked down the street and grinned broadly. "You're behind the times, sir," he said. "London is where all the important things take place." Stuart adroitly dodged a burly man pushing past and said, "But in all truth I'm not too fond of it myself."

Claiborn Winslow, now in his later years, was lean and quick and he dodged the man almost as easily as Stuart had. "I'm not sure we're on the right street. Someone could put up signs marking streets. How is a fellow supposed to find his way?"

"By hit or miss, I suppose," Stuart answered.

The two men threaded their way down the crowded street, dodging others who were bent on coming up. Carts and coaches made such a thundering, it seemed that all the world went on wheels. At every corner they encountered men, women, and children, some, arrayed in the gold and gaudy satin of the aristocracy, gazing languidly out of their sedan chairs borne by lackeys with thick legs. Porters sweated under their burdens and peddlers scurried like ants about the two men making their way through the human tide that flowed and ebbed on the street.

"Watch yourself, Son!" Claiborn Winslow grabbed Stuart's

arm and jerked him to the middle of the street just in time to avoid a deluge of slops that someone was throwing out of an upper window. "Nearly got you that time. At least the city has put a drain in the street so that the rain will wash away this garbage." He waved his hand at the ditch about a foot wide and six inches deep that ran down the center of the cobblestone street. "That carries all the slops and garbage away quite nicely. It's a wonder what a change modern improvements make, isn't it? Why, most cities just let the garbage and slop pile up—but London won't put up with that."

"I think that's what we're looking for," Stuart said. He pointed at a sign that was faded and almost obliterated by smoke and weather. *Jared Pounds, Solicitor.*

"Doesn't look very prosperous, does he?"

"No, but I suppose he's as good as any other lawyer. I don't trust the breed too much myself."

Going in, the two men walked up a flight of rickety wooden steps and then down a dark corridor. Stuart knocked on a door, and a man stood there before him.

"Ah, Mr. Winslow, is it?"

"Yes, Mr. Pounds," Claiborn answered. "This is my son, Stuart."

"Come in, come in. Have a seat. We'll have something to drink here. Will it be ale or wine?"

"Ale will be fine," Claiborn said, and Stuart nodded his agreement. They looked around the room as the lawyer scurried about and poured ale into flagons. The heat was oppressive inside the office, which looked as though a storm had swept through it. Books, books, and more books everywhere, papers stuffed into crevices, three tables covered with documents.

Pounds simply shoved the contents of one table aside and nodded toward the chairs. "Be seated, gentlemen. Be seated. I think you'll like this brew."

As Claiborn watched the lawyer, he was not favorably impressed. Jared Pounds was an apple-shaped man of fifty. Everything about him was round. His big eyes, his thick neck, his fat stomach, even his thick legs filled out his hose until they nearly burst the seams. However, he was by all accounts a clever man, and Claiborn had learned not to judge a man by his looks.

"Well, sir, does the ale please you?"

"Very good," Claiborn nodded.

"Very well. I suppose you're ready to get down to business. I wanted to see you to talk about Lord Edmund's will." Pounds shuffled through papers, tossing some aside like a small storm, and came up with a document. "Ah, here it is." He glanced over it and said, "Your brother Edmund is eighty-six. Is that correct?"

"Yes, sir, he is," Claiborn said.

"And you are seventy-nine?"

"That's correct."

"Well," Pounds said, studying the will, "this is as clear as I can make it. Since Edmund has no children, you are his heir, sir. All will come to you, including the title, on the death of Lord Edmund."

"So I understood."

"Your brother. Is he in good health?"

"No, I'm sorry to inform you he is not. But one good thing—he has become a follower of the Lord Jesus in his old age. He's actually happier now than he's ever been in his life, despite his illness."

"Well, I'm happy to hear it, then." Pounds tossed the remark away as a man will toss aside the peel of an orange, picked up a pen, and turned his round eyes on Claiborn. "It's time for you to make your own will."

"Well, I don't really have enough property to make a will."

"You have some property, I trust, and I would guess you would rather your son and your family have it."

"Well, of course, that's true. I hadn't thought of that."

"And besides," Pounds said, leaning back and folding his

hands over his enormous stomach, "when your brother passes on, you will have the entire estate and the title as well. But I must insist that you need two wills. The will that's in force now will take care of your family in case you die before your brother. The second will be written so to take effect if you have already received the estate and the title."

"That seems wrong to me," Claiborn murmured. "I don't like to think of that."

"We all must go sometime. All that lives must die, passing through time to eternity. If you died the day after tomorrow, you'd have no will, the court would make the decisions. Don't trust the courts, sir—" Suddenly alarm flitted across Pound's face. "Never tell anyone I said such a thing."

"Well, I would want my son, Stuart, to be master of Stoneybrook with the title."

"That's easy enough. And you have a grandson, I believe."

"My son, Brandon," Stuart said.

A silence fell on the room, and Pounds' eyes narrowed slightly as he watched their faces. "I have heard that he is—irresponsible." The pause was noticeable. His eyes went from one man to the other but came back to Claiborn. "Irresponsible, that's all I say. But he is working on his studies, correct?"

"He is a student at Oxford."

Pounds nodded. "Very good. Perhaps he simply needed to sow his wild oats. And what profession is he preparing for?"

"He's . . . looking for a profession," Claiborn answered stiffly.

Pounds stared at his visitors and obviously deduced that all was not well between Claiborn Winslow and his grandson. "And what would you like to do with your property?"

"I would like to divide what property I have now between Stuart and his brother Quentin."

"If Lord Edmund died, you would have the title."

"Yes, and when I die, Stuart, as the eldest, of course would be lord of Stoneybrook."

"Very good, sir. Now, then," Pounds said, "let's see to the business of these two wills."

ꝏ

It was now late afternoon. "It's too late to go home tonight," Claiborn said. "We'll have to stay at an inn."

"Yes, and I'd like to have something to eat. I'm starved."

"Well, the Red Lion is a little further than most, but it's worth the trip. They have good meals. I've eaten there several times."

The two men made their way through the crowded streets.

The inn's sign portrayed an animal painted a brilliant red.

Stuart grinned and said, "It looks more like a house cat."

"Not a very impressive lion."

"Come on. Let's get something to eat."

The two men went inside and seated themselves at a table. Soon they were served hot eel pie, fresh bread, and some very good ale.

"I never could understand why eel tastes so good when the bloody things look so awful," Stuart remarked.

"They don't look any worse than some other things we eat."

The two men ate slowly. Finally Claiborn said, "I need to buy some gifts for that grandson of mine."

"You've always spoiled Brandon."

"Well, perhaps." He leaned over and stared into Stuart's face, so much like his own. "I wasn't able to give you much, Son, as you were growing up. So now perhaps I try to make it right with Brandon."

Stuart suddenly gripped his father's forearm in a rare gesture of affection. "You gave me all I needed, Father. No man ever had a better father."

Claiborn was touched and shook his head. "We had some hard times during those early years. There wasn't always food on the table, not good food."

"We survived, Mother and I and you—and Quentin, too, of course, though he missed the hard part of growing up."

"What will you do while I look for some gifts?" Claiborn asked.

The two men were about ready to leave when Stuart looked up to see a tall man enter the room. "Why, there's Orrick. What's he doing in London?" He called out, "Orrick, over here," and when the man came to stand before them, he asked, "What's wrong, Orrick?"

"It's Lord Edmund. Mrs. Winslow said to tell you he's taken a very bad turn. She wants you to come at once."

"He was all right when we left."

"Yes, sir, it was all very sudden," Orrick said. "And she sent Nap to Oxford to bring Master Brandon home."

"I hope he will come," Claiborn said.

Both men had the same thought, but neither spoke it aloud. Orrick muttered, however, "Well, she sent to Nap to get him, but he'll have a time finding him."

5

The afternoon sun was fast falling in the west as Derward Carstairs looked up from where he was seated with his back to a huge yew tree. His eyes narrowed and he nudged his companion. "Look there, William, what do you make of that fellow?"

William Short had been dozing. He awoke confused and said irritably, "Don't be digging your filthy elbow into me, Derward!" He looked across to where a man leading a handsome black mare was pulling up a beautiful bay. Short, being a lover of horseflesh, said, "I'd like to have those two horses!"

"You're not likely to. They'd bring a pretty price anywhere."

They watched while the man, who was tall and almost emaciated, stood looking irresolutely around. "He doesn't know what he's looking for." Derward grinned. "Come on. Let's find out who he is."

"You're always poking your nose into somebody's business."

Carstairs merely laughed and got to his feet. He was slightly under middle height, and the academic robe Oxford demanded of its students covered him thoroughly. He approached the man and asked, "Well, my good man, are you lost?"

The newcomer appeared to be the sort of lean, lanky man who eats like a starving shark and yet never seems to gain an ounce. He had obviously put on his best clothes for the trip to Oxford, but they were not much. He looked at the two men before him and tugged off his hat.

"I beg your pardon, sirs. I ain't lost, but I'm looking for a man."

"Will just any man do?" William Short laughed. He leaned closer to Carstairs and whispered, "Look there, the fellow's got one blue eye and one brown eye. Now that's odd. Don't know that I ever saw it in a man."

"I had a dog like that once," Carstairs said quietly. "Who is this fellow you're looking for?"

"Master Brandon Winslow. That's who I need to find, sir."

Short demanded, "What in the world do you want with him?"

"Don't know, sir," the man said. He obviously did know but did not care to share the information. He chewed his lower lip thoughtfully and waited while the two men studied him. "Do you mind where I might find him, sir?"

Carstairs shrugged. "This time of the day he won't be studying. You can be sure of that."

Short laughed and nodded his agreement. "Or any other time, for that matter. I don't know why he came to Oxford. He certainly didn't come to learn anything."

The man shifted uneasily, catching their tone of disrespect.

"Well, fellow, I suppose you might try the Yellow Parrot."

"The Yellow Parrot, sir? What might that be?"

Both men smiled, and Short said, "Why, it's an inn, a place where one can get a meal of sorts. But most of all it's a place where one can find some—ah, female companionship."

"Oh, that kind of place, is it?"

"I'm afraid so. Go on into town, and you'll find it at the end of the longest street there."

"I be thanking you, sirs."

Despite his ungainly appearance there was a sort of grace

about the fellow, and as they watched him mount the larger of the two horses and move away, Carstairs said, "I doubt if he'll get much sense out of Brandon. He's probably been drunk all day."

"I don't see how he does it. If I drank as much as he did, I wouldn't be able to hit the ground with my hat."

The horses disappeared around one of the buildings, and Carstairs shook his head. "It's too bad about Winslow. He could do anything he wanted to."

"If only he wanted to do something other than drink and chase wenches."

"He succeeds at that well enough."

"He's good enough with a sword and a bow."

Carstairs widened his eyes and nodded once. "I'd hate to have him come at me. Even drunk he can defeat most men. Well, come along. Let's find something ourselves to drink."

Polly Townsend put four tankards of ale on the table, which was littered with markers and chips. The four men who sat there were all drunk to some degree, but Brandon, she saw, was so drunk he could barely sit in his chair. She leaned over and whispered to him, "Get out of this game. You ain't fit to play."

Brandon Winslow stared at her through bleary eyes. He was eighteen years old but looked five years older. "Oh, come on, Polly. I can beat these fellows with one hand tied behind my back."

All three of the other players grinned. One of them, a burly man dressed in fine clothes that did not conceal his lower financial status, said, "Leave 'im alone, Polly." He picked up a tankard of ale, drank quickly, then set it down. "Come on. Let's 'ave another hand."

"Sure," Brandon said. His movements were slowed down by half, and Polly was certain he was thinking at a similar speed.

He leaned toward her and smelled her perfume as she leaned over him. "What do you want, Polly?" He reached up, grabbed her, pulled her down, and kissed her, almost missing her mouth. "You won't leave a fellow alone, will you?"

Polly said, "You need to go to bed, Brandon. You ain't slept in forty-eight hours."

"I can . . . go on like this forever."

The three other men winked at each other with broad grins. The burly one named Matthew Smith said, "Yer right, Winslow. Now c'mon. Let's 'ave another hand."

The card game started again, with Winslow losing.

It was interrupted when a tall, skinny man came in and looked around, hat in hand. Polly went to him at once. "You want something to eat?"

"No, miss, I'm looking for Master Brandon Winslow."

Polly studied the tall fellow. He was obviously a servant. His hands were rough and his face was weathered. "What do you want with him?"

"I got a message from his family."

"Well, that's him over there in that chair."

The man nodded; he had already spotted young Brandon Winslow. He moved over quickly to the table and said, "Master Winslow?"

Brandon looked up and had to blink and shake his head before his vision cleared. "Who is that? Why, that's you, Nap."

"Yes, sir. Message from your family."

"Well, what is it?"

Nap looked at the other gamblers and Polly. "Maybe we'd better go outside."

"No, tell me what it is." Winslow's voice was slurred.

"Your father says for you to come home at once."

"Why, I can't leave."

"It's your uncle, sir, Lord Edmund. He's about to die, they think."

The words startled Brandon. He straightened up and looked as if he meant to shake the cobwebs out of his brain. "All right," he said. "I'll come."

Smith protested at once, "Nah, you ain't going nowhere until you pay up."

"I've told you, Smith, I'll have to get the money from my father."

Smith suddenly leaned forward. "All right. I'll take that ring until you bring the cash back."

"No, you can't have the ring."

Smith's eyes narrowed. "I say I will." He reached over. Brandon's reactions were slow. Smith grabbed his wrist with his left hand and jerked the ring off with his right. He tossed it up in the air and said, "Might be worth half of what you owe. You come back when you get the money, and you can have it back."

Drunk as he was, Brandon managed to lurch to his feet and move around the table. Smith grinned when he saw him coming. "You're not going to hurt me, are you, Brandon?"

"Give me that ring!" Brandon threw a blow that missed the big man's face by a foot. Smith struck him a stunning blow on the forehead. The blow sent Brandon down, and by the dazed look in his eye, Polly knew he was seeing stars and colors. He rolled over, pushed himself up, and staggered. Nap grabbed one arm and Polly the other. "Come on, Brandon. You're too drunk to fight."

"I'm gonna have that ring!"

He thrust himself back at Smith, but the fight didn't last long. Smith was a rough character who had bludgeoned many men to the ground with his huge fists. He now took pleasure in driving blows into Brandon, who resorted feebly to trying to block them. Finally Smith gave one last blow to Brandon's mouth and laughed as he fell. He was about to kick him, but Polly jumped between them. "Leave him alone, Matt."

"Oh, I forgot he was your sweetheart. He ain't no man,

Polly." He laughed roughly and then tossed the ring in the air. "Right pretty bauble."

He looked down at Winslow and said, "When he wakes up, you better tell him I'll have the rest of my money or I'll take more than this ring from him."

The world seemed to be made of nothing but thick darkness. Brandon came out of what appeared to him to be an ebony pit with no light whatsoever. He opened his eyes and moved his head. His lips were swollen, and his ribs ached as though a mule had kicked him.

"Are you feeling pretty bad, Brandon?"

The words came from his right. Brandon turned his head and immediately winced. He felt exactly as if someone were driving a red-hot stake through his temple. He waited for a moment with his eyes closed until the pain lessened and then opened them. "What happened, Polly?"

"You were a fool is wot happened." Polly Townsend was an attractive woman, if you liked well-padded, rosy-cheeked women. And she had formed an unmistakable affection for Brandon Winslow. She put her hand on his forehead and said, "You need to go back to sleep. No way through this but through this. Best you try and do it without waking."

"How long have I been here?"

"All night. It's almost dawn now."

Memory came flooding back to Brandon then, and he struggled to sit up. He was in a bed and fully dressed. "Where's Nap?"

"The fellow who brought you the message? He's probably asleep."

"I've got to get home, Polly."

"You know what Smith said. He's going to have his money or he'll take it out of your hide. I did, however, get this back for you." She held out his family ring on the palm of her hand. He groaned and leaned over to take it from her.

Polly took a cloth, dipped it in a pan of cool water, and dabbed at his face. It hurt, but he said, "You're a good woman, Poll."

"You're a fool!"

"I well know that, but I've got to go home."

"You're in no shape to travel. You need to rest today. Go tomorrow."

Brandon looked up and tried to smile, but his lips were so swollen from the blows he had taken that it was a sorry effort. He reached up and put his hand on her cheek. "Thanks, Poll, for taking care of me like this."

"Look. I've got some money. I've been saving up. Let's go away somewhere."

"Go away? Go away where?"

"Anywhere. We can find a better place than the Parrot."

"Maybe we'll do that, but I've got to go home first and see about my uncle." He got to his feet painfully and swayed. "The room seems to be moving around," he murmured.

"Don't go," Polly said. She put herself against him and pulled his head down and kissed him gently on the cheek. She whispered, "We could have a good time, you and me. We get along."

Brandon Winslow felt a moment's compunction. He was not an insensitive young man, but women were so drawn to him that it seemed impossible to keep them at bay. He had taken what they had to give but had never given anything of himself. "I have to go," he said, "but I'll come back."

Polly drooped and started to turn away.

"I'll come back," he insisted, seeing her face.

"No, you never will, Brandon. You never go back to nothin'."

Brandon saw he had hurt her and said quickly, "You'll see, Poll."

"I'll get your servant and fix you something to eat," she muttered, "before you go."

"Just something soft, Polly. I can't chew much."

Half an hour later, after eating a breakfast, he followed Nap out to the horses. Polly stood in the door. Nap said, "That there's a fine-looking woman, sir. Taken with you, ain't she, now?"

"Be quiet, Nap."

Nap glanced at him with surprise, for they had always been good friends, as far as a servant can be friends with one of the nobility. "No offense, sir. I can see she likes you."

His words cut Brandon. He knew he had behaved badly, and he tried to put the woman's face out of his mind. *I'll come back,* he thought, but he knew that he never would.

"Let's go on to Stoneybrook, Nap."

"Yes, sir, and we'd better do it in a hurry. Mr. Claiborn he said it didn't look like your uncle would make it."

As the two men rode away, Brandon thought of the money he had lost, and his opinion of his own merits, which was never very high, dropped further. "I'm no good," he muttered. "I'm no good for anything at all."

ॐ

Stuart and Heather stood back from the bed where Edmund Winslow lay, and waited silently. They had been summoned by Claiborn. Claiborn leaned forward and picked up his brother's hand. He was somewhat bent with age now but had good health and a clear mind. His elder brother, on the other hand, had a face the color of putty and lips that were already pouting outward, as happened to so many in death.

"Can you hear me, Brother?" Claiborn asked.

Edmund Winslow's eyes fluttered and for a moment they were clear and aware. Then he whispered, "Yes—Brother."

"How do you feel?"

"I want—to tell you something before I die." The words came

in short gasps on labored breath, and Claiborn knew that his brother was on the very threshold of death. He remembered a line of poetry by John Donne: *I tune the instrument here at the door.*

"You were always—the good brother—and I was the bad one."

"Don't say that, Edmund!"

"True enough." Edmund's eyes opened wide, and he seemed to see beyond the room where he lay in his bed. He had no wife now. He had been married, but the woman had betrayed him, and none of them knew where she had gone. He began to breathe more shallowly, and his chest heaved, and Claiborn thought he was gone. But then Edmund whispered again. "You—were always the—good brother . . ."

"You had a hard time for a while, Edmund, but you changed. You know the Lord now."

His words seemed to bring great comfort to the dying man. "That's right," Edmund whispered. "I know Jesus now, thanks—to you."

"I wish I could do something for you."

"You have." The words were barely audible "You brought me to know the Lord. I can meet Him now without fear."

Claiborn stood beside the bed, holding his brother's hand. He felt the hand tighten and then loosen, and then a single gust of air was expelled from Edmund Winslow, and Claiborn whispered, "Farewell, Brother. You'll have no problems and no pain and no regrets from here on." He sat for a long time holding the hand of his dead brother, and finally Stuart moved to stand beside him. "He's gone, Father."

"Yes. He went easily, calling on the Lord."

Stuart put his hand on his father's shoulder. "That's your doing. He loved you very much, sir."

"And I loved him."

Stuart was silent for a while, and then he said, "And you'll be lord of Stoneybrook now. You have the title."

"It means nothing to me except, perhaps, that I can do some

good for my family." He stood up slowly. Looking down at his brother's face, he said, "He looks calm, doesn't he?"

"I believe he is."

"Well, we all must go. As the scripture says, 'It is appointed unto man once to die.' My time is not far off."

"You're a strong man, Father."

"Well, I can't have many years left. And since I lost your mother, I've been anxious to go to her and to my Lord. One day you'll have the title, Son." He suddenly asked, "No sign of Brandon?"

"No, not yet."

Claiborn did not speak. He was thinking how different his son and his grandson were. Stuart steady, reliable, faithful to his God and his family, to everyone. And then there was Brandon, faithful to nothing except his wild, undisciplined impulses.

"We can't wait on him. We'll have the funeral as soon as possible."

"Yes, Father. I think that will be good."

❧

Stuart and his father were in the fields. They had been talking to Orrick, who was now supervisor of all the lands that composed Stoneybrook. He was not a young man any longer, but still the outdoor life had given him endurance, it seemed. He looked up and said, "Look, sir, there's Nap, and I believe he has your son with him."

Stuart and Claiborn both turned around, but neither said anything. They waited until the two men pulled up their horses. They saw that Brandon was the worse for wear. His clothes were dirty and worn, his face was puffy, and a raw, unattended cut on his jaw had been bleeding.

Stuart said nothing but waited until his father spoke, anger and disappointment strong in his voice. "You found him, I see, Nap."

"Oh, yes, sir, I found 'im." Nap looked from the lords of Stoneybrook to Brandon and then hung his head.

"I'm sorry I'm late," Brandon said.

"Late?" Stuart thundered. *"Late?"* He strode over to his son and pulled him from the saddle. Although Brandon was the taller man, he didn't fight. He refused to look his father in the eye. "You could've been here, Brandon. In time to say farewell to Uncle Edmund. But no, you were—what? In a fight of some kind?" He leaned closer and smelled him. "You reek of beer and women. Is that what you were up to as your uncle lay dying?" He pushed the young man back to his horse. "The funeral will be tomorrow," he spat out. "Go and catch your rest and a bath before your mother has to see you."

Brandon stood there, obviously ashamed, not wanting to stay, not wanting to go.

Stuart frowned and shooed him off. "Go! Go and make yourself presentable."

"Yes, sir." Brandon turned and left. Claiborn turned to Stuart. He started to speak but shook his head sadly and followed Brandon away.

Stuart moved over to where Nap was holding the horses.

"I hate a talebearer, Nap, but I need to know what happened."

"I—I don't like to say, sir."

"I know you don't, but I need to know."

"Well, sir, he was in a card game, and he got into a fight with one of the men. Got pretty badly beaten."

"What else?"

"Well, sir, you knows Master Brandon. The ladies always like him. A woman took care of him, patched him up, don't you see."

"What kind of a woman?"

"Just a barmaid. Her name was Polly."

"Keep all this quiet, Nap. But then I know you will."

"Oh, yes, sir. I always liked Master Brandon."

"Everybody does," Stuart said grimly. "That's his misfortune. He knows how to make people like him—and it's hard to thrash someone you like."

ℑ

"Your father wants to see you, Master Brandon."

Brandon had been sitting outside enjoying the morning air. He looked at the maidservant who had brought him the message and said heavily, "All right, Betty." Getting up, he went into the house and found his father behind the big desk where he conducted his business. He had a sheet of paper in his hand. It had been sealed. Brandon could see that the seal was broken.

"This is a letter from Oxford," Stuart wearily said. "You've been expelled."

"I'm not surprised, sir."

Stuart wadded the paper up and threw it across the room. He was usually a calm, even-keeled sort of man, always had been, but Brandon was clearly driving him to the point of desperation.

"I have no idea what to do with you, Brandon. You have everything a man could want. Good looks, a fine mind that you never use for anything. You have everything except honor."

"I can't argue with that, sir."

"There's a verse in the Bible in the Psalms. I was reading it the other day, and I thought about you. The psalm says, 'I will not lay my honor in the dust.' And yet there you are, laying the family's name—our honor—God's honor—in the dust. What am I to do with you, Brandon?"

Brandon had been dreading this interview and he had been thinking of how he would answer his father. He was bitterly ashamed of himself and had slept little. "I learned one thing at Oxford—"

"Well, I'm glad you learned something! What is it?"

"I've learned that I'm no man for the law or the church. And I'm no businessman, as you know well enough. But there's one profession I can master and do well in."

"And what is that?"

"The same as I've always said—the army."

"The army? You still want to go into the army? I thought you'd given up on that nonsense."

"I know I'd be a good soldier, sir."

"You have no discipline, Brandon. That's the first thing a soldier has to have."

"I think they could put it into me. If I like a thing, I can do it. You know that, sir."

Stuart looked down at his hands. Then his face softened. "Alright. You'll get your start, and then perhaps you'll come to your senses."

"I'll do whatever you say, Father. I'd even go as a common soldier."

"No, your mother would never sleep at night. I want you to be an officer."

"Thank you, sir."

"It's my last gift to you, Son, until you prove yourself."

"Yes, sir. I appreciate what you're doing."

"Go see your mother."

"Yes, sir." As soon as Brandon was outside the room, he drew a great sigh of relief. "Well, that's an unbelievable turn of events! I wouldn't have been surprised if he had kicked me out." He made his way down the hall until he came to the room his parents shared. He knocked on the door, and when he heard his mother's voice he went in. Heather Winslow was standing beside a window. Brandon could clearly see the sadness in her. There was a gentleness in this woman, and Brandon had always loved her dearly. He was so ashamed that he could not meet her eyes now, but he managed to say, "I've made such a mess of things, Mother."

"Yes, but you're still my son, and you're your father's son."

"Not much of either of you in me, as far as I can tell. I can't do anything right. I never have."

"I gave you to God, Brandon, the day you were born."

"God? Why, Mother? God won't have me."

She ignored his harsh words. "I have his promise that you'll serve him some day. That you'll bring him honor."

"I wish I could believe that." Brandon shook his head, a miserable expression etched on his features. "I wish I were like Father and Grandfather."

"Your father had a difficult time finding his way when he was your age."

Brandon steeled himself and said, "Father and I have spoken. I'm going into the army."

She wavered, looked to the window, then back to him. "I'll pray for you every day, Brandon. You are not as lost as you feel."

She lifted her hands, and he took them and kissed them. "Thank you, Mother. I'll try to be a better man—the man you believe me to be. I must get ready to leave now."

He made it to the doorway before she said, "Brandon?"

He turned and looked her in the eye. "Yes?"

"I plan on wearying God with my petitions for you. You know that, right? You are fighting him now. But you can't fight him forever."

He looked to the floor, searching for something right to say. In the end, he simply walked away.

6

Brandon Winslow ran his hand down the bare back of Alice Poplin and idly thought, *It's 1553. I've been a soldier for two years.* He laughed aloud; it was a strange thought for a man engaged as he was. He was lying beside Alice Poplin, the wife of his commanding officer, Major Cecil Poplin. Softly he stroked the silky skin of Alice's back, and it amused him that a wayward thought could interrupt such a delicious activity. But then, he had a strangely active imagination, which frequently made such strange leaps. He had been carrying on a torrid affair with Alice for three months and was beginning to tire of her. She was an attractive woman with a tempting body, but she had no more mind than a mouse.

As these thoughts came to him, he continued to stroke Alice's back, and she wiggled and cried, "You will drive me mad!" Alice turned over and faced Brandon. She put her arms around his neck, drew him closer, and kissed him passionately. "Love me," she whispered. "Love me as you always do."

Brandon grinned and drew her closer, but at that instant a banging on the door drew his attention away. "Who can that be?" he muttered.

Alice froze and stared in horror at the door.

Brandon knew that he had taken a terrible risk in bringing

Alice to his room. If word got out that he was having an affair with the major's wife, there would be trouble he didn't need. During his months of service as a soldier, he had done well in every aspect of military expertise. But despite his excellent record in the field, he had stayed in trouble most of the time for breaking the rules. Now he called out, "Who is it?"

"It's me—Caleb."

"Go away, Caleb."

"Open the door, Brandon. Quick. There's trouble!"

Throwing the cover back, Brandon padded over to the door. He opened it a crack but was shoved backward as Caleb Carter came in. Carter was a big man with blond hair and deep-set blue eyes. He glanced at Alice. "Have you lost your mind, Brandon?"

"If you've come to preach at me, take your sermon somewhere else."

"Don't you know the major has come back?"

Brandon stared at his friend. He and Carter had hit it off from the beginning, which was strange, considering that they were so different. Carter was always the good soldier, obeying orders, keeping within the lines drawn for him in His Majesty's army while Brandon had delighted in trying to redraw those lines. "He was supposed to be gone for three days," Brandon exclaimed.

"Well, he's not. He's back, and he's looking for his wife."

Alice's face turned pale. "Brandon, he'll kill us!"

"He won't kill anybody."

"You're a fool, Brandon!" Caleb cried. "If he catches you, he'll call you out."

"A duel? Don't be stupid. He'd never challenge me. I'd cut him into pieces."

"You may be the best man with a sword or with a pistol in this company, but if you fought a duel with your commanding officer you know what would happen. You'd hang for it."

"All right. Get out now, Caleb."

"I'm telling you that you'd better get that woman out of here." Caleb cast a disgusted look at Alice. She had slept with more than one of the soldiers under her husband's command. "You're risking your career, your life, for nothing—worse than nothing."

Brandon grinned broadly. "Oh, come, now. Alice is worth a little risk. Now, you go on. I'll see you later."

With a look of despair Caleb shook his head, then turned and left.

Brandon locked the door and turned back to Alice. The heightened intrigue had made his pulse race, and desire for his mistress once more flowed through him.

"I should go, Brandon," Alice said, moving to the edge of the bed.

"No, we have time. Come, darling. This might be our last chance." He pulled her closer and promptly put all thoughts of Major Cecil Poplin out of his head.

❧

"The major wants to see you, Brandon."

Brandon, who was lying flat on this back and staring up at the blue sky, replied sleepily, "What does he want, Caleb?"

"How should I know? You'd better hope it's not about his wife."

"He's a fool. He can't see what's going on under his nose."

"No, he's not a fool. He's simply sly, hiding his emotions. You'd better hurry and find out what he wants. He looked upset about something."

"All right. I suppose I must." Brandon came to his feet in one easy motion and slapped Carter on the shoulder. "What do you say we take a break, Caleb? Take a run to London and see what's going on there."

Caleb didn't smile back. "You go see what the major wants."

With a sigh Brandon made his way to the major's tent.

When he entered, he found Major Poplin speaking to one of his men. Poplin was a small man, and at the age of forty-five he had gained weight. He had tried pulling his clothes tighter, but that only emphasized the fat on his stomach. He peered at Brandon with close-set eyes and then glanced at the other man. "We'll talk about this later. Please excuse us."

"Yes, Major."

As soon as the lieutenant left, Poplin said, "We've got a crisis, and I'm sending you to take care of it, Winslow."

"What kind of a crisis, sir?"

Poplin put his hands behind his back and glanced furtively up at Brandon. Apparently it infuriated him that he had to look up at the young man. Brandon stifled a smile. Poplin had seen to it that he had difficult tasks, but never had he failed to meet his commanding officer's demands. He was studying Poplin carefully and expected to see some sign that the man suspected betrayal, but there was nothing there.

He's a fool. Brandon thought. *A disgrace to the uniform. He can't fight, and he can't keep his wife happy.*

"King Edward is dead."

The blunt words didn't surprise Brandon. "The king has been ill for years. Everybody knows that."

"Well, there's difficulty ahead—issues with the succession."

"Can you be specific, sir?"

"Princess Mary is next in line for the crown, but she may not get it. You know her, don't you?"

"Yes, sir. My father took me to visit her, sir, and Princess Elizabeth, too."

"Well, Princess Mary is in considerable trouble."

"How can she be in trouble?"

"The Protector, Lord Northumberland, well knows that if Mary becomes queen she'll bring Catholic persecution to the whole country. So he talked King Edward into naming Lady Jane Grey queen when he died."

"Who is she?"

"Oh, she's the granddaughter of King Henry's sister Mary. Northumberland forced Jane to marry his son, Lord Guildford Dudley."

"Why, he can't do that!"

"He *has* done it, lieutenant! Now Northumberland is leading a force to take Mary captive. If he does, she'll be executed."

"But, Major, we can't let that happen!"

"No, we can't. I have a message here that's come by courier. It's from Queen Mary." He looked up and shook his head. "You must have made quite an impression on her, Winslow. She wants you to lead the force assigned to turn Northumberland back. I think it's a mistake. You are not yet prepared for such a task."

"I think I am ready, sir. We need to send all the men possible."

"Well, I can't disobey my queen. She may bring Catholic persecution, but if Lady Jane is queen Northumberland will rule the country, and he is a devil if there ever was one! I'm sending the largest group of men we can get together. There's going to be trouble among the officers who think they ought to lead this, but Queen Mary has demanded that you lead the group. I want you to leave today. Time is of the essence."

"Yes, sir. Give me the orders, and I'll see that they are carried out. You have my guarantee Northumberland will not touch our queen."

"See it is so, then."

ꕥ

"May I be of service, my queen?"

"You have been of service already, my dear subject." Mary put forth her hand, and Mason kissed it. He had been Mary's faithful friend for years.

"You must move very quickly, Your Majesty," he urged.

Mary nodded, then accepted his help to climb into a tiny carriage. A small body of followers and knights surrounded it, all determined to reach their refuge, Framlingham Castle.

"It's a strong fortress," she had explained to her advisors. "It's close to the coast in case I have to take flight."

All along the road traveled by Mary and her entourage the people followed. They had heard the news that the king was dead, and there was outrage at the rumors that were flying that Lady Jane Grey would be queen. Most of them had never heard of her, but they had known of Mary since her childhood. Cries of "Long live Queen Mary!" followed her wherever she went, and by the time she reached Framlingham she found she was encouraged, despite the coming danger.

Some of the nobility came to Framlingham, bringing with them both townspeople and farmfolk. Mary listened as they vowed to fight to the death.

"But they are not able to fight against trained armed soldiers, are they, Lord Jerningham?" She turned to eye her host.

"Alas, no, but there will be others who will join your cause."

The next day Mary walked the parapet of the castle and waved to the people who had gathered in her support. They were passionate, but her heart faltered. Without trained soldiers they could not stand against Northumberland's army.

She looked to the horizon and saw a large band of soldiers coming, and her heart faltered.

"Northumberland—and we have no defense!" She stood still, considering how she might die with dignity if it was God's will. But as the soldiers drew closer, she recognized their leader. "It's Brandon Winslow!" she cried.

When Brandon looked up, she motioned to him and called out, "Come up, Winslow! Come up at once!" She descended to the parlor to wait for him.

It was not long until Brandon came in. He dropped to one

knee and said, "Queen Mary, we have come to fight your battles."

"I knew you would come, Brandon! Your father would do the same if he were in your place."

"He will still come. So will every true Englishman. You are the queen of England, and we will not abide any other."

Mary pulled him to his feet. "You have grown into a fine young man, Winslow." She looked up into his face and smiled as relief flowed through her. "I remember how you came in with your father and how we played chess and you and Elizabeth became close friends. I never doubted that you would come to me if I called."

Brandon smiled. "We'll make short work of this traitor."

And, indeed, that was the way it turned out. The nobility, for the most part, flocked to Mary's standard, and Northumberland saw almost at once that he was a lost man. He came finally to the castle and lifted up his hat and shouted, "Long live Queen Mary!"

That was the end of the revolt, and Northumberland was sent to the Tower. Throughout it all, Mary kept Brandon close. As they watched Northumberland led off in chains, Brandon said, "You're safe now, Your Majesty."

"No, a queen is never safe, nor a king. I will need you and your loyal support."

"You have it."

"Are you a loyal Catholic, Brandon? I don't remember you ever saying anything about religion."

"Alas, Your Majesty, I am a sorry example. If you want true religion, you must go to my father or my uncle. They are both men of great devotion."

"But what about you?"

"I'm afraid that I'm the lost sheep."

Mary reached out, and he took her hand. "I will pray that God will touch your heart."

"I would not displease my sovereign, but I must tell you my father and my mother and my uncle have prayed for me for years. I think I have sinned beyond the day of grace."

"No, you will be found. I know it!"

ᴥ

Months after Queen Mary had been crowned, Major Poplin stood at the second-floor door of the Lion Inn and eyed the four soldiers that accompanied him. "I shall go in first," he said quietly.

"Don't attack him, Major. He's a master swordsman."

"You think me an utter fool? I know that. Be ready to advance upon my call."

Cecil Poplin had succeeded in the army not because of prowess in arms or courage but because he was shrewd. He well knew that he could trap the man who had made him a cuckold only by taking him by surprise. He flung open the unlocked door. As he had been told, there was his wife in bed with Brandon Winslow.

"You'll die for this, Winslow!" he cried. He drew his sword. Brandon rolled out of bed. His sword was hanging from the top of the bedstead. He whipped it out. "Don't be a fool, Major. I'll kill you."

Poplin advanced, slashing the sword in a great arc. He knew he had no chance, but the shame that Brandon Winslow had brought upon him ate at him like acid into his soul. There had been others before him, he knew that, but Winslow had laughed at him, mocked him, and scorned him, telling everyone in the inn, the night before of his exploits with Alice. He advanced in a frenzy of strikes against the younger, stronger man, but Brandon coolly parried each one. Brandon's cold steel suddenly whipped across Poplin's chest, cutting through his uniform and making a shallow wound. Poplin gaped at Brandon as he felt the slice burn across his chest. "Sergeant! Sergeant!" he cried.

Instantly Brandon Winslow found himself facing four hardened soldiers all with swords drawn. He tried to fight them, but he was overwhelmed. When his sword was knocked from his grasp, he took a minor wound in his right arm. Two of the soldiers took him down to the ground. Poplin smiled down at him in triumph. "Brandon Winslow, you are under arrest for attempting to kill your superior officer."

At that instant Brandon knew that he had surpassed his most foolhardy moment. His bragging words the night before in front of so many in their company had obviously caught up with him. He had been caught before, but this was different. One simply did not draw a sword against a superior officer. It was not only the end of a career; it could be the end of his life. Hanging was a common enough punishment for such an offense, despite the honor and glory he had received at the side of Queen Mary.

"Lock him up and keep close guard over him. Put him on bread and water."

"Yes, sir. Come along, Winslow."

Brandon did not look at the woman who had caused his downfall, did not turn when she called out his name. He was, for the first time in his life, aware that he was no better than the village idiot. But as soon as the door shut, he heard Alice screaming, and the sergeant chuckled beside him. "I'm afraid your sweetheart there is taking a beating for her indiscretions, Lieutenant."

Ordinarily Brandon would have tried to defend Alice, but he knew that she was beyond help now—not that he could have done anything with four men guarding him. He'd brought himself this trouble—and Alice too. If only he had listened to Caleb, walked away! His mind leaped ahead to imprisonment, to a trial, to the look on his parents' faces when they heard. And the skies seemed bleak indeed.

ఌ

The trial was brief. Brandon had absolutely no chance. The commander, General Lester Stevens, was head of the court. He was old army, and the very thought of a lowly soldier wounding his commanding officer was anathema to him. He listened to the evidence and stared into space while Mason Stevens, the man appointed to handle Brandon's case, pleaded for clemency.

Finally it was all over. Brandon stood at Stevens's command. "You deserve to be hanged. If I had my way, that's what I would do. Unfortunately we have received orders from the queen that we will not be permitted to punish you as you deserve. That sentence will be set aside. But you will be stripped of your rank, dishonorably discharged from the army, and will receive fifty lashes."

Brandon did not say a word. Stevens glared at him. "Do you have anything to say?"

"No, sir."

"I should think not! Take him away. Major Poplin, you see to the punishment."

Poplin smiled and nodded. "I will do my best, sir."

Indeed, the lashing, which came later that day, was a masterpiece of cruelty. Poplin appointed one of his sergeants, a big, burly man with the strength of an ox. He had been known to kill men under his lash, and he had grinned when Major Poplin said, "Get the cat with the metal barbs in the thong. Strip his flesh from his bones, Baines."

"Yes, sir. I'll give him the best the house has to offer."

Brandon was led out, and one look showed him that Cecil Poplin had seen to it that the audience was large. As far as he could see, every soldier in the regiment was there and many civilians as well. Brandon said nothing but removed his jerkin, and Baines stripped the thin shirt from his back. Baines leered at him as he fastened Brandon's hands to a post and said, "I hope you enjoy this as much as I will."

Brandon did not reply. He waited.

Poplin said, "Let him have it, sergeant."

The first blow drove the breath out of Brandon's body. Lines of fire, it seemed, gained heat with every moment. With each blow he had to grit his teeth to keep from crying out. Mercifully he passed out, and as he lost consciousness, he thought, *I'll die at this. He'll kill me.*

❧

"It's a wonder he didn't die." The surgeon, a tall, thin man with salt-and-pepper-colored hair, shook his head. "Look at his back. I don't see how he lived through it. It's the worst I've ever seen."

Caleb could hardly bear to look down. "He'll bear those scars the rest of his life."

"He's lucky," said the surgeon, whose name was Clemson. "He'll heal up, but he's a fool. He'll carry the scars inside as well. I've seen it before. When a man takes a beating like this, he may heal up in the flesh, but his spirit will always be raw."

Caleb said, "He'll need some care, won't he?"

"Oh, yes. He won't be able to tend himself for a while." He glanced over his shoulder and then back to Caleb. "I'm sorry, but he can't stay here. According to the commander, we're to cast him out the gates now."

"Don't fret over it," Caleb said. "I'll see to his care. Thank you, sir."

❧

For the next two weeks Caleb gave short shift to his own duties, and he had the surgeon come and treat Brandon's wounds at an inn where he had secured a room for him. He was relieved to see Brandon's skin finally begin to heal, but it was as the surgeon had said. Something had gone out of Brandon Winslow, and it was a dismal thing to see.

Caleb made his way to the inn early one morning two weeks

later wearily rubbing his eyes. He had been up the night before, thinking through Brandon's situation, trying to see what might make him whole again. *Brandon must put this behind him. I'll have to get him back to his family.*

When he entered Brandon's room, with one look, he knew his friend was gone. Even his few belongings had disappeared. Stepping outside, he hailed the innkeeper below. "Have you seen anything of Mr. Winslow?"

"No, sir. I've been up since dawn. Nobody came out since then."

Caleb asked around, and finally the truth sank in.

Brandon Winslow had left under cover of darkness because he did not wish to be found.

❧

Caleb Carter stood before Stuart and Heather Winslow. He had given them his report and softened it as much as he could, but he saw that they were heartbroken. "I'm very sorry, sir, and you, madam. I tried to help Brandon all that I could."

"I thank you very much for helping our son and telling us what you know. You'll stay with us tonight before you go back."

"No, sir, I must go back at once. I really would be in trouble if I stayed." Caleb shook his head. "He has so many gifts. So many talents. And he's thrown them all away."

He immediately regretted his words. Heather slumped, and Stuart narrowly caught her. She wept, broken, as lost for a moment as her son, it seemed.

"It's all right, Heather," Stuart murmured. "Somehow, God will see it right again."

PART TWO

Lupa

7

Lupa Valerik watched as the skinny man took the glass. Her eyes gleamed when she saw his hand trembling so violently that some of the liquor sloshed out onto his wrist. She took his hand and guided the glass up. “Drink deep,” she said, and forced the man to drink, but after a while he turned his head away. “Can’t . . . drink any more.” Lupa took the glass from him, and watched him, holding a glass in each hand. *I’ve given him enough to drug three men. I hope he doesn’t die. That would be trouble.*

The man slumped slowly forward. Lupa shoved him to the bed. He fell back on it, mumbling incoherently, and she laughed. Putting the two glasses on the table, she came back and noted with satisfaction that the drug had done its work well. The man’s eyes were rolled half upward in his head, and his lips moved, but no sound came out. Working efficiently, she removed the rings from his fingers and put them into a hidden pocket in her dress. She found a bag containing his gold and silver under his coat. It had a good heavy weight to it, and her broad lips curled upward in a smile. She found another bag with a silver hairbrush, a comb, and a small silver flask. “Easy to pluck as a dead chicken, aren’t you?” After wrapping her findings in a shawl, she came to stand over the man. For a moment she fingered the knife hidden under the folds of her dress and thought of ending his life, just in case he remembered her, but she put the notion away.

Leaving the room, she made her way down the unlit staircase. When she stepped outside, she saw that the dark sky was filled with scattered clouds drifting toward a silver moon. The fall of 1553 had been harsh, and the moon looked pockmarked and weary. She shivered and drew her shawl closer about her, then paused and waited. It was very still, and she thought about the man that she had just robbed. She felt no regret, only disgust for him and all men like him. He had approached her at the inn, as she had known he would, and she had led him on. Now he would wake up without a farthing in his pocket—or anything of worth at all. Lupa smiled. It pleased her to think of him begging the innkeeper for help.

"Did he give you any trouble, Lupa?"

Lupa started as a man suddenly appeared from the shadows. Rez Fabin could do that sort of thing, appearing and disappearing like a ghost, but even after two years of knowing him, it still frightened Lupa. She lifted her chin. "No more than your average drunken sot."

Fabin was a lean man with a sharp face and pair of deep-set hazel eyes. He was, Lupa knew, a totally immoral man with a vicious streak that appeared from time to time, but he had never treated Lupa badly. In fact, he had once rescued her from the gypsy camp, fighting off Duke Largo, the leader of the band, to win her freedom. It had been a bloody affair, and while Largo had survived, he was in no condition to come after them when Rez took her away. After a time she had broken off their affair, but Rez didn't care, for he could always get a woman. He was different from Duke that way. Duke had wanted to own her.

"Did he have much on him?"

"Yes. He had some rings and some gold and silver."

"Good. Give me my share."

"No, you'll just lose it gambling."

"That's my business. You give it to me now. Or next time you'll see how well you can find that potion that can put a man out so handily."

Lupa sighed and pulled out the bag of coins and rings. She kept the bag with the silver brush, comb, and flask hidden in the folds of her skirts. Wearily she counted out the coins, handing Rez his share. He slipped them into a bag at his waist, grinning in the moonlight. "Well done, lovely. Well done. Now, come on. I want to show you something." He led her from the side door of the inn to the stables, where a wagon was already hitched to two horses. "How do you like those horses?" Fabin said.

Lupa frowned in confusion. "Why, they're brown. What happened to the white ones?"

"That's them." Fabin laughed. "At least until the first rain. Whoever buys them will get a shock."

"Why did you go to all that trouble?"

"Because I want to sell them, and as soon as your jilted lover in there wakes up, he'll have the law out looking for white horses. By that time we'll have sold them and have the money. Come on, now."

"Where are we going?"

"London, I guess."

"No, let's go to Bath."

They argued, and Fabin finally said, "I suppose there are plenty of pickings in Bath for a woman with your looks. And I like the gambling there."

"If we get any money, you'll lose it all gambling. You're no gambler, Rez. When will you realize that?"

"Shut your mouth, Lupa! We split down the middle. I don't ask you what you do with your money, so keep your mouth shut about my cards." Fabin grinned at her in the moonlight. "I've got to have one fault, lovely. What if I was to die? I've got to have at least one sin to repent or Saint Peter will find my arrival a bore."

She laughed at that. "You've got more than one sin to repent, Fabin."

He merely laughed at her and said, "Here. Put that stuff inside. You can ride in there if you want to. The team is rested."

Lupa agreed. She climbed into the back of the wagon and arranged some of her clothes and blankets into a makeshift bed. She was tired, for she had missed all of one night's sleep and part of another. She waited until she felt the wagon sway as Fabin mounted to the seat and listened as he spoke to the horses. They moved forward at a slow walk. One of the wagon's wheels had a squeak, but it had a rhythm about it, and the sound of the horses' hooves made a counterpoint. Closing her eyes, she thought about the haul that they had made and what might be ahead for them in Bath, but then she put it out of her mind. Rez would figure it out. He always did.

Rez Fabin was good for her. He was protection, for one thing. And a lone woman needed that. As she grew more sleepy, she thought of how they had made their way across the south coast. They made a good team. She drew men by her exotic looks, and if any of them tried to hurt her, Rez Fabin was there to prevent that. It was a hard life and a dangerous one, but Lupa dropped off to sleep thinking that at least for tonight all was well.

Lupa slept deeply, even though the road was rough. But when she heard Rez calling out to the horses, she pulled herself up and looked around. "What's the matter? Why are you stopping?"

"Man down beside the road. He looks dead, but maybe he's got something worth taking."

At once Lupa rose and swung over the side. She waited until Fabin came near with a lantern in his hand. The moon had grown brighter, it seemed, and she could clearly see the man in the pearlescent light. After a nod from Rez, she carefully approached.

She leaned over and waited for the man to move. Was he even breathing? "What's wrong with you?" she asked, but no answer came. She drew her knife and with her free hand she rolled the man over. He was limp, and the only sound he made was a painful groan. Lupa leaned forward and studied his face. She had become an expert in reading the expressions of men, for she had seen the most vile and evil things in them since she had come of age. This man looked different. His face, she saw, was not harsh, and it was hardly the face of a working man.

"Is he dead?"

"No, he's not dead." Lupa sheathed her knife and picked up the man's hand. His palms were softer than the hands of a working man, and yet he had calluses, as if he were a fighting man. A soldier? Fabin drew alongside Lupa and stared down. "What's the matter with him? Is he drunk?"

"I don't think so. I think he's hurt."

"Get his goods, Lupa, and let's get on with it."

Lupa leaned forward and smelled the man's breath. "He's not drunk." She put her hand behind him to move him, and he groaned again. She felt something damp and rolled him to one side. His back was bleeding. She let him roll back again with another groan and searched through his jerkin pulling out a packet containing a letter along with a small bag of money.

Fabin reached forward and took the ring from the man's finger. "Any coinage?"

"Yes. But hold the lantern close. There's a letter here." She scanned the old, worn letter and then said, "It says here this man's name is Brandon Winslow. His father is a nobleman." She had been taught to read as a child, but Rez had not.

"Oh, this one's a lord, is he?"

"Well, his father is."

"Let's get away from here, Lupa. If someone found us with 'im, it'd be prison for us and maybe the noose."

But Lupa continued to study the letter. "We're taking him with us," she said abruptly.

"Not bloody likely!" Fabin stared at her. "What do you want to do that for? Get his bag of money and let's go."

"No, not without him."

Rez hesitated. "He's a pretty fellow, but that don't mean nothing to you."

"I'll find a way to use him." Lupa smiled, and there was cruelty in her expression. "I'll use him, Rez, like I do all men."

"He's a son of a rich man. He could be trouble."

"No. You'll see. He'll be a benefit to us both. Now, come on. Help me get him into the coach."

❦

The sharp pain in his back brought Brandon out of the dark pit he had fallen into. He'd had bad dreams and at times thought he heard voices, but he could not identify any of them. He tried to remember what had happened, but he caught only fitful brief scenes, mere flickers in his memory. He remembered leaving the camp and getting on the road. He remembered growing feverish and stopping and his back hurting more and more. Now it frightened him that he didn't know where he was. Try and try as he might, he could not remember where he was or how he had got here.

He knew that he was in a bed. When he opened his eyes for a moment, the room seemed to move. He closed them quickly and realized that his back was not as painful as it had been and that there was something cooling on it. He opened his eyes again and found himself looking into a face.

It was a woman. He tried to think if he knew her. Her hair was as black as ebony, and her eyes were large, dark, and well-shaped. She was wearing a dress made of some emerald-green material, and around her head was a crimson neckerchief that had slipped back to reveal her raven hair. He watched her move and then heard the sound of water pouring. Suddenly he was aware of a raging thirst. Gently she lifted his head and said, "Here. Drink." He greedily guzzled the water. It ran out of his mouth and down his neck, but he ignored it. When he had drained the mug, she set it aside and then turned back to stare at him. "So, you are awake. How do you feel?"

"Where—where is this place?" he managed to ask. His lips were still dry, and his tongue seemed to have swollen. "What am I doing here?"

"My . . . cousin and I found you on the road. This is the first inn we came to. It's called the Silver Fox. You want some more water?"

"Yes." He drank again. She was close enough for him to smell a strong scent, like violets. She put the mug down and then leaned over him. He guessed she was in her late twenties. She had golden olive skin, and her eyebrows were beautifully arched. There was a fullness in her lips that any red-blooded man would find stirring—not that Brandon was in any condition to do anything about it. "Why did you bother to pick me up?"

"You would have died if we had left you there. Are you hungry?"

"Not very."

"You'll have to eat. My . . . cousin will soon bring us food."

He stared at her, and then memory came flooding back all at once. How he had made a fool of himself over Alice Poplin—a worthless woman if there ever was one—how the major had seen him beaten, how Caleb had had to see to his care. What a mess he'd made of things.

What now? Where? He could not go home. He could never go home again—not until he had redeemed himself.

He looked up at the woman, who was watching him intently. "What's your name?" he asked wearily.

"Lupa."

"Just Lupa? No last name?"

"Lupa is enough for now."

He stared at her and started to respond, but at that moment the door opened and a man came in bearing food. He was strongly built, dark-skinned, and had gold earrings dangling from both ears. Brandon said in wonder, "You're gypsies."

The man laughed. "Well, he's got his sense back at least. Yes, we are gypsies. Here. Something to eat. I'll add it to what you owe us. Let me help you up."

Brandon struggled to sit upright. Surprised, he said, "My back is better."

"I'm a healing woman. I put some ointment on it. We'll put it on for several days, and you'll be well."

"Who gave you such a lashing?" the man asked.

"Don't ask so many questions, Rez," Lupa said. She handed Brandon a bowl and asked, "Can you feed yourself?"

"Of course." He took the bowl and began to eat rapidly. He finished the soup and felt better. As Lupa took the bowl he asked, "Why did you bother with me?"

"I like good-looking men." He stared at her, not knowing what to make of that. "I read the letter from your father. He's a great lord, is he?"

"He has a title, yes." He stared at them. The man looked like a villain. As for the woman, she had an exotic beauty that men would fight for. Suddenly a thought came that amused him. "Well, I was running away from one trouble, and it seems that I've landed in more."

"What makes you think we'll get you in trouble?"

"You look like trouble to me," Brandon said.

"We'll help you, then you can help us," Lupa said quickly.

Brandon's mind was working now. He shook his head and said as firmly as he could, "You won't get a reward from my family for helping me."

Lupa touched the letter. "He sounds like a good man. He wants to help you."

"He is a good man, but I'm not. That letter is quite old. And much has . . . transpired since he wrote it."

Fabin laughed suddenly. "That's coming right out with it. What have you done that's so bad? How'd you get your back torn up like that?"

"It's not a very original story. I was a soldier in the army, and my commanding officer had a witless but pretty wife. She liked me, and the major caught us. He managed to arrange it so I'd get fifty lashes and be drummed out of the army."

"Were you a good soldier?" Lupa asked curiously.

"Yes. But apparently I was better with women and playing the fool."

Lupa laughed, and her eyes seemed to glow. "Most men don't know that until it's too late."

Brandon cocked his head. "I had some money, but I'd wager you've taken that, so I can't pay you. So . . . what is it you want?"

Lupa leaned closer. "You can go home and get some money, and then you can pay us."

"I won't do that. Once my parents know what I have done, they will disown me." He smiled, but there was no amusement in it. "You know, I met Princess Elizabeth once."

"Who's she?" Lupa asked curiously.

"Well, she may be queen of England one day if enough people die. She asked me if I was a good man, and I said, 'No, I was born in sin from my mother's womb.'"

"Me too," Fabin grinned. "We're brothers, then."

"We'll help you, Brandon," Lupa said. "I'll find a way to put you to good use."

"That's probably what you do with all men."

"You're right about that." Fabin grinned, a pirate among comrades.

"So you'd use me, would you, Lupa?" Brandon asked, eyeing her.

"Yes. I would." She stared back at him.

"Well, you're an honest woman—which is rare."

She reached out and put her hand on his chest. "Continue to be honest with me and I shall be honest with you."

"I'm in debt to you," Brandon said soberly. "Rest assured I'll pay my debts, Lupa."

❧

The weather had warmed up, strangely enough, during the two weeks that Brandon had convalesced at the Silver Fox Inn. Lupa had taken good care of him. She sat now at a table, watching a card game between Fabin and Brandon. He had insisted she teach him Spanish, and she had been amazed by how quickly he picked up the language. She asked him, "How can you learn so quickly?"

"Always found it easy to learn languages," he replied.

"Which ones do you know?"

"Latin. French. A little German. A little Greek."

From time to time, in the midst of the game, she would give him a Spanish phrase or word for something, and he seemed to lock it into a box that he called a memory. She noticed with disgust that Fabin was down to the last of his money, gradually losing to Brandon. Finally he lost his last farthing, cursed, and threw the cards on the table. "You are lucky, Englishman!"

"Sometimes I am, but if that doesn't work, I cheat. I'm very good at cheating, Rez. Never been caught, at least at cards. Now, you're a cheater," Brandon said. "But, Rez, you're not a good cheater. Look. You mark the ends of the cards with your thumbnail. By the time we had gone through the deck, I had every one of them memorized, so I know what you had as well as you did." He laughed and shoved all the money back. "Never gamble with me, Rez."

Lupa laughed. "If you can convince him that he is a sorry gambler, you'd be doing him a favor. I've never been able to."

Brandon gingerly leaned forward in his chair. "We can't go on like this."

"What do you mean?" Lupa asked.

"You and Fabin paying all the bills. I'm nothing but a lazy loafer."

"We'll get our return, in spades."

Brandon looked at her in amusement. "How will you do that?"

"We'll set you up as a rich man, buy you expensive clothes. You'll use your ring, and we've got some more. When we get to Bath we'll get you into a game with rich men. Do you think you can win?"

"I always win."

"Will you do it, then?" Lupa demanded.

"I owe you, Lupa, and I have one virtue. Probably only one. I always pay my debts."

"Good," Fabin said. "I'll go see about getting you some expensive clothes. You'll have to make quite a splash in Bath. Be aware, they're pretty sharp there. If they find you cheating, they'll cut your throat."

"They won't catch me." He picked up the cards and began shuffling them as Fabin left the room. He shuffled expertly, fanning the cards and shuffling them again. He noted that Lupa was staring at him. He put the cards down and leaned back, wincing as his healing back met the back of the chair. "Why are you looking at me like that?"

The Englishman was a puzzle to Lupa. She knew a lot about men, but this one did not seem to be like any other. Finally she said, "Why have you not yet tried to make love to me, Brandon?"

Brandon frowned and glanced away from her with some embarrassment. "I don't know. I'm pretty sure it's not because I've become a good man. I'm not good and never was. But you saved my life, Lupa. I'm already tied to you for that. I don't . . . wish for another reason."

Lupa stared at him. The answer was not what she had expected. He had the most unusual face. He was handsome, of course, with a wedge-shaped face and wide mouth. A generous mouth, she thought. His eyes were a shade of blue she had never seen, very light, almost like the cornflowers that appear on the hills in the spring. His nose was straight, and his face bore no scars. His hair was a rich auburn color. But it was not his good looks that troubled her. She had founded her whole philosophy on the fact that all men were pigs, only out to use a woman, but Brandon, although he'd had many opportunities, had never once offered to put a hand on her. His answer disturbed her. "I don't think there are any good men," she said at last.

"There are some good men, Lupa. I know some. And some good women too. I'm simply not one of them, but my father is and my uncle. What you need to find is a good man."

"No chance of that."

"You'll find one. Now, teach me some more Spanish."

* * *

"Well, do I look respectable?"

Lupa studied Brandon, who was dressed in his new clothes. "You look very handsome and very prosperous."

"Just don't lose our money." Fabin grinned. "If you do, I'll cut your throat. We've put everything we had in getting you a stake together and those rich clothes."

Lupa walked around him and leaned over to pull his sleeves down. "I can't believe I set this up. It took all our money. I must be losing my mind to trust a man."

"It's usually not a good idea for a beautiful woman to put her trust in a man."

Lupa studied Brandon in his new clothes. "You really mean that?"

"Do I mean what?"

"You think I'm beautiful?"

"Never was a question about it, Lupa."

Fabin laughed. "You lose my money, and I'll mess up your own pretty face, Winslow. Then you won't be so pretty anymore."

"I won't lose."

Both Lupa and Fabin were impressed by the calm confidence that Brandon Winslow exhibited. His confidence was like an iron bar, both of them saw. He laughed at their expressions. "I won't lose," he repeated.

Lupa said, "All right. We'll be waiting for you."

He left, and the two of them watched him go with uncertainty.

"He can win," Rez muttered, "but if he wins, he could leave us here."

"You think he'd do that?"

"I don't know. He's not like anyone I ever met, but I don't know many lords." He stared at her, then turned his head to one side. "He doesn't try to bed you. Why is that? Every man I ever saw wanted you."

The same thought had troubled Lupa, despite Brandon's explanation. "Maybe I'm losing my looks."

"No. It's not that."

Lupa shrugged. "Anyway, I swore I'd never trust any man other than you, and here I've done it." The two stared at each other. Each was troubled.

Fabin shrugged, "Well, he's got us, Lupa."

Lupa did not answer. She paced back and forth, reflecting that it would be hours before Brandon Winslow returned—if he ever did!

❧

Fabin had drunk too much wine and was depressed. "He's not coming back. Not this late," he mumbled.

"He'll be back."

"What makes you think so?"

"I just know," she repeated. But deep down Lupa was disgusted with herself, fearing the worst. She had subjected herself to another man, something she swore she'd never do again.

Lupa resumed her pacing and Fabin his drinking. Finally they heard steps, then the door opened, and Brandon entered. Seeing the expression on their faces he laughed. "You thought I'd forsaken you?"

"Yes," Fabin mumbled numbly, obviously shocked by Brandon's return.

"You came back," Lupa said, and found gladness that a man in her life had kept his word.

"Well, you gave up on me. I'm disappointed. I told you, Lupa, I won't hurt you. I pay my debts." He pulled out a heavy leather bag and dropped it on the table. Fabin pounced on it and poured out coins and goods on the table.

Lupa picked up one of the rings and looked at it, then at Brandon. "You won all this and you came back?"

Fabin began counting the loot. His eyes were gleaming, and the gold earrings in his ears glittered as he swung his head from side to side. "We'll go to London where the big games are. That's what. We'll get rich!"

Lupa saw that Brandon was amused. "Tell me about how you won it."

"I'd rather learn Spanish."

"Then tell me in Spanish."

He began speaking, and Lupa leaned forward, her eyes fixed on Brandon's face. A faint hope that she had thought long dead stirred in her, and her lips parted as she listened to him tell in halting Spanish how he had succeeded.

8

Heather had seen the rider coming down the road and watched as he stopped in front of Stoneybrook, evidently asking directions. He nodded and then came riding up to the front door of the castle. She saw Stuart come out to meet him. The rider gave Stuart a paper. Stuart gave the rider a coin. The rider turned and rode away.

Heather watched as Stuart opened the sealed paper. She could see his face clearly. *Something's troubling him.* The thought saddened her.

She waited. She heard his steps, and then the bedroom door opened, and he came in with a sheet of paper in his hand.

"Well, I have news, Heather."

"Good news?"

"I am uncertain." Stuart had a rather puzzled expression on his face. "It's an invitation for me to come to the royal palace."

"For what purpose?"

"An audience with Queen Mary next Monday."

Heather blinked in surprise. "Why would she send for you, I wonder?"

"I have no idea." Stuart looked up at her, and his expression softened to one of concern. He came over and put his arm around her. "You look tired."

"I'm alright."

She knew Stuart was trying to think of some way to comfort her, but they were both sick with fear and disappointment over Brandon's disappearance. He hugged her tightly and said, "Perhaps she simply needs some advice."

Heather reveled in his embrace. She loved to feel the lean strength of his body. He was fifty-two now, but he had the body of a man much younger. "It's been a troubling time since King Edward died, hasn't it?"

"Yes, it has. People don't know what to expect from a woman as ruler."

She looked up into his eyes, clear as they had been the first day she had seen him. "You told me once that she's a strong Catholic."

"Oh, yes. She got that from her mother, Queen Catherine." Stuart bit his lower lip and added, "She wants me to bring Quentin with me. Now *that* I don't understand. He's never met her that I know of, and I'm sure I would have known it if he had."

"What could she possibly want with Quentin?"

"Not sure, but he'll have to go, of course."

Heather frowned. "Would it have anything to do with the fact that he's become quite a popular preacher?"

"I don't believe his Protestant faith—or his popularity—will endanger him," Stuart said slowly. "But it is puzzling."

"Will you be gone long?"

"Oh, I don't think so. Probably only for a day or two." She rested against him and he sighed, "Heather, try not to grieve over Brandon. We must try to remain hopeful."

"I'm sure you grieve as much as I do, Stuart."

"I'm not sure about that. A mother's love is somehow stronger than a father's."

Heather put her hand on Stuart's cheek. "I love you," she said, "and we've agreed in prayer that God is going to bring our son back to us, and I believe that he will."

❧

Stuart had been sitting in Christ Church for some time. He and Heather attended as often as possible for they both loved to hear Quentin preach, but today he was troubled by the queen's command to bring Quentin to the palace. And that is what it was, a command. Mary had always said she wanted England to return to the Catholic Church, but over and over she had expressed her desire to do so by invitation and encouragement rather than violence. But then why demand Quentin accompany him? There were rumors . . .

The service began. As always, Stuart drew himself into an attitude of prayer and worship. The splendid music was his brother's doing. Quentin himself was a fine musician, an accomplished singer, and able to play several instruments. The voices seemed to rise to the top of the church and fill the building, and the congregation felt their power.

Finally the worship was over, and a cleric stood up and read from Scripture. Quentin glanced around the building, an old church going back to Roman times. He noted also that the church was full and that many of the worshippers were poor men and women worn by toil but with faces alight as they took in the singing and now the reading of the Scripture.

Quentin entered the pulpit and greeted the congregation. Stuart had always loved the simplicity of his brother's preaching. Many preachers read from a manuscript, but Quentin seemed to have the Bible memorized and gazed out over the congregation with eyes alight. He had one of William Tyndale's bibles in his study, Stuart knew. Stuart's heart warmed as he thought of the part that he himself had played in smuggling bibles from Europe to England at the behest of the great translator. He remembered Tyndale's death with a pang, and knew that the man would ever be a part of his life.

Quentin began to speak and Stuart leaned forward to catch

every nuance of his brother's voice. "Christ views the sinner not as he is in himself but as he is in the purpose of redemption." Everyone's attention was riveted on Quentin, captured by his abrupt beginning. "His whole head is sick, sayeth Christ, but I can cure him. His whole heart is faint, but I can restore him, and I will do it. His feet have gone astray, his mouth as an open sepulchre, his eyes are windows of lust, his hands are stained with blood; but I will amend all that and make him a new creature meant to be a partaker of the inheritance of the saints in like."

Total silence, almost palpable, lay on the congregation as Quentin continued, "Jesus looks, you see, not so much to what the sinner is in himself, but to what he can make of him. He sees in every sinner the possibility of making a glorified saint who shall dwell with him forever and ever. He chose you, poor sinner, before all worlds were made and bought you with his blood. He sees you not as you are now but as you shall be when he has perfected you."

The words flowed from Quentin. Stuart again marveled at the breadth of his brother's knowledge of scripture. And even more he marveled at how simple the sermon was. Quentin's sermons always centered on Christ. Jesus was in almost every sentence, and Quentin's eyes glowed and his whole face lit up as he spoke of the glory of Jesus.

"Sinner," Quentin continued, "thou art so ashamed of thy sin that thou darest not approach a minister, but you can approach Christ. There is no pride in him and no cautious reserve such as we might rightly expect in dealing with him. Though you could not tell your own father about yourself, you can tell it all to Jesus. You could not tell the story of your sin to the wife of your bosom, but you can tell it to Jesus. There's no music that he loves so much as the voice of a sinner confessing his sin. There are no pearls that he prizes so highly as those pearly tears that repentance forms in the eye of the soul that trembles at his word. Do not imagine that he is hard to please, for he loves sinners. Don't think it's difficult to obtain access to him. Like the father in the parable, he can see a sinner when he's a great way off, and he will run to meet you and give you a hearty reception and a loving welcome."

Stuart marveled at the passion, the genuine emotion that possessed Quentin as he spoke. Many preachers spoke dryly with no sign of emotion, but not Quentin Winslow! There were actually tears in his eyes as he spoke of what Christ can do with a heart of a sinner who had come to him.

As the sermon came to an end, Quentin's voice quivered slightly. "'Oh, but he would never receive such a sinner as I am!' You might say that, but how do you know? Have you ever tried him? There is not even in hell itself a sinner who will ever dare to say that when he came to Jesus, Jesus refused to receive him. There is not a lost soul in the pit who could look up to God and truthfully say to him, 'Great God I asked for mercy through the precious blood of Jesus,' but you said, 'I will not give it to you.' No! That can never be. Neither on earth nor in hell shall there ever be one soul that trusted in Christ and then perished. I beg you, no matter what your sin is, no matter what your life has been, the Lord Jesus Christ is able to make you a new creature. May the Lord bless you and enable you to find your way to his cross and be washed forever in his blood."

A choruses of amens swept through the congregation. Stuart rose as the final prayers were said. As soon as they were done, Stuart stood back, observing the people trying to get close to Quentin. He saw one very old woman who could barely walk reaching out to him. He saw Quentin take her hand, hold it firmly, and smile down at her as he gave her his blessing. As the old woman turned away, her face alight, Stuart thought, *If I could only bless people the way Quentin does, I'd call myself a real believer.*

Quentin slowly threaded his way though the crowd and put

out his hand. Stuart took it and said, "A fitting sermon, Quentin. How are you?"

"I am well, Brother." Quentin hesitated and then asked, "No word of Brandon?"

"No."

"He'll find his way," Quentin said. "God will not let him fall to the ground."

As the two men left the church, Stuart told Quentin about the "invitation" from Mary. "She wants both of us to come to Whitehall."

"Well, you know her, Stuart, far better than I. Why would she send for me?"

"I don't know, Quentin," Stuart said, "But I do know it's a dangerous time here in England. Mary's in a position to do a great deal toward healing old wounds."

Quentin sighed deeply. "Well, there has been much bad blood between Catholic and Protestants. What do you think she will do?"

"I don't know. Mary is . . . different of late," Stuart answered, troubled. "The last few times we visited, I found it hard to read her intention clearly. And, of course, it's been some time since our last visit."

Quentin said, "Don't worry, Brother. At any rate, I'll be happy to meet her."

☙

Stuart and Quentin knelt to Mary, who greeted them with a smile. They had entered the apartment where she and her ladies spent the afternoons. Mary was dictating something to a scribe, but she brushed him aside, and he scurried away quickly. "Rise, Stuart, and you, Reverend Winslow."

"We are honored to be here, Majesty."

"I've heard so much about you, Reverend Winslow." She extended her hand, and Quentin kissed it.

"I'm gratified to meet you, Your Majesty. My brother has told me so much about you."

"Has he told you that he was my playmate for years?" She smiled.

Stuart was glad to see her smile. "I think so often about those early days with you."

"As have I, Stuart. How is your family?"

"My wife is very well."

"And Brandon? He's a favorite of mine, you know."

"I'm afraid the news isn't good. I am in your debt, Majesty," he said with a nod, "for sparing his life. I understand that if it hadn't been for your intervention, he would've served a far greater sentence."

"It was the least I could do," Mary said sadly. "He came to my aid when I called for him. But his failures grieve me. He has many talents."

"Yes, but he's had his . . . Moral problems have proven to be his downfall."

"Well, surely he has grown out of that, after losing so much. You must bring him to see me. Together we can steer him to a proper role in society," Mary said almost playfully.

"I appreciate your interest, Majesty."

She turned her head to Quentin and began to question him about what people were saying about all sorts of matters—"I must know what my people are thinking and feeling"—but she carefully avoided the subject of faith.

"Surely you've heard their cries as you've passed through the streets. Cries of joy," Quentin said carefully. "The people are very glad to have you as their monarch."

Mary said tentatively, "You know my mother raised me in the true faith." The words were innocent enough, but Stuart saw that Quentin reacted strongly to them.

"People wonder, Your Majesty, what you will do as far as religion is concerned," Quentin said. "Much has transpired since your father's days on the throne."

Mary answered "I am not my father. I don't intend to force my faith on anyone. People will be free to choose between the new learning and the old faith. My father executed those who disagreed with him on religion, even his dear friend Thomas More. How I wept over that man's death! I will never do such a thing as that! I want the love of my people, and you must help me. Quentin Winslow, may I have your loyalty?"

"Always, Your Majesty. I pray that you will be given wisdom to lead this country along the pathway that will please God."

It was the correct thing to say. Mary smiled graciously. "That was well said. I've always had the friendship of your brother, and I will treasure yours as I treasure your brother's." She turned to Stuart and said gently, "And I will pray for Brandon. Where is he now?"

"We are uncertain, Your Majesty. We have not gained word of him in some time."

Mary was clearly grieved at this. "I will try and learn his whereabouts, Stuart."

"I would be most grateful, Your Majesty. But I fear that Brandon will not be found until he wishes it."

Finally she dismissed them.

As they left, Quentin said, "I didn't expect her to seem so kind. I don't know why."

"She's under pressure to bring back the Catholic faith. Pray that she will not listen to those who are not so kind-hearted."

"Stuart! Stuart Winslow!"

Both men turned, and Stuart smiled. "It's the Princess Elizabeth."

The two men advanced to where Elizabeth had detached herself from a group of young women. They both bowed and Stuart introduced Quentin. Elizabeth said, "You must come with me.

The queen told me you were coming. I've prepared some refreshments."

"We would be delighted," Stuart said.

"I always gave your brother a hard time, Reverend Winslow," she said to Quentin. "Since you're a minister, I'll have to be very careful to be good."

Quentin studied Princess Elizabeth. She was an attractive young woman, slender, with the red hair of her father and a clear, translucent complexion. There was a liveliness about her that was lacking in her sister Mary. "Are you always good when ministers are around, Princess?"

"Oh, certainly!"

"Then perhaps you should hire a minister to stay in your presence always."

"Oh, that would cut down my enjoyment considerably, begging your pardon, Reverend. Come along with me."

She took them to an inner room and soon the three of them were seated at a table, eating delicious cakes and drinking ale. "You're a minister, Reverend Winslow. What will you do under the new rule?" All sense of play was gone. Stuart tensed, awaiting his brother's answer.

"The same as I have done under the old rule, Princess. Serve Jesus with all my heart."

Elizabeth seemed to feel a rebuke, and she lowered her head for a moment, then said more soberly, "That is sometimes difficult."

"It's always best to serve Jesus no matter what the cost, don't you think?" Quentin asked gently.

"Of course you're right."

"What do you think your sister will do, Princess?"

"I cannot say. It's unsafe to make predictions in these days."

"Well, the queen has told us that she intends to force Catholicism on no one," Quentin said. "That's good news."

"I hope that it is so. But enough of such sober matters. Tell me about Brandon." As Stuart related the story of Brandon's downfall, she seemed genuinely disturbed. "I hope he'll change his ways. He has good blood in him. He'll come back, I'm sure."

She rose, and the two men knew they were dismissed. As they left the palace and mounted their horses, Quentin said, "I'm encouraged and hopeful. Queen Mary seems to have a good heart."

"I think she wants to do the right thing, and that she will try," Stuart agreed.

The two men were silent. Quentin finally brought up the subject of Brandon again. "What have you done to find him, Stuart?"

"Well, I've hired a man to look for him, but he's not been successful."

"It must be very hard on you."

"Harder on his mother," Stuart said grimly.

"He'll come back home, I'm sure."

"I pray he will. He's all we have, Quentin."

"No, you have Jesus."

Stuart smiled. "Yes. You are right. We have Jesus."

9

Lupa had persuaded Brandon to accompany her to buy some material for a new gown, something she had failed to do until now. She was puzzled by him and this troubled her, for if she knew anything, Lupa knew men. And out of all those she had known, only Rez and Brandon were deemed of any use. Brandon was an asset with his expertise with cards. He brought in a steady income that soon far surpassed what he owed them. They moved from city to city once he became known as such an expert player that others refused to play with him. Nevertheless, his skill, along with other schemes that Lupa and Rez concocted, kept them all in ready coins.

Lupa thought of the two months that had passed since they picked Brandon out of the ditch and felt a glow of achievement: she had been able to make a steady source of income from him. He was an unknown quantity, however, and as she looked at the bolts of cloth at a shop, she glanced covertly at Brandon, who sat in a chair, patiently waiting. He was wearing the latest in fashion, the dress of a wealthy man, and Lupa was well aware that the woman of the shop could not keep her eyes off him. She had noticed this about women before, and also saw that Brandon seemed to be oblivious to them. This both pleased and troubled Lupa, for he seemed oblivious to her also. She was not accustomed to having men ignoring her charm. She turned now to the woman.

"That fabric would look very well indeed on you, my lady."

Lupa smiled at the title that she had been granted. She had never been called such a thing before, but now she accepted it without argument. "It is rather nice."

"Why don't we drape you and discuss the design you wish? You have a lovely shape. There are many options."

"That would please me." She followed the woman into the back of the shop, and as she quickly undressed, she knew that the woman had gone back to talk to Brandon. "I'll claw her eyes out if he shows any interest in her. She's interested enough in *him,*" Lupa muttered. But then she was there beside her, quickly showing Lupa design after design. Lupa chose one, and the woman immediately cut the fabric and pinned it, taking measurements down on a piece of paper as they worked. "Shall we see what your gentleman thinks?"

Lupa gaped at her and then shrugged. Feeling awkward, she made her way to Brandon. "It's not finished, obviously, but you get the idea of what it will look like," Lupa said, hating the nervousness in her belly. "Do you . . . do you like it, Brandon?"

"You look like a queen."

Lupa laughed. "No one ever called me that before."

"Well, they should have." Brandon leaned back, crossed his arms, and stared at her. His bright blue eyes were alert, and he ran them up and down her body. "I don't know whether we ought to get it or not."

"Why not?" Lupa cried. "It'll be beautiful."

"Every man in town will follow you." He smiled at the woman, who had reappeared, adding, "No, I think you'd better remake her old ragged gown a little bit dirtier if possible. I'll smear some of the dirt on her face. That ought to keep the men away."

The woman laughed. "I'm sure she wouldn't agree to that. And, sir, the gown is perfect for her."

"How much is it?" Lupa asked.

"For you twenty pounds."

"Oh, that's far too much!" Lupa cried. "I never paid that much for a gown in my life."

"Lupa, it's done," Brandon said. "We get so few things in life that give us pleasure, dear. We need to grab what we can. Can you have it done tomorrow?" he asked.

When she came out, the woman was standing close to Brandon, looking up at him with a tantalizing smile. Lupa quickly stepped between them and took Brandon's arm. "I'll have my servant come by tomorrow to fetch it."

"We will have it ready for you," she said, but her eyes were on Brandon.

Outside it was almost dark. Lupa's mind was still on the recent scene. "That wench was making up to you, wasn't she?"

"I didn't notice."

Lupa shook his arm. "You did notice! You couldn't help it. She was practically glued to you."

"She was simply being amiable."

"Amiable! I'll show her amiable!"

Brandon glanced down at her. "Why, I do believe you're jealous."

"Why should I be jealous?"

"Because you're afraid somebody will get part of me that you can't have."

His answer was given with a smile, but it troubled Lupa. "Let's hurry," she said shortly. "I want something to eat."

They went to an inn that Lupa knew, and as they entered, the owner of the inn came to greet them, wiping his hands on his apron. "What may I do for you today?"

"We're very hungry," Brandon said. "What are you serving?"

"We have some very fine beef today. Does that sound like something you'd like?"

"Bring us the best you have."

The innkeeper led them to a table set in an angle of the room. It was a pleasant enough inn, well lighted with lanterns hanging from the ceiling. The smell of cooking food left them salivating. The room was filled with the sound of talk and laughter from the those who were already there. Lupa waited until Brandon pulled out a chair for her and then she sat down. It was just a little thing, but it was a custom she had not known before meeting him. As he took his seat, she watched him. He was looking around the room in a leisurely fashion. For a time, until the food came, she talked about the gown and how much it pleased her. Suddenly she reached across the table and put her hand over his. "You never want anything, Brandon."

"Of course I do. I want something to eat. Something to wear. A place to sleep."

"I mean you don't seem to care about how much things cost."

"Oh, I think I do at times."

Lupa studied him carefully. He was a tall man and he sat easily in his chair, limber and yet with a suggestion of sleeping strength. His widely spaced blue eyes were half hidden behind the lids, and there was a benign, complacent smile on his lips. His auburn hair was neatly cut. As she sat before him, she admired the ease about him and admired his sun-kissed face. Despite his good looks there seemed to be, she thought, a dark preoccupation in his expression. She had seen him angry once, and then his eyes were as hostile and bright as broken glass. Now, though, they were not. He did not move his hand from hers. But fugitive shadows chased in and out of his eyes and somehow hid the man within.

"I know why you don't care about having fine things. You've had everything. Your family is rich. What do you want?"

Winslow moved his hand away and passed it across his face, as if to brush away something that troubled him. "I'm not sure what I want, Lupa, but I do know this. It has nothing to do with money or clothes or food."

At that moment the innkeeper set the steaming food on the table, and as she picked up her fork she said, "Did your family pray over food?"

"Always."

"But you don't."

"They're better people than I am, Lupa. I'm hardly a fit man to pray." He began to eat. As always, Lupa took careful note of how he handled his fork and his knife. This made her more careful with her own manners.

When they were finished, she said, "Are you ready to fleece our sheep?"

"Not really."

This surprised her somewhat, but not altogether. He had never shown any excitement or interest or pleasure in the games that she dreamed up, just a willingness to go through the motions. Her games always included robbery.

"The fool's half in love with me," she said, referring to her latest conquest. "He'll follow me anywhere. Why are you hesitant?"

"I don't know."

His answer displeased Lupa, and she said, "He's running around like a boy and yet he's a middle-aged fool. He deserves to be taken." When Winslow did not answer, she said, "I'll have him in his room at the Green Lantern Inn. Be there at eight o'clock. He'll be trying to take advantage of me."

Brandon lifted his head, and Lupa met the full force of his eyes. "No man's going to do that, Lupa. You won't allow it."

"What makes you say that?"

"You're too hard. A diamond wouldn't make a scratch on your soul."

Lupa's eyes narrowed. "My life has hardly been like yours, your lordship," she cried defiantly. She looked around, embarrassed that he had roused such a reaction from her. "You don't know anything about me."

"I think I know a little."

Lupa made a dismissive gesture. "Just forget it. But you'll do it, won't you? Come to the Green Lantern when I give the signal? Or should I get Rez?"

He sighed and pushed his plate back. "I've come to that, it seems."

"See that you do." She stood up and stared at him with a hard expression. "You've never had to fight for anything, but I have."

Brandon was in a dark mood. He sat in the inn after Lupa left, drinking heavily and thinking of his family. He tried to avoid this as much as possible, because thoughts of them brought him pain. The barmaid came and managed to push her hip against his shoulder. He looked at her and saw that she was smiling at him. She was a blonde woman with a tremendous shape, and there was an invitation in her eyes. "What's your name?"

"Mary."

"Do you have a fine family, Mary? A mother and a father?"

The woman was surprised. She stared at him dully. "I had a bad father who got his jollies beating on me and on my mum. He got killed. No loss to me or anyone else."

"What about your mother?"

"She went on the streets. Died a year ago."

"What would you do, Mary, if you could do anything you wanted?"

Obviously no one had ever put this question to the barmaid. She stood silently for a minute, and then, eyes opened wide, she said, "I'd buy me a gold bracelet that cost five pounds."

Brandon reached into his pocket and pulled out a bag of coins. He took out two of them and said, "There's ten. Buy two bracelets."

He put the money in her hand, and the woman stared at him. "You want me to do something for this?"

"No. Just enjoy the bracelets." He got up, put more money down to pay for the meal, and then made his way to the door, moving somewhat unsteadily. He turned back and saw that the barmaid was watching him. "Enjoy the bracelets," he said thickly, then left the inn. He walked down the street to the Green Lantern, which was only a short distance away. He heard the town clock striking ten as he climbed the stairs, and when he got to the door of the room that Lupa had told him about, he heard her voice. She was crying out, speaking loudly. A man's voice was muffled. For a moment Brandon stood there and almost decided to leave, but he had allowed Lupa to get into a bad position, and he had to get her out. He opened the door and saw what he expected. Lupa, wearing only a shift, was being pushed onto a bed by a skinny man, who wore only his smallclothes.

Brandon pulled a pistol from beneath his heavy doublet "That's my wife," he said.

The skinny man was clearly half drunk. When his eyes fell on Brandon's pistol, his jaw dropped and he began to babble. "Don't—don't shoot me."

"What do you mean, coming here with my wife?"

It was an old scene for Brandon. He had done it four times, and each time he had been successful. Brandon watched as the man retreated from the bed and backed up against a wall. He was pathetic and skinny as a plucked chicken, and as he begged, suddenly he began to cry.

"Here. Take what I have. Just don't kill me." He seized a leather bag from a table, and thrust it toward Brandon.

Brandon looked at the bag, then at the man's terrified face. "You stay away from my wife, do you hear me?"

"I promise. Never again!"

He shoved his coins at Brandon, who took them and stared at them, a bit dazed. "Go home to your wife," he said roughly.

"Come on, Lupa." He turned and walked out of the room, and Lupa, now dressed, followed him. She shut the door behind her and took his arm.

"Well, that was easy," she laughed. "How much in the purse?"

"I don't know." Brandon gave it to her. "Share it with Rez."

Lupa looked up at him, obviously shocked. "No. You deserve a share."

"I don't want it."

She had been excited over the little drama that she had dreamed up, and she said, "Why won't you take it?"

"I feel sorry for the poor fellow."

Lupa was angry. Obviously she had not thought to feel sorry for anybody in so long that it came as a novel concept to her. "You think you're too good for such things?"

"No, I'm not." He paused for a few moments and then he added, "I'm no good for anything. But my father wouldn't do it. He's a good man."

Lupa had no answer for that. She took his arm and pulled at him. "Let's get some wine. That's what to do when you're feeling bad."

He stopped suddenly and took her by the arms. She felt the strength of his hands and for a moment was actually frightened of him, but he merely stared at her with an inscrutable expression in his blue eyes.

"Lupa, there's not enough wine in the world to make me feel good about myself," he said miserably.

It was the second day of the new year 1554. Queen Mary had called a meeting of the Privy Council. She spoke in hushed tones to Simon Renard in a small room adjoining the room where the council would meet. Mary could feel Renard's eyes upon her. He was the emissary of Charles V, Holy Roman Emperor, King of

Spain, master of most of Europe and much of the New World. His dominion stretched from Spain through Italy, where he was duke of Milan and king of Naples and Sicily, all the way up to the Low Countries. Treasure ships brought him gold and silver from the mines in the ruined empires of Mexico and Peru, and no one up to this point had dared to challenge his strength.

Renard was not the typical flamboyant ambassador. He was small and thin, but there was an electricity about him. He had dark hair and darker eyes, and his English had a pronounced Spanish accent. Mary knew he had been sent to investigate the possibility of a marriage, but there seemed to be something else beneath the surface.

"What are you going to say to the council, Your Majesty?" Renard asked Mary. He watched as she thought about her answer. He knew her well. At thirty-seven, she was short of stature with a thickened body. She had brown hair and a sallow complexion. Her eyes were of a peculiar hazel color, very large, and her nose was wider than desired. There was about her, Renard had noticed long ago, a defiant attitude, but he did not dislike this at all. He knew that she would need it to rule over this land. He approved of her love of expensive, elegant clothing that alternated between the close-fitting, trailing gowns worn by many English noblewomen and the French gowns with a looser bodice and huge full sleeves. She loved rich, ornate fabrics with gold and silver woven through them and took great delight in her jewels.

Renard thought, *Her love of finery is the only sign of self-indulgence I see in her. She's led a severely disciplined life, and even as queen she keeps it up*. This was encouraging, for he knew that Charles's plan would require diligence from her.

"I have been thinking about marriage, Renard."

"Of course you have. You've been thinking about it for years."

Mary smiled, but there was little humor in it. "You're right.

My father offered me to half the princes in Europe. I felt like a prize heifer being auctioned off!"

Renard blinked at the bitterness in her tone. He knew that her father had treated her terribly but was surprised that she remained so bitter now that he was gone.

"Pray tell, Majesty, what have you been thinking?"

"I have been praying about what you mentioned to me three weeks ago."

Renard felt a surge of joy. "And what is that, Your Majesty?"

"I have decided to marry Philip, the emperor's son."

Instantly a thrill of triumph shot through him. This was actually what he had been sent to accomplish. There were tremendous handicaps, but there were also tremendous advantages. If Mary, who was a staunch Catholic, married Philip, who was even stauncher, the Catholic hold on England would be secure again. There would be problems, but this was a major victory.

"I think you have made a wise choice, Your Majesty."

"I have prayed about it, and God has told me to marry Philip. And what God plans never fails."

"That is very true, but many of your people have hopes for Elizabeth, and there are those who say that she has enough support to overthrow you. You have enemies, Your Majesty."

"Which do you mean?"

"I mean, my lady, the duke of Northumberland, the kings of France and Scotland, and even Princess Elizabeth. They are dangerous."

"You need not mention Elizabeth."

"But she's not Catholic."

"She will be. I will teach her myself. I will bring her, Renard, back to the true faith."

Renard did not argue, but he knew Princess Elizabeth. He knew she was wily, intelligent, quick-witted and knew well how to hide her true feelings. "She is clever, my queen."

"She will do as I say, Renard. I will see to that, and you will be convinced."

❧

Elizabeth entered the room, fell on her knees, and said, "Your Majesty, thank you for allowing me to see you."

Mary took Elizabeth by the hand. "Rise. We must talk. There is much we have to say. You appear to be in good health. You are over your sickness?"

"Almost, Your Majesty. It was a very frightful sickness."

Mary tucked Elizabeth's hand in the crook of her arm and they strolled down a palace hallway. "Elizabeth, I am concerned for you."

"I'm glad of your concern, Your Majesty. You have always been good to me, and I have never ceased to be grateful." This was true; Elizabeth remembered the time when she, much younger than Mary, had looked to her almost as a mother. But that time was past; a huge wall was between them now, with the crown teetering on it.

"What is it you wish to say to me?" Mary asked.

"Your Majesty," Elizabeth said, "I feel very badly. I'm deeply grieved."

"Why are you grieved?"

"I fear," Elizabeth said carefully, "that you have lost your love for me, and this is a grievous thing to me indeed. We have always loved each other. If I have done anything to offend you, Your Majesty, pray let me know and it will be amended."

Mary's face grew almost stern. She was a very direct woman when the necessity called for it, and she said, "I have expected you to help me in my task, which is to bring Catholicism back to our country. You have not been faithful in attending Mass."

Elizabeth answered meekly, "I have not your advantages. You grew up under the tutelage of your mother, who was a Catholic, but I had no one like that."

"No, you certainly had no mother fitted to instruct anyone!"

Elizabeth knew this was no time to argue. "I was brought up in the reformed faith," she said quietly. "I know no other."

"I know that is true, and that is why I am offering you someone to instruct you."

Elizabeth answered, "I would appreciate any help you might give me. I must have instruction. Perhaps, Your Majesty, you can assign some learned man who will understand that one brought up and tutored in one form of religion must have help to make the transition to another."

Mary stared hard at Elizabeth. "I will see that the best comes to you at once."

Elizabeth fought to return her sister's gaze; she well knew what that hard stare meant. *She doesn't believe me, but she must—otherwise I'm lost.* She made herself smile. She bowed and curtsied. "Thank you so much, Your Majesty. I will apply myself as best I can."

Mary's expression cleared. She leaned over and kissed Elizabeth. "We are sisters. Let us be friends."

"Always, Your Majesty." Elizabeth left, and as soon as she was out of the door, she put her back against it and closed her eyes. *That was very close, but I must be careful. Any love that once was between us is certainly gone now.*

Late in January of the same year in which Elizabeth had promised her sister to study the Catholic faith, the word that the queen meant to marry the prince of Spain brought a flood of outrage. The English people did not like Philip. They felt that all Spaniards were thieves, and their excesses with women were well known. Many of the Protestants swore that they would die before they would submit to the reign of a Spaniard who would, in effect, be king over them if Mary married him.

This feeling was widely felt across England and finally brought forth an actual rebellion. Mary heard of it early one morning, when she was informed by the Privy Council. It had called a special session, and the head of the council said, "There is a rebellion, Your Majesty. It is led by Sir Thomas Wyatt."

"Who is he?" Mary demanded.

"The son of a poet and a close friend of Anne Boleyn, probably her lover. He's been a man to watch, and now he's raised an army of sorts, and we have word that he's going to march on London and remove you from the throne."

"He could not fight our army."

"Your army, Your Majesty, is scattered at the moment, called to too many fronts. We have no time to gather it and turn Wyatt back," he said. "It is a desperate situation. You must leave."

"No. This is my capital city. I shall not abandon the throne simply because rebels dare to attack. What sort of monarch would I be? And where would it leave me? Constantly a target."

The councillors argued mightily but Mary refused to leave.

Then Renard brought word that Wyatt was advancing with four thousand men. "We've sent messages to him asking him to state his demands, but it has not slowed his pace. Your Majesty, you don't fully understand the danger."

But Mary did understand the danger. She was wise about such things. She kept her head, and enough of her loyal subjects—and a sizable remnant of her army—came to her defense. Wyatt had no real strength. By the time he got to London, most of Wyatt's men had faded away. Wyatt's attempt failed miserably.

Bishop Gardiner, Mary's lord chancellor, came to tell her. "Wyatt is arrested and is now in the Tower. You should send Elizabeth there too."

"Elizabeth! Why should I send her there?"

"We have evidence that she was involved in the Wyatt's rebellion."

"What evidence?"

Gardiner seemed uncertain. "You must send her there. She's dangerous."

There was a lengthy argument, but finally Mary agreed. On March 17 Elizabeth was arrested and sent to the Tower.

❧

Stuart stared at the messenger, Charles Freeman, who was, he knew, a loyal friend of Elizabeth. "Princess Elizabeth in the Tower! Impossible!"

"I'm afraid not, sir. I saw her myself. She was taken through Traitor's Gate. It was pouring down rain, and she refused to go in. But at last she was persuaded."

After Freeman left, Stuart went to Heather, told her what he had heard, and said, "I must go to Princess Elizabeth."

"What do you intend to do, Stuart?"

"I've always been friendly with both the princess and the queen. Elizabeth must be frightened out of her wits, fearing she'll be beheaded next. I need to do what I can to encourage her."

"Mary may turn on you."

"She may. I'll have to chance it." He kissed her and said, "I'll be back as soon as I can. Don't worry about me."

"I will not worry, but I will pray that you will find favor with the queen."

❧

Elizabeth was in a dark corner of her cell. She had been deprived of all her servants except one old woman—who was no help at all—and had been questioned many times already by various members of the council, all determined to prove that she was involved in the plot. She had been kept in close confinement and given nothing but the coarse food of the rest of the prisoners. Hearing the sound of the door of her prison open, she stood up, expecting and dreading another interrogation. Her heart leaped slightly when she saw it was Stuart Winslow. He came to her at once and knelt before her and took her hand, which she held out. "Princess, I've come to give you what poor comfort I can."

Elizabeth kissed his hands, and he felt the tears fall on them.

"You must not lose hope," he said. He took a liberty that he would never have dared taken in other circumstances. He put his arm around her as if she were his daughter and said, "God will not allow you to perish."

Elizabeth said, "Your coming encourages me, Stuart. I can offer you very little in the way of refreshment."

"My refreshment is to see you cheerful and full of faith."

"You do me good, Stuart Winslow! You have always been good to me and to my family."

"I hope so. Now, tell me all that has happened."

Elizabeth had no one to confide in, and she poured her heart out to this man who had been, indeed, like a light in a dark place. She had learned to love him and trust him as, perhaps, she trusted no other man in England.

When she had finished, Stuart said gently, "God is in control. He is sovereign."

"That's true, isn't it?"

"Yes. He pulls some down and he raises others up, the Scripture says. Heather and I and Quentin will pray, and we will ask others to pray."

Elizabeth felt the tears rise again in her eyes. "I never weep, but I can't help it now."

"Weep then, but inside your heart you must have faith."

Elizabeth, Princess of the Realm, held on to Stuart Winslow's hands, and as he poured comfort into her, she vowed, "I will never forget this devotion, Stuart Winslow—never!"

10

"There is a gentleman to see you, sir."

Quentin looked up from the book he was reading. "Who is it, Mark?"

"He's a soldier, sir. His name is Caleb Carter. He wishes to speak with you."

"Show him in, please."

"Yes, sir."

Quentin knew the name well. His brother had told him Carter had brought news of Brandon's disgrace and disappearance. He knew Carter had been a good friend to Brandon. Might he have gained further word of his nephew?

As soon as the door opened, Quentin went forward and put his hand out. "Come in."

"I appreciate you seeing me, sir."

"Please sit down. I'll have a servant bring some fresh cake and something to drink."

"That would suit very well."

Quentin moved to the door and called out, "Mark, bring some ale, please, and some of that cake I favor."

"Yes, sir."

Quentin seated himself and studied his visitor. Carter was a tall man with a wealth of brown hair and warm brown eyes. There was a neatness about him that one expected in a good soldier, and his complexion was tanned from outdoor living. "I want to express my thanks to you. My brother told me how much trouble you went to and what a friend you tried to be to my poor nephew."

"Well, it was not much, Reverend."

"Oh, don't call me that! I hate titles. It was indeed very much appreciated by our whole family."

"I wish I could have done more." Carter shook his head. "I did everything I could, but as you know, he's a stubborn fellow."

"Yes, I have reason to know that."

Carter cleared his throat. "I don't know if I'm out of line or not, sir, but I thought you might like a word about Brandon. Perhaps I should have gone to Brandon's parents, but I thought you might do that. It might be best for them to hear it from kin."

Quentin asked alertly, "You know where he is?"

"Why, yes, sir, I do."

"We've tried everything to find him."

"Well, I can tell you where he was two days ago. I assume he's still there."

"And where is that, Mister Carter?"

"Dover. He's in Dover."

"In Dover? I would never have thought of looking for him there. I thought perhaps he had left the country. We've been terribly worried."

"So have I, sir."

"Is he ill?"

Carter shifted uneasily in his seat and seemed reluctant to answer. At that moment Mark came in with a tray of ale and cakes. "Will there be anything else, sir?"

"No, this will be fine. Thank you, Mark."

As soon as Mark left the room, Quentin said, "Help yourself to the cake."

Carter seemed to be glad of the distraction, as if he hesitated to say what he had come so far to say. He took the ale and tasted the cake, which he pronounced to be very good indeed.

Finally Quentin could no longer endure the suspense. "What is it that's troubled you? Something about Brandon, I assume."

"Well, sir, the good news is that Brandon isn't sick. As I understand it, he had a hard time. He was beaten rather severely, and when he left the inn he wasn't completely healed. I was at a gaming house in Dover. I gamble a little myself, nothing very seriously. A soldier doesn't make enough for that—"

"And you saw Brandon there?" Quentin interrupted.

Caleb nodded. "Yes, sir, I did."

"What was he doing?"

"He was playing cards, as you might expect in such a place."

"How did he look?"

"Better than ever. He was more finely dressed than I had ever seen. Of course, I'd only seen him in his uniform, but you could tell. He had an expensive ring on his finger and fine clothes."

"Did you speak to him?"

"Oh, yes, of course I did. I waited until the game was over, and I went up and greeted him. He was glad to see me, or at least he seemed so."

"There must be something more. Tell me what you learned."

"You won't like it, sir."

"I gathered that, man. Now out with it."

"I'm afraid, sir, that he's taken up with a gypsy woman and he's become a rather infamous gambler. He never loses, or almost never, and he's almost been called out by several men he's beaten. There are some who call him a cheat."

"He was always good at cards. What about this woman?"

"Well, she's very beautiful, and there's a man in the picture somehow. Both gypsies. The man wears gold rings in his ears, just as you'd expect, you know. Anyway, Brandon wouldn't say much about himself, and when I asked him about his family, he cut me short. He said, 'I haven't talked to them. They don't need a chap like me.'"

"I tried to reason with him and tell him how much his family cared for him, but he wouldn't listen. The woman listened, though. She hated me. I could see that. I'm sure she had a knife on her, and she would have used it if I had talked Brandon into coming with me."

"So he wouldn't listen at all?"

"No, I'm afraid not. I didn't know what else to do, so I came here. And facing Mrs. Winslow . . . I simply could not find it in me."

"I'm very grateful to you, and my family will be too, in time. Leave it to me to talk to Heather. She'll take comfort from the fact that her son is alive, but you are right—it will be difficult for her to learn what has become of him."

"I hope you can do something with him. The gossip is pretty rank about him. He's not only gambling. He's been involved in some shady deals. I couldn't get the details, but he's gone downhill, sir, I'm sorry to say."

"Thank you. You've done a good deed. Stay with us overnight. I'll see that you have a good place to sleep, a good meal tonight, and a good breakfast."

"Thank you, sir. That would be very fine, and I will occupy my time by praying that you'll have success with Brandon, where I could not."

❧

As soon as he had made provision for Carter, Quentin went to Stoneybrook. He found Stuart and Heather, and without preamble, told them his news.

"Thank God he's alive!" Heather cried.

"Yes, I've been fearing the worst," Stuart said.

They listened soberly to the rest of the story. Heather wept when she learned that it was widely assumed that Brandon was involved in dark deals. "I think you need to go see him, Stuart. Maybe you can change his mind."

"I don't know whether I can or not, but I'm going to try."

"And I'm going with you," Heather said, wiping her eyes and lifting her chin.

"That may not be best, dear."

"He's my son. I'm going, so don't argue."

"When you marry, Quentin, be sure you meet a woman with a strong will. You won't have to worry about what she's thinking." He put his arm around Heather and squeezed her. "Very well. We'll go together."

"Let me know as soon as you get some kind of word, will you, Stuart?"

"Of course I will. This could be good news. We'll pray it is."

"Where's Rez gone?"

Lupa looked down at Brandon, who was slumped in a chair. "He's off on one of his horse-stealing trips." She reached down and took a cup from him. "You're drunk, Brandon. You're drinking too much." She felt a twinge of guilt, for she had been encouraging him to drink for some time.

"What difference does it make, Lupa?"

"You don't appreciate what you have. I don't think you've ever noticed how you've been blessed."

"Blessed by whom? By God? You don't believe in God, do you, Lupa?"

"Sometimes I do."

"I would never know it."

"Don't you believe in God?"

"I certainly do, and the dread of my life is the day I have to face him when he's my judge, and I'll have to confess what a rotten sinner I've been."

He got up slowly, as if he were an old man, and started to leave the room. "I'm going out to get some air."

"I'll go with you."

He did not argue, but neither did he invite her.

It was a windy night in March, and the stars were out. Neither of them spoke as they went down the street. Finally they came to what seemed to be a communal garden and they stopped.

"I love gardens," Brandon said. "My mother loves them too."

Lupa said, "We never had a garden. We never stayed in one place long enough to plant."

"Where did you live?"

"We lived in a wagon, a caravan you'd call it. It sounds romantic, but it's not. Everybody hates gypsies. I've been run out of many towns." As she continued telling him her life, she saw that he was watching her with a peculiar expression. "Look at me," she whispered. "I'm crying like a baby. I don't cry."

"What is there to cry for?"

"I never had anything good." She suddenly reached up and put her arms around him. "You are good. You must see that I care for you, Brandon."

"Well, Lupa, I'm not good for you. I'm lost, wandering."

"Sounds like a gypsy to me. We're both lost, so we should make the best of it." She pressed herself against him and whispered, "We have each other, Brandon. We can have that much at least. Come on back to the room. I need you to love me."

"That's not love, Lupa."

"It's as close as we can get."

She pulled at him, and Brandon reluctantly followed. As soon as they were in their room, she closed and locked the door. She came to him and said, "We'll have each other. That's better than nothing."

And Brandon surrendered. "I'll probably regret this and so will you," he whispered, then accepted her kiss.

"No regrets," she said pulling him down onto the bed. "What's to regret in love?"

Three days later, Brandon and Lupa walked along the cliffs. Brandon smiled at her and appeared happy for the first time since he had met her. In truth, she had comforted him, at least in a physical way.

The famous white cliffs of Dover impressed them, and Brandon said, "This is a beautiful sight. As beautiful as anything in England. I think we should—"

Suddenly he heard his name being called. He whirled quickly, and his eyes widened. He saw his father and mother hurrying along the pathway along the top of the cliff, and could not, for a moment, think of what to say.

"Who is that?" Lupa said, looking from him to the figures still twenty paces off.

"My—my parents," he whispered.

Brandon had no chance to say anything else. His mother rushed ahead of his father. She came to him, and he had to catch her in his arms to keep her from falling. She was weeping. She pulled his head down and kissed his cheek.

"Mother, what are you doing here?"

Stuart answered, "Brandon, we heard that you were here, and we came to see that you were all right."

Brandon was filled with shame, for he knew that he had never been the son they deserved, less so now than ever.

He glanced toward Lupa, standing behind him, and saw the antagonism in her face, then back to his parents. "When did you arrive?" It sounded inane, and he barely heard their reply.

"Do you have a room yet?"

"Yes. We have a room at the inn."

"Go back there then. We'll meet you for dinner tonight."

"All right. We're at the Anchor and Albatross Inn. It's so good to see you, Son," Heather said. Her eyes drifted to Lupa, but then she turned and she went back along the cliffs with Stuart.

Brandon turned to Lupa. "Forgive me. I didn't mean to

ignore you," he said. "I was so shocked to see them . . . But you'll meet them tonight."

"You won't want me there."

"Yes, I do," he said.

"Are you certain?"

"I am. Please, come with me."

They walked along the path again. Brandon looked out over the Channel, and for one brief moment he had an insane desire simply to throw himself off the cliff and be done with his problems. But that would only put one more arrow in his parents' hearts.

Lupa had dressed with care, but she was deeply afraid of Brandon's parents. She had become part of him physically, but she knew she had never touched his spirit. She had seen the quality of the couple and knew that she was on the verge of losing this man who had come into her life and made her feel as no other man ever had.

"You look fine," Brandon said. "Let's hurry."

"Are you sure you want me to go?"

"Of course. Come along now."

The two of them went to the inn and found Stuart and Heather waiting for them. They sat down and ordered a meal, and Stuart began to tell Brandon about the situation in London, obviously eager to fill the uncomfortable silence among them.

"You've heard of Elizabeth's trouble?"

"I heard that she was put in the Tower. But she's done nothing, has she, Father?"

"Absolutely not. Mary's listening to some of Elizabeth's enemies. Have you heard about Lady Jane Grey? She was involved in Wyatt's Rebellion, and she's been executed, along with her husband. I think she was innocent. It appears that Mary is adopting her father's ways—eager to believe lies."

"I hear that Mary's going to marry Philip of Spain. Is that true?" Brandon asked.

"She's made it very clear. It's not a popular decision, and it's going to mean a great deal of heartache and danger for some of us."

"You think she will be hard on people who aren't Catholic?"

"I think she will."

Such talk went on throughout the meal.

Then the two men left the women alone, going outside to look at the horses that Stuart and Heather had brought. As soon as they were gone, Heather tried to show at least some politeness to Lupa, who had said absolutely nothing. She asked a simple question about Lupa's parents, about her history, and Lupa flared out at her. "You think I'm not good enough for your son, don't you?"

"Why, I hadn't thought of that."

"Yes, you have," Lupa said flatly.

Heather asked simply, "Do you love him, Lupa?"

"Yes, but I know you'd never have me as a daughter."

"You don't know that because I don't know it."

"I'm a gypsy. I know people hate gypsies."

"It's not what you are. It's what you become. I want Brandon to find God, and I want the woman he marries to be a woman of God. That's all I want for him."

"I can never be that." Lupa turned away.

Brandon came back with Stuart, but he did not sit down. Stuart shifted from one foot to the other, obviously agitated. He was flushed at the neck. What had they been discussing?

Brandon looked at his mother and said, "I appreciate the visit. But now I want you to give up on me. You, too, Father."

Stuart said at once, "We won't give up on you until God does."

"He already has. Come, Lupa."

11

By the first of June, 1554, Queen Mary had decided to have Elizabeth released from the Tower. This decision did not please Simon Renard, who said bluntly, "I think, Your Majesty, it is a grave error permitting Elizabeth to leave the Tower."

Mary stared at Simon Renard. She trusted him, but since he was not an Englishman, she doubted his wisdom in some matters, especially those concerning her family—mainly Elizabeth. "I cannot leave my sister in the Tower, Renard. She is innocent. I am convinced of it."

"Some of the traitors involved in Wyatt's Rebellion accused her."

"Yes, they accused her under torture. People will confess anything under torture. Besides, Wyatt himself never accused her. At his execution he was almost deformed by the tortures he had undergone, but he steadfastly refused to admit that Elizabeth had ever contacted him. I cannot ignore such testimony."

Renard stared at the queen, but said, "I think it's a mistake, but you are the queen. She's here to see you. I saw her in the outer room."

"Have her brought in, Renard, and you may leave us alone."

"Yes, Your Majesty."

Mary went to the window and stared outside. Wyatt's Rebellion had shaken her. She had been only a hair's breath away from being deposed. She had said Mass four times a day since that close escape from death. She was convinced that God had saved her. A beautiful summer had come to England after a hard winter. She watched a group of sparrows on the ground beneath the window and saw a tremendous fight begin, the small birds rolling in the dust and pecking as if to kill.

"Even birds don't agree! How could human beings possibly live in peace?" Mary whispered.

Hearing steps at the door, she came to stand in the middle of the room as Elizabeth entered. She saw that Elizabeth looked pale, her sojourn in the Tower had had its effect on her. *How could it be otherwise,* Mary thought, *when each day she might have been taken out to share her mother's fate?*

"I greatly regret," Mary said, "it was necessary to send you to the Tower."

"I appreciate Your Majesty's regret. But I say again what I have said all this time. I am innocent of any plot of any kind, and I know that your love would never allow harm to come to me."

"It's your future that I'm thinking of, Elizabeth."

"Yes, I know that, Your Majesty," Elizabeth said quickly, "I would like to leave here and go to the country, to my house there, to Woodstock. It's always been good for me."

"You're no longer a child. I have a proposition for you."

"A proposition?"

"Yes, indeed. It's time for you to think about taking a husband." Mary saw Elizabeth turn pale. "I will be married soon, and it is time for you to marry. Why have you turned pale? Emanuel Philibert, the duke of Savoy, would be a worthy match."

"I—I have no desire to marry, Your Majesty."

"Nonsense! You must marry. It's what every woman must do."

"Not every woman, if you please. I would prefer to remain unmarried."

"Elizabeth, you speak of matters of which you have no knowledge." Mary frowned. "Well, I cannot force you, but I think you're making a serious mistake. You may go to Woodstock."

"Thank you for your gracious kindness, Your Majesty."

Elizabeth curtsied deeply.

As soon as she was gone, Mary paced back and forth. Talk of marriage brought to mind her own upcoming nuptials. Renard entered but did not speak. Finally Mary turned to him. "Renard, I am excited. I'm going to marry. I will have a husband who will love me and care for me, and it's true I'm almost too old for childbearing, but it's not impossible. I want children. I want to become a mother. I tell you, Renard, my happiness at just the thought of my coming marriage to Philip brings great joy to my heart."

"I am happy for you, Your Majesty," he said, then added cautiously, "We must keep a watch on Elizabeth."

"Of course. Send for Sir Henry Bedingfield. He's been a loyal supporter of mine. Charge him with watching Elizabeth closely. He's faithful. I think he will serve admirably well."

"Yes, Your Majesty."

Mary returned to the window and peered out. She did not speak for some time, but finally said in a low tone, "I am at a great disadvantage, Renard."

"And how is that, Your Majesty?"

"I know nothing of—of marriage."

"But you have been engaged to be married many times."

"But I have no knowledge of—" Mary lowered her head and she flushed. "I have no knowledge of what it's like—the physical side of marriage."

Renard seemed somewhat taken aback, and Mary was immediately sorry she had mentioned it. "That will come, Your Majesty. I am sure you will be happy."

"Very well. I will find someone to counsel me, some faithful woman who has been married."

"That would be well. I think you should see to it."

❧

Philip, son of Emperor Charles V, stood looking out over the prow of his ship. Several of the young courtiers who had accompanied him from Spain were gathered around him.

"There it is," he said. "England."

"Yes, land of your bride." The speaker was Pedro Devine, a handsome young man of twenty-five. He winked at the other young men and said, "I am certain she is young and beautiful."

Philip frowned at Devine. "Do not mock me, sir. By all accounts she is not beautiful. And she is no longer young."

"But she is the queen, sire." Devine answered. "You will be king not only of Spain but also of England. It is what your father most desires, and you are wise to do as he bid."

Philip shook his head. He was wearing brilliant clothing, a gorgeous doublet and a coat of gray satin with white velvet lining. Gold and silver bugles adorned the gown, and gold thread was applied so thickly that the cloth beneath was all but hidden. Along with these Philip wore jewels at his wrist and around his neck and the gold chains that he liked to wear around his shoulders and around his hat. Indeed, he was magnificently adorned, but he had an air of apprehension.

"I do not know how this will go."

"What do you mean, sire?"

"We both know that the English will not welcome a foreign king."

"It is not their decision," Devine said flatly. "They will accept whoever the queen designs, and she has chosen you, my prince."

Devine continued to comfort the prince and encourage him.

As soon as the ship docked, the visitors got into two royal

carriages that had been sent for them and set out for the meeting of Philip and his bride to be.

However, they stayed in Southampton for three days and slept late each morning. During those days they met with Mary's council and other lords. Philip made a formal speech to all of them, assuring them that he had come to England not to enrich himself but because he had been called by the divine powers to be Mary's husband. He promised in many ways that he would be a good and loving prince.

Philip was well aware that his every word and gesture were being weighed and that they would be reported not only to the queen but also to the rest of the court. He gave every appearance of being a carefree young man looking forward to his wedding day. But behind that façade he was troubled. Things were not going well in the war that Spain was carrying on with the French, and word had come from his father that it was absolutely necessary for the marriage to take place. Finally Philip and his companions arrived at Winchester in the midst of a rain so hard that the horses were splashed with mud up to their eyes. It was dusk when he arrived, and there were few to meet him. He was led to his quarters in the castle, and after a change of clothes he was taken to meet his bride to be.

When Philip entered the room, his eyes went at once to the woman who was standing in the center. She was not what he had expected. There had been some hints that Mary was attractive, but she was not. She was wearing a black velvet gown, a petticoat of frosted silver, and a headdress of black velvet lined with gold. She was short, and her youthful shapeliness had become a thick-set middle-aged appearance. Her complexion was sallow, and he could see that she was nervously twisting her lips.

Quickly he went forward, took her hand, and kissed it. "Your Majesty, at last we meet. I cannot tell you of the happiness in my heart." Philip could not speak English, so he spoke in French, which he knew Mary understood. He saw her eyes light up and knew that this woman was hungry for love. She was eleven years older than he, but he had not come to find a woman who would please him in the bedroom. He could see that pleasing her would be easy.

Philip kissed Mary on the mouth. She was taken aback. Philip laughed. "I understand it is the custom in your country for men to kiss women. It is a most happy custom."

"I must learn some Spanish so that we need not always confer in French," she said. "It is such a beautiful language. Come. You must sit down and have refreshments. Bring your companions with you. I want to hear about your trip."

The rest of the evening passed slowly for Prince Philip. He was a man capable of playing a role, and he played his role well. He saw that Mary had a desire for love, and he could provide that—or at least the semblance of it.

After the meal and some entertainment, when they were then left alone for the first time, Philip said, "I am delighted with you, Your Majesty. I hope you find me acceptable."

"Oh, yes, Philip. Of course I do." She looked almost attractive as her eyes lit up again. "Our dream will come true."

"Our dream, Your Majesty?"

"That England will be returned to the true faith, the Catholic faith. Between us we will do that."

"That is my desire and also the desire of my father. It will not be easy," he warned.

"It must be done."

"It may even take some force."

"I once wished for a peaceful transition, but I believe now that even if we must resort to force, God will be with us."

Philip saw that Mary was thinking more of weddings and unions than the future of her country's faithful. He smiled and said, "We will talk of this a great deal, but later. I am so happy to be here. With you."

"I'm glad you've come, Philip. Our marriage will be a happy one."

"I know that is true. Now, I bid you good night."

Brandon and Lupa were at an inn for the evening meal when a man approached their table and said, "I congratulate you on your companion, sir."

Brandon casually observed that the speaker was a tall, thin man with a narrow face and a pair of eyes somewhat too close together. He was dressed in a lordly fashion with jewels sparkling at his fingers and around his neck. His clothes were of the finest, and Brandon, who had learned to read men rather well, saw that he was a fop. "You are impertinent."

"My name is Sir Leo Summerville." Summerville waited for recognition to come to Brandon, but it did not. His face reddened and he said, "As I say, you have an attractive companion."

"And I say you may leave, sir." Brandon did not even sit up straight. He was indolently leaning back, holding a goblet of wine in one hand. He glanced over at Lupa and saw that her face was tense. "I'm sorry, my dear, that you have to put up with such a lout. Perhaps I will speak to the owner about keeping the riff-raff out of this place"

Summerville sneered at him. "I know you. Don't think you're getting away with anything."

"You don't know me."

"Yes. I remember you as a boy. You are a son of Sir Stuart Winslow and nephew of the preacher Quentin Winslow."

"I prefer to not discuss my family."

Summerville was infuriated. He was clearly used to getting his own way and having people bow before him. He sneered and placed his hand on the hilt of his sword. "Your uncle is one of these new religion people."

"Whatever he is, sir, is no concern of yours. I've asked you twice to leave. I will not ask a third time."

Summerville laughed. "We have a Catholic queen now, and we'll have a Catholic king soon. Your uncle has been brave enough until now. That'll change his tune."

"No, he won't."

"Then he'll lose his head."

Brandon swiftly came out of his chair. He grabbed Summerville by the nose, twisted it hard, and then pushed. Summerville went cartwheeling backward, fell into a table, and a pitcher of wine spilled across his chest.

He scrambled to his feet and drew his sword. "I'll kill you for that!"

By the time Summerville had finished that statement and was plunging toward him, Brandon had drawn his own sword. With one quick blow he struck at the hilt of Summerville's weapon and drove it out of his grasp. With the next motion Brandon struck him on the forehead with the butt of his sword and drove him to the ground. Instantly the point of Brandon's sword was at the throat of his fallen foe.

"Confess that you are a liar."

"You'll hang for this!"

Lupa took his arm quickly. She was pale, which was unusual, for she was a courageous woman. "Let him go, Brandon."

"Why should I? He threatened my family and insulted you and me."

But Lupa pulled at his arm. "Come. Let's leave here."

Brandon kept the tip of his weapon on Summerville's throat. "If I were you," he said pleasantly, "I would not pursue further discourse. Otherwise you will be a dead fop." He walked away with Lupa, and Summerville scrambled to his feet and shouted curses and threats at their backs.

Lupa said nervously, "He's a powerful man. I've heard of him."

"He'll be a dead powerful man if he tries to touch my uncle."

"That won't happen."

"It could. There're rumors that Philip and Mary are going to make it a capital offense to preach anything except Catholic doctrine."

"They should know the English will never put up with that."

"I think, from what my father's told me of Mary, that she doesn't take kindly to any advice. She was raised by a woman who was a devout Catholic and poured this doctrine into her."

"But she wouldn't dare touch your uncle. He's the brother of a nobleman."

"She'd better not," he said. "I wouldn't put up with it."

Lupa pulled him to a stop and faced him, her face lined with anger. "You don't know yet what it means, do you? To be forced to flee? How to discern real danger? This is real danger, Brandon. Life-threatening." She put her hands on his arms and looked up into his eyes. "You must not get involved in this."

"If the queen touches my uncle, I'll get involved. You can believe that, Lupa!"

❧

The marriage of Mary, Queen of England, to Philip of Spain took place on July 25, 1554.

A sullenness fell over the people afterward. Once upon a time, Mary had been cheered by the populace when she was carried through the streets. "God bless Queen Mary," the cries rang out. But now that she was Philip's wife, that was seldom heard. The months rolled by, and not until the second month of 1555 did the true intention of Mary and Philip show itself. They had the heresy laws revived, and almost at once people were arrested for heresy. A shock ran through the entire country, and none felt the grim shadow that had fallen over England more than Brandon Winslow.

"I must go to my uncle, Lupa."

"Why? Is he sick?"

"No, but he's in danger. I had a letter from my father. The queen has arrested three members of his parish on the charge of heresy. They'll be executed."

"Well, how does that involve your uncle?"

"It means that he could be accused as well. I must go to him."

"Are you so close to him?"

"He gave me comfort when I needed it," Brandon said. "I was only a boy, but I had got into trouble. I couldn't face my parents, I was so ashamed. But my uncle came to me and made me feel that I wasn't a complete loss. I've never forgotten that, Lupa. I must go to him."

"I'll go with you."

"No. You wait here with Rez. You have plenty of money."

"But how long will you be gone?" Lupa demanded.

"I don't know, but I must go to be sure that my uncle is safe."

"But if he's arrested by the queen—"

"I'll get him away somehow. There are other places to live besides England."

Lupa pleaded, but Brandon was adamant. He left early the next morning before she was awake.

Brandon made a fast trip back to Quentin's church in Winchester and fortunately found his uncle at once.

Quentin was surprised. "Why, it's you, Brandon! At long last!"

Brandon saw lines in Quentin's face, lines of tension, and said, "I wanted to see what was going on for myself. These people from your parish that were arrested—are they traitors?"

"Of course not! They're simple people. None of them is a danger to anyone. They are fervent Christians. They speak out for the Lord Jesus, and evidently that has become unpopular with the Crown."

"What can be done?"

"To get them free? Nothing. Everything has been tried. Your father even went and received an audience with the queen. He begged her to talk to these people at least. He told her that she would see that they were no danger. But she's so enamored of Philip that she wouldn't listen."

"Do you think Philip has brought this on?"

"Not really. Mary's always been a strong Catholic. The difference is that once she didn't have any power but now she does."

"What are you going to do, Uncle?"

"Right now I'm going to visit the poor souls that are in the Tower. Try to give them some comfort."

"You can't go alone."

Quentin smiled. "Well, then, you come with me. Come along. I'll send word to your parents that we will be along to Stoneybrook as soon as our task in London is completed."

The Tower was frightening to most people, and Brandon, for all his courage, was somewhat intimidated. It seemed that there was an odor of fear. He mentioned this to Quentin.

"This place has a terrible smell. I don't know what it is."

"The smell of misery, I think, Brandon. So many have died in this place. Others have been tortured beyond human endurance. I wish the earth would open up and swallow it, but until that happens, we must do our best."

They were following a guard down a musty-smelling corridor. Another guard opened a steel door with a key attached to a belt around his waist. "They'll all die tomorrow. Don't try giving them weapons, sir. It wouldn't do 'em no good."

"I don't have any weapons," Quentin said. He stepped inside the cell. Brandon followed him.

A high, narrow, barred window gave a feeble beam of light. Brandon stood back. He saw Quentin go to the prisoners and embrace each of the three men. He listened as Quentin spoke of hope and the world to come. One of the men, a simple enough fellow in his forties, began to cry. "What will happen to my dear wife and my little one, pastor?"

"You need not worry about that. The church will take care of them. I'll see to it myself. They will always have food and shelter and care."

"Thank you, sir! Thank you!"

Brandon did not say a word, but felt somehow strange as Quentin sat down and talked with each of the prisoners. They all hung on his words—mostly verses of hope and promise. He stared at the men thinking, *They'll be dead soon. What would that be like, I wonder? Better to get killed in battle when you don't know it's coming than to sit here and wait for it to come and take you!*

The visit lasted a long time. Quentin embraced each of the men again and said a prayer over each one.

As soon as they were outside, Brandon took a deep breath. "I've seen battle, but nothing was as bad as this. Is there no hope at all, Uncle?"

"Yes, there's hope. There's hope in Christ, but no earthly hope, I'm afraid, for these three. They will be with their Beloved tomorrow." He turned to Brandon. "I need you with me tomorrow, Nephew. I need your strength."

"Uncle Quentin, I hardly—"

"Will you attend me?" Quentin pressed him. "It will take everything in me to see these dear folk at heaven's gate."

Brandon closed his mouth and looked him in the eye. Hadn't he given enough in being with him today? But Quentin gave him no quarter.

"I will be by your side, Uncle."

❧

Brandon slept very little the night before the execution at Smithfield. The two men shared a room. Quentin seemed awake all night, often on his knees in prayer. Perhaps that was the reason Brandon slept so little. His uncle did not pray loudly, but from time to time a groan would issue from the darkness. *It's almost as though his soul is being pulled out of him,* Brandon thought. *He has a passion and a love in him that I know nothing about, something I'll never know.* The thought left him hollow.

Finally the dawn came, and the two men, neither of them having an appetite, went at once to the prison. Quentin was admitted, but Brandon was told that only the pastor could visit the condemned.

For two hours Brandon wandered about Smithfield, torn by strange feelings. He had seen men die in so many ways on the battlefield, but in almost every instance it was quick and in that sense merciful. Even those who did not die at once did not linger long.

He came to where a large crowd of unruly people were gathered. Out in an open field were a number of stakes and two cartloads of wood drawn by donkeys. Brandon tried to force himself to be calm, but cold perspiration came out on his forehead as his imagination put him against one of those stakes with the fire consuming his feet, his body, and the agonizing pain that would ensue.

A muffled cry went up from someone in the crowd, then many voices were speaking. Brandon turned quickly to see the prisoners being led from the building where they had been kept. A shock ran over him as he realized that there were four prisoners—and one of them was a woman!

Accustomed as he was to the shock and horrors of the battlefield, the idea of a woman being burned at the stake shook Brandon more than he had thought possible. He could not take his gaze off her. She was an elderly woman in her sixties, probably. Her hair was white, and her face was lined with care, but to Brandon's shock and amazement he saw that she was smiling. "What in the world can she have to smile about?" Brandon whispered under his breath.

Then he saw that Quentin had accompanied the prisoners, and as they stopped just short of the stakes, he watched as Quentin went to the four, and despite a protesting guard, began to pray. His voice was loud and clear on the air.

"Oh, Father, all things are in thy hands that made the world and all that is therein, all that swims in the great seas, all that flies through the air, all that walks the earth. You who care for the sparrow that falls, care for these who come today to make their home with thee. They leave their earthly home, and they will now come and be in your arms in peace and joy and perfect bliss forever. I pray, Lord, that you would show mercy and give them a death that is as painless as such a thing can be. And, Lord Jesus, as you appeared to Stephen, as he looked up into heaven and saw you, Lord Jesus, I pray that your holy presence might be made known to each of these your children—"

The prayer was cut off when a burly man wearing a snuff-brown doublet shoved him out of the way with a curse. "Get out of here with blasted prayers. It's too late for that," he snarled. As Quentin stepped back, the executioner said, "Tie 'em up! We'll have us a burn here."

Almost paralyzed, Brandon could not take his eyes off the scene. He was shocked to see seven ravens that had been circling in the sky come down and alight near one of the stakes. Evidently, there was grain scattered about; they pecked at it and they chattered as they moved about the ground, searching for more. Something about the sight of these ebony birds shook Brandon, and he turned away and looked out over the horizon. It was a beautiful day. The air was clear and pure—a jarring contrast to what was about to take place.

Quickly Brandon forced himself to look as the victims were tied to the stakes. He watched with mounting disgust that was turning to rage as one of the guards tightly bound the old woman, making her cry out in pain. "Hush up there, granny. You'll make a bright light, you will."

I'd like to get you alone and make a light out of you! Brandon thought.

When all the prisoners were tied to the stakes, the wood was unloaded from two wagons. The guards piled it around the feet of the victims, and a fat man standing next to Brandon said to his companion, "Well, that won't be easy. Look at it. Those faggots are green. It'll be a slow death."

When the sticks were in place, a torch was brought, and the executioner took it. He started with the oldest of the three men. Since the wood was green, it was hard to get it started, and he cursed. As soon as it began to burn, he called out, "Here, help me with this. Light 'em up."

Two more men picked burning branches from the fire and lit the wood at the feet of each of the condemned. The wood began burning reluctantly. A slight breeze sprang up, which made the flames burn higher. Brandon could clearly hear the crackling of the wood as it started to burn in earnest, and then from the second wagon dry wood was added. The fires sprang up, and one of the men cried out, "Oh, Jesus, have mercy on me and receive my soul!"

The new wood caught quickly, and soon all the victims called upon the name of Jesus, and when the flames suddenly caught and curled around the oldest of the men, his clothing caught fire and his head went back and in a short time his tongue was so swollen that he could not speak and his lips were shrunk to the gums. The fire swirled around him, consuming the flesh. He cried out one more time, and then the ropes burned away and his body, burned black, fell forward.

Quentin appeared beside him then, tears streaming down his face. Brandon searched for a way to comfort him, but there were no words. Despite himself, Brandon looked to the woman. The fire had begun to burn her legs and consume her clothing. He expected to see horror on her face, but instead her face was turned upward, and to the shock and amazement of Brandon

Winslow he saw that she was smiling. She cried out in a clear voice, "Blessed be the Lord! Take me to yourself, Lord Jesus!"

Brandon could stand no more. He whirled and shoved his way through the crowd, some cursing at him as he shouldered them aside. He stumbled blindly away, and Brandon, who was not a crying man, found his eyes blurred. He was breathing heavily, as if he had run a great distance. "Oh, God, how can you let this happen? What beasts have been created in this world?" He walked quickly, half-running, holding his hands over his ears, but he could not shut out the crackling of the wood or the dying prayers and cries of the prisoners.

"I could not do that! I could never endure a thing like that!" he cried aloud and knew that there were horrors yet in this world that he had not dreamed of and some inexplicable, mysterious power in serving God.

12

"Sir, your brother and son are here to see you and your father."

Stuart looked up from the book he had been reading and nodded. "Bring them into the front parlor, where my father is sitting, will you, please?"

"Certainly, sir."

Stuart opened a door to the next room. "Heather, Quentin and Brandon are here." He smiled, "Good to see you, Father." He felt the pressure of Heather's eyes on him and nodded. "You're worried. Well, so am I."

"You must make him listen to reason. He's in dreadful danger. And Brandon . . ."

"It's not a *reasonable* matter. It's a matter of faith. Quentin feels that he can't betray what he believes in order to please the queen. But I will try."

Heather lowered her eyes so that he could not see the pain that was in them. Nevertheless he knew. She had slept little, and the two of them had been bearing a double burden. They were, as always, praying with a sense of desperation for Brandon. That was a burden that never left them night or day. But now this danger to Quentin Winslow occupied their minds with almost equal desperation. It gave them some small consolation that Brandon had come to Quentin's aid.

Quentin came in, with Brandon and Claiborn close behind. He smiled and came over and clasped Stuart around the shoulders. "Good to see you, Brother, and you, Heather." He embraced her and gave her a kiss on the cheek. He said, "It's always a pleasure to kiss a pretty woman."

"You wouldn't know much about that," Stuart growled. "You'd be better off if you would start chasing some woman rather than riling the queen."

Quentin laughed and then stepped aside, hands clasped, as Brandon went to his mother and kissed her on both cheeks, then to Claiborn, then shook hands with Stuart.

"It's good to see you, Son. And it means so much that you came to be with your uncle in his time of need."

"It's for him that I am here," Brandon said. "I thought that together we might talk some sense into him."

"Ah," Quentin said. "It all depends on what you consider logical. I think you'll find my views quite cogent."

Stuart gestured toward two chairs and said, "Please, both of you, sit down." He sat down beside Heather on a stuffed couch covered with a fine leather and kept his arm around her. He knew it must be a struggle for her to have their wayward son here and stay silent, to say nothing of the danger that her brother-in-law now faced. Claiborn was sitting beside the fire in his favorite chair, a blanket across his legs.

"Well, what about it?" the old man asked. "Tell us what's going on."

"I suppose you know more about what's going on at the palace than I do, Stuart," Quentin began. "From what I hear, the queen is besotted with Philip. She can't blow her nose without getting his permission."

"I'm afraid it's as they say. I wasn't even allowed to see her this last time. They have her surrounded by those loyal to Philip."

"She's a woman who thinks she's found love for the first time in her life," Heather said. "She's how old now? Thirty-eight? Thirty-nine? And as far as I can tell, she's never had a romance. A woman's heart is a tender thing."

"I fear you are right," Stuart said. "Her father used her as a pawn, hoping to marry her to this duke or that king or some other prince, and most of them young enough to be her sons or old enough to be her grandfather. She's never had a romance, and now she thinks she's found it."

"What do you think of Philip? You've met him, haven't you, Brother?" Quentin asked.

"Just once briefly, and some years ago. It's difficult to tell. He's one of those men who hide everything behind an agreeable smile. And now the people are in an uproar."

"As far as Dover," Brandon put in, "people are saying nasty things. They claim that Spaniards are thieves, a natural enemy of the British, that there are more Spanish than English in the streets of London. England for the English is what they cry."

"Even in London," Stuart said, "children shout insults as the royals go through the street and even throw stones at them."

"What was Mary thinking?" Heather shook her head. "She must have wanted a husband dreadfully."

"So she did, and I believe she still harbors the dream of having children," Stuart said.

"She's far too old for that," Heather said.

"It's possible." Quentin shrugged his shoulders and gave Heather a direct look. "Women in their forties in my flock routinely give birth. And it would give England an heir who would be entirely Catholic. If that occurs, the current uproar will seem like nothing in comparison with what is to come."

"I don't know what's to be done," Stuart said. "But I want to ask you to do something, and please don't say no."

"I will do anything I can for you, my brother, of course. Now, what is it?"

"I'd like you to take a holiday, go on an excursion. There is some Stoneybrook business that I hoped you would resolve for me."

"A holiday?" Suddenly Quentin's eyes narrowed. "You want to get me out of the country until this matter of burning of parsons and Protestants is over."

"Yes, I do," Stuart said adamantly. "Go to Ireland or the Low Countries. You've been working hard all your life. It wouldn't hurt you to take a year's absence."

"I'm not sure a year would do it, Stuart, but in any case, I can't go. You already know that."

"You must, Uncle," Brandon said. "Men—and women—are being arrested everywhere. Most of them are ministers of the new religion."

"They're called protestants now," Quentin said. "But I cannot flee. I must stay here and do what I can to help others during these trying times."

"Think, Brother. Think!" Stuart said. "Mary is far too aware of your affiliation with the protestants. I can only believe that she has spared you so far because of our family's long-term friendship with her. I think your four who were executed was a warning shot. She will not keep her dogs on a leash for long."

"I am aware of the danger. I choose to place my life in the hands of God."

Brandon leaned forward, his head in his hands. "Uncle, those people yesterday placed their lives in the hands of God."

"Yes, they did." He smiled. His eyes had a far-off look in them.

"It's so dangerous, Quentin," Heather tried. "Please, do what Stuart has asked."

Quentin's smile faded. "I appreciate your concern. But you all must think back. Think back to when Stuart was smuggling bibles into England for William Tyndale. Even Father and Uncle

Edmund took part. You, Heather, endured the intrigue and danger then. Did we falter? Did we fail our God then?"

"No, we did not." All eyes turned to Claiborn, who had remained silent until now. "We believed in what you were doing, Stuart, as God's will, just as I believe Quentin is now under his will."

The argument went on for some time, but in the end, as they feared, Quentin refused to even consider a retreat.

Stuart and Heather saw the men to the door.

"Brandon, you could stay the night," Heather suggested.

"No," he said, shaking his head. "I'm sorry I came. In the end I was of no use."

"No use?" Quentin said. He looked up at his nephew. "You gave me strength, man, standing beside me."

"But I came for you, to help you, Uncle. If all this did nothing to spare your life—"

"Our lives are not our own," Quentin said, looking about at the three of them. "How many times must I say this? And you, Brandon, your very presence brings me succor."

"I—Forgive me, Mother, Father. Obviously I have brought you pain."

"It is good to see you, Son," Stuart said. "Your mother and I wish to see you whenever possible, for whatever reason. Please, will you not stay the night? Resume your journey in the morning?"

Brandon shook his head. "I must be off."

"God be with you," Quentin said. "God be with us all."

Winter fell across England like an iron curtain. The skies were iron gray, and snowflakes as large as shillings shook loose from the clouds and covered the countryside in white. It made a beautiful scene, but it also made life difficult, especially for the poor. With no money to buy fuel, many foraged for anything that would burn.

The weather seemed to cast a deeper chill within Brandon. Lupa had known something was wrong with him ever since he had come back from his visit to his family. She suspected that the executions that took place daily intensified his fears. She had tried to talk to him about these moods, but he had simply refused to discuss the subject. She watched him now as he walked along a path that led to the open fields.

Rez was standing to one side by the fire, warming himself. "He's not himself, is he, Lupa?"

"He's shut tight and won't say a word."

Rez was gloomy too, for he hated the winter weather. "We ought to leave this place. We could go to Spain. It's sunny there most of the time. And business might be better."

"Yes, they're always so kind to gypsies in Spain, aren't they," Lupa said sarcastically. "No, I can't leave here. But you could go, Rez."

"I couldn't make it now without you and Brandon."

His words found a refrain in Lupa. She leaned closer to the window. The snow was at least eight inches deep and even deeper in drifts. Brandon was looking down and paying no attention to any of the activities that were going on around him. "I don't know what we're going to do. I'd like to get him to go with us somewhere. Somewhere where gypsies aren't hated."

"I'd like to know where that is," Rez said, with a short, bitter laugh. "Heaven maybe. You think gypsies have a standing in heaven?"

Lupa managed a small grin. "You don't have to worry about that. You'll never see heaven."

"Me? Well, why not? I'm as good as some of those popes that go there."

Lupa shrugged and turned back to stare blankly out the window.

Finally Rez asked, "What are we going to do? He don't care

about gambling no more. He just does it enough to see that we have cash."

"I don't know, Rez. I thought I could make any man forget his troubles, but he's different from other men."

"He's a deep one, he is. I didn't think so at first. Seemed right shallow. But now you can see he's wrestling with something deep inside. Think it's that uncle of his?" Rez came over and joined her at the window. "Look at him. He's all stooped over like he's got the world on his shoulders. Worried, he is. You can see it on him like a blanket."

Lupa did not answer, but she knew this was the truth. "I'll fix us something to eat."

"That's right. Maybe some meat in his belly will help him."

Lupa was a good cook, and by the time Brandon came in, she had the meal ready to put before him. "Look, fresh beef, and I made you an eel pie. You always like that."

"It sounds good," Brandon said.

His voice was cheerful, and he had a smile, but Lupa saw that it did not go all the way to his eyes. "Sit down here," she said.

"All right. Where's Rez?"

"Out trying to find our next game, I suppose."

"You ever think about God, Lupa?" Brandon asked abruptly.

She hesitated. "I try not to."

"Would you be afraid to die?"

"Of course I would. Only a fool's unafraid of death."

For a time Brandon was silent. He cut up his meat into small pieces but merely picked at his food. Lupa didn't comment, knowing there was no sense in urging him to eat. She desperately searched her mind for some way to give him comfort. All she had was physical love, and he already had that. He was the only man she ever saw who seemed to want more from her, but she did not know how to give it, and now she simply waited. To her relief he began to speak.

"I was never afraid on the battlefield, men falling all about me, but for some reason it never occurred to me that I might die there—or if it did, it didn't matter. But while I was visiting my uncle, I went to one of the burnings at Smithfield. They burned four people, one of them an old woman."

"I hear they are burning even children now."

A savage look crossed Brandon Winslow's face. "I'd like to take them apart, those that are responsible."

"You'd have to take the queen apart, then. It's her and that Spanish husband of hers who are behind it all. You can't fight them, Brandon."

Brandon did not answer. He picked up a mug of ale, took a swallow, and then put it down. "I suppose that's true. I think I'll go visit my parents again. Would you want to go?"

"Do you want me to?"

"It might be a change for you. Pretty grim in this place."

"They might not want to see me."

"They'll be glad enough. I'm the one they probably don't want to see. It's not you who's failed them, Lupa. It's me."

She leaned back in her chair and studied him. "Yes, I'll go with you." Better to be beside him than to sit back here, waiting and wondering if he would ever return to her again.

ꕥ

December brought a break in the bitter-cold weather. By the time Brandon and Lupa arrived at Stoneybrook, much of the snow had melted. It left the roads a soft, gooey mud, which made it hard on the horses. They arrived at Stoneybrook late in the afternoon, and at once, as they dismounted, James Campbell, the head groom, came up to them with a smile. Campbell was a short, muscular man in his midforties. He had black hair without a gray hair in it and sharp, dark eyes. He was always glad to see Brandon, for the two had been companions in poaching. Campbell's eyes lit up as he said, "Well, now,

Master Brandon, a pleasure it is to see you, sir. And you, too, my lady."

Lupa obviously liked 'my lady.' "Thank you."

"Is my father at home?" Brandon asked.

"That he is, sir. Let me take the horses. I'll groom them and see that they get a good feed. You go on in to meet your family." He turned to the horses, and then a sorrowful expression crossed his features. "I'm worried about your uncle. I'm afraid he's in for trouble."

"You mean because of his religious stand?"

"That's what it is. There were eight burnings right over in Canterbury yesterday. All of them were preachers. If you can, talk to you father about getting Master Quentin away from here."

"I'll do my best, but you know how stubborn he can be sometimes, James."

"I know, sir, but it may be a real matter of life or death." He led the horses away.

Twenty minutes later the visitors were greeting Brandon's parents, who were clearly overjoyed by his visit, even though he had Lupa in tow. Brandon was torn. He knew he would probably cause his parents less pain if he disappeared and remained away; but more and more, he couldn't resist the call to come home.

Claiborn came in next, looking a bit more feeble than last time and leaning hard on his cane.

They chatted for some time about Stoneybrook, about politics, but carefully avoiding any reference to Brandon's or Lupa's life in Dover. Indeed, Stuart and Heather didn't even ask where they were living now, perhaps not wishing to know.

Eventually Stuart said, "I've got a new bird I'd like you to see. A peregrine falcon."

"Against the law for anyone to own a peregrine except an earl. You haven't become an earl, have you, sir?"

"Not very likely," Stuart said, with a boyish grin. "That law is probably the most violated law in England. Come along. Maybe tomorrow we'll take him out, and you can fly him."

The two men left at once, and Claiborn dozed in his chair by the fire.

Lupa had great difficulty in meeting Heather's eyes. As a rule she had a fierce dislike of aristocracy, but Brandon's parents were different from what she expected. She knew that not all nobles and their wives were as gracious as these two, but it gave her an odd feeling to be in this situation.

Heather said, "It's good to see you, Lupa. You're looking so well."

"Thank you, ma'am."

"I've been hoping you'd come. As you must know, we're terribly worried about Brandon."

"I know you are." She hesitated, then said, "I'm worried about him, too."

"Worried about him? In what way?"

"He's not himself. He's changed. Something happened to him on his last visit to you, I think, when he went to see his uncle. When he came back, I could hardly get a word out of him. He's unhappy—miserable really. I thought maybe you knew why."

"I think it has something to do with the experience he had."

"You mean watching the people burn?"

"Yes. Did he speak of it?"

"Only once, and when I tried to question him, he told me he couldn't talk about it."

"How do you feel about Brandon, Lupa?"

Instantly Lupa grew defensive. "I know you'd rather he had never met me," she said.

"I never said that. You deserve something good, Lupa."

"He'll never marry me."

"Nobody knows about things like that."

"Would you ever accept me as a daughter-in-law?" Lupa said,

and her dark eyes burned as she stared at Heather. "You'd probably be ostracized for having a gypsy in your family."

"I want the best for Brandon, as every mother does. I want to see you both find something good in your life, and as far as I can tell, the best comes from serving God."

"We have different thoughts on that." Lupa managed to meet her eyes but not for long. She quickly turned her head. There was something essentially good in Heather Winslow, and to Lupa goodness was a rather frightening thing. She had always denied it existed. It had been the way she justified her own immoral life. But now she knew . . .

❧

Out in the mews where the falcons and hawks were kept, the two men were talking. They talked about the birds for quite a bit, and then Brandon said, "Father, you must do something about Uncle Quentin."

"What would you propose? Short of kidnapping him and spiriting him away in chains. He's as stubborn as—well, as stubborn as I am. Even as stubborn as you are, Son."

"I can't understand why he deliberately would court death. Such a horrible death."

"He's doing what God is telling him to do."

"But what if he dies? I haven't ever been able to get over that execution."

"I know it must have been terrible."

"The old woman! She reminded me of Grandmother. She had a sweet face. She went to her death with a smile. I couldn't do that."

"We'll do all we can, but now's the time that God wants our prayers."

Brandon shook his head. "You know I can't pray, Father."

"I know you'd better start praying. Everybody in England had better start praying or we're a lost nation."

They went back into the house, and the rest of the visit was almost meaningless to Brandon. He had thought it would help to see his father and mother, but it simply sent his spirits spiraling down. They had a faith he did not have, the same kind of faith, he knew, that could send them to the stake themselves. But it was Quentin who was in ever-present danger. When he told Lupa about it, he said, "They'll kill my uncle. They'll burn him just as they did the other people I saw."

"You can't do anything about that, right? What did your father say?"

"He said that God lets his favorites go through hard times. He said the blood of the martyrs is the seed of the church. I don't understand that, but I'll tell you this, Lupa. If my uncle is arrested, I will do something."

"They'll kill you if you try."

"Would it matter if they did?"

"Yes," she said, wrapping her arms around him. "It would. To me, Brandon."

He sighed and gently extricated himself from her embrace. The last thing he needed now was a woman in love with him. No one should love him. He was untrustworthy. A failure. A liar and a cheat. And considering the steadfastness of his family, utterly lost.

❧

Mary clung to Philip. She did not know if she pleased Philip in bed or not. He was a young man with the lust of a young man, and she was an older woman, too old to begin learning the secrets of a marital bed. But for the first time in her life she was in love.

The two of them walked along a garden path despite the inclement weather. Philip talked platitudes and of things that were taking place in the court and back in his native Spain, but when they returned to the house, she turned to him as they stood before the fire to gain some warmth. "We're making headway, Husband. We're destroying Protestantism."

"The people don't like it—your people, I mean."

"They don't understand. I've come to understand my father and the decisions he made. Heretics must be executed. They must face the fact that they are not serving God unless they are Catholic."

"Have you considered this?" Philip asked. "When the people see someone go to his death praising God as he is consumed, maybe they think he has something of God already?"

"That's impossible. They are heretics, Philip, and the only way that we're going to see England return to the old ways, the older religion, is to give them no quarter. We must make them see it's death to do anything else."

"What are your plans?"

"My council and I are making a list of prominent churchmen who have lost their way. They'll have a chance to repent, to give up this new religion and come back to the true faith. If not, they'll go to the stake."

This was what Philip and his father wanted, but he had seen the English people and the emperor had not. "The people are stubborn, my queen. Once you start something, it may not be as easy to bring it to a halt."

"God has put me on the throne to turn England back to the true faith, and that is what I will do." She hesitated, then said, "I have something else I must tell you."

"Something of the court?"

"No. Of us. For you and me, but for the court too."

"I don't understand you, Mary."

"I think I am with child."

Philip turned to her, eagerness in his movement and in his eyes. "Are you certain?"

"I have good cause to believe it."

"When will it be?"

"I can't be certain. But when we have a child, that will change everything."

"Yes." Her handsome husband smiled. "Yes, it will change things indeed. I'm happy for you."

"I'm happy for both of us."

February was nearly past and an early spring seemed nearly upon them. Lupa and Rez had been gone for a week, determined to make some money on their own, and Brandon sat by the window day after day, staring outside. He had just forced himself to shave and dress when Polly, one of the maids, knocked on the door and said, "Master Brandon, there's a gentleman to see you."

"What's his name, Polly?"

"Don't know sir, but he's a fine gentleman."

Brandon went down the stairs, and in the large room where meals were served he saw a tall man, obviously of the nobility. "I am Brandon Winslow, sir."

"My name is John Fairfax." He put out his hand and Brandon shook it.

A shock of memory ran through Brandon. He had heard of the Earl of Fairfax often from his father and from others. He was a powerful member of the Privy Council, and for one brief moment Brandon thought, *He has soldiers outside and he's come to arrest me.*

"May I be of service to you, Lord Fairfax?" he asked, willing his voice to be steady.

"Yes, you could." Fairfax wore a large diamond ring and he held in his hands an ermine fur hat that was likely worth a great deal. He was fortunate that Lupa was not at home or he would've had a cold head on his ride home, Brandon thought. "Is there some place private where we might speak?" Fairfax asked.

"Yes, of course. Perhaps we'd better go to my room. It will be private there."

"I would very much appreciate it."

"Innkeeper, bring us some hot mulled wine to drink. Will you have something to eat, my lord?"

"No thank you, but a hot drink would go down well."

Brandon nodded and led the way upstairs.

"Please, sit down. The drinks will be here shortly."

"Thank you, Mr. Winslow."

Brandon sat down, his mind alert for the first time in what felt like weeks. Why he should be arrested he had no idea, but he had done plenty of things that could bring an arrest.

"I know you were not expecting me, and I have something to say to you, Mr. Winslow, that may come as a shock." The earl's voice was pleasantly moderate. He was a handsome man of some fifty years, as far as Brandon could judge. There seemed to be no threat in him.

"I'd be interested to hear it, Lord Fairfax."

Brandon started when a maid knocked at the door. He took the tray from the girl quickly and shut the door again. He handed a mug to Lord Fairfax.

"I have a story to tell you, and I would appreciate it if you would simply listen until I finish. Then I will be glad to answer any questions."

"Of course."

"My wife and I wanted many children, but we had only one, a daughter. She was the light of our life. We named her Eden. Until she was four years old she brought great joy to us." He hesitated, then picked up his ale and sipped it. This was, Brandon saw, something difficult for him to talk about.

"To make a long story short, we sent my daughter and her governess on a sea journey to be with my brother. I had to make a diplomatic journey for the king. My wife came with me. It was the worst mistake I ever made." He rubbed his temples and shook his head. "Before they reached shore, the ship was attacked in a raid by Spanish pirates. As far as we knew, everyone on the ship was killed, including our daughter's governess. It nearly broke my wife and me, too."

"I'm very sorry to hear it, my lord."

"Thank you, Mr. Winslow." Fairfax leaned forward, and a light came into his eyes. "A month ago a man came to me with some startling news, which I did not believe at first. He said that my daughter had not been killed, that she had been taken captive by the captain of the band of pirates. The man who came to me freely admitted that he was one of the crew."

"My first thought was natural enough, that he was out to get money from me, but I listened to his story. There were points in his story that I could verify easily enough. I began investigating, and I found out that, as far as I can determine, he is telling the truth. His name is Francisco Diaz and his story amounts to this. That same pirate chief Jaspar Mendoza who attacked the ship on which my daughter sailed is now a man of some wealth, but is still searching desperately for respectability. My agents have discovered that the young woman who he calls his daughter appeared sixteen years ago almost magically. Her description would fit our daughter perfectly. Blond hair and blue eyes. Not a drop of Spanish blood in her. And that is why, sir, I wanted to see you."

Brandon was completely mystified. "To see me, Lord Fairfax? Why would you want to see me?"

"Because I need someone who is crafty, determined, and absolutely fearless."

"Your agents must know my reputation."

"Those are all good qualities for my purposes."

"Then you also know that I am immoral. Your agents probably told you that as well."

"Indeed they did. Including your bad experience in the military and the fact that now you are a cheating gambler living with gypsies and certainly headed one day for the noose."

"True enough. But why are you telling me these things?"

Sir John leaned forward, his eyes sharp and eager. "I want you to go to Spain and bring my daughter back."

Brandon laughed. "Well, there are two problems. The first is it probably can't be done, and the second is I'm not the man for a noble gesture. Whoever goes for you will probably lose his head after being tortured to near death."

"Yes, I'm aware of that, but I think you'll agree to go."

"I won't take your money, Lord Fairfax. It's an impossible thing you're asking."

"Are you aware that I'm a member of the queen's council?"

Brandon stilled. "Yes, I am. I've heard my father speak of you several times."

"My daughter is eighteen years old now. My wife and I want her back, and you are the man to go and get her. I will pay you well for the task, but perhaps this will be more of an incentive for you to undertake the mission."

Brandon watched as Fairfax pulled a paper out of his inner pocket and handed it to him. "What is this, my lord?"

"It is a list of men and women and even children who are going to be arrested and in all probability burned at the stake if they do not relent and accept the Catholic way."

Brandon ran his eyes down the list and suddenly straightened. One name jumped out at him.

"My uncle's name is on this list!"

"Yes. That's why I'm here."

Brandon felt a coldness creeping over him. His eyes flicked up to meet Fairfax's. "You're telling me you can save him?"

"I can't promise that I will save him permanently, but I can . . . protect him for a time. I can have his name taken off this list. I have that much influence with the queen. I'll have to lie, of course, and your uncle will have to do some cooperating."

"I doubt he'll do it."

"In any case, that's the proposition. It will be up to you to talk sense into your uncle. But I'll do my part."

"How soon are these people to be arrested?"

"Some of them will be arrested by nightfall. If you agree to accept this charge, I must hurry back to the palace so as to use my influence with the queen. She owes me a favor."

Brandon considered, but he knew what he had to do. "I think it's a fool's mission, Lord Fairfax, but I will do my best."

He stood up and Brandon stood with him. They shook hands. "I accept your word, Winslow."

"Then you are a fool. Even you said you knew I was a liar and a cheat."

"I believe your father is Stuart Winslow, and he is a man of honor. Your uncle is Quentin Winslow, a man whose honor nobody doubts. Some of that must be in you, Brandon Winslow. I only hope you can use your less sterling qualities to aid you in freeing my daughter. We'll have to make careful arrangements." His smile was chilly. "To see that you are not apprehended and your head chopped off."

"That wouldn't be so bad, but to be burned alive . . . I don't want anyone I care about to face that—including myself."

Lord Fairfax hesitated. "You realize, Winslow, that she'll be well guarded. You'll die if they catch you trying to kidnap her. I don't know how you will do it, but I'm putting my hope in you and God."

"I don't know God, Lord Fairfax, but for once in my life I am going to offer myself to him as I do to you."

"I pray that God will reward you for your bravery. Come, then. Get your things together and we'll leave at once. I'll go to the queen, secure more time for your uncle, and then we will meet some of my men at the estate. There we will formulate your plan."

"I'll be ready in an hour." Brandon wrote a quick note for Lupa, gathered some of his clothes, went downstairs, and found an ornate carriage waiting outside the inn, his horse tethered behind it. Brandon climbed into the carriage and sat down across from Lord Fairfax.

"I'm ready."

❧

As Brandon approached the outskirts of Dover several days later, the snow was swarming into miniature tornadoes with the breath of the wind. He had not yet been able to absorb the shock of his meeting with Lord Fairfax and had paused only once on his way back to Dover to think about what he had agreed to do in two weeks' time. Even now his mind seemed to buzz as if filled with swarming bees. He pulled his horse to a halt and stared at the city before him. He noted that snow had covered the rooftops and every sharp angle was now a soft, rounded curve. The trees were rounded too, molded into foreign forms by the snow. The sun brought forth a glitter so that Dover seemed like a city of tiny flashing diamonds beside a wash of blue sea.

His thoughts went to the life he had led since meeting Lupa. As always disgust filled him when he considered how futile his life had become. He had struggled to find a way to change his life, to get away from Lupa and the life that he had been leading. He had often struggled with the temptation simply to ride away and leave everything behind, including Lupa, but could never see where he was to go. Now, as he sat looking at the city, he felt a surge of hope for the first time in years. Deep down he longed to find a trace of honor in himself, despite the life he had been leading, a reason to hold his head high again.

"Come on, boy, let's go." Despite his misgivings about the life he led with Lupa and Rez, he still owed them a debt. They had saved his life. And Lupa, God bless her, loved him, despite all his faults. He could not walk away without at least saying good-bye.

Brandon rode into town, noting the strange snow-driven silence that cloaked the world, and brought his horse to a stop before the Anchor and Albatross Inn. As he dismounted, a hostler came out of the stable across the street.

"Stable your horse, Mr. Winslow?"

"Yes. Grain him and rub him down, Paul." He reached into his pocket, pulled out a coin, added another. "I've ridden him far of late, so be good to him."

"Aye, sir. That I will."

Tiny flakes of snow stung Brandon's face like miniature needles. Reaching shelter in the inn, he pulled off his hat and cloak, shook them out, and hung them on a peg. Moving to the huge fireplace, he held out his hands to the warmth.

"So you're back, are you, Master Winslow?"

Brandon gave the innkeeper a faint smile, "Yes, Jones, I am." He had grown to know Byron Jones fairly well. In his youth, Jones had been a fighter and brawler in inns, and he bore the scars of his ancient battles: his nose was crooked, one eye drooped, and large gaps between his teeth could be seen when he smiled. He was still, even at the age of fifty, a formidable man and did not need to hire anyone to keep order at the Anchor and Albatross.

"Will you be having something to eat, sir?"

"Yes, whatever you have."

Jones nodded. "Yes, sir. I'll get you something very good." He started to speak again, then seemed to cut off the words. "I'll get your food, sir," he muttered. Brandon wondered what was on the man's mind. He put the matter out of his own, and when he was thawed out, he went over to a table in a corner and sat down. The room was illuminated by lanterns and candles, and there were only four customers, two of them sitting at a table and two sitting alone. He sat alone and facing the fireplace, deep in thought, until Jones brought him a trencher full of smoking meat. "Got some hot punch for you, sir."

"Looks good, Jones."

Brandon started to sample the punch and then glanced up. He saw a wrinkle in the innkeeper's brow and knew that something was on his mind.

"What is it, Jones?"

"Well, sir, I was wondering how Miss Lupa is doing."

"Lupa? Why, I've been gone for a few days. Why are you asking about her?"

Jones wiped his hands on the filthy apron that hung from his waist and shook his head. "You ain't 'eard then, 'ave you, sir?"

"Heard what?"

"Well, she's been hurt, sir. Hurt pretty bad, so I hear."

Brandon straightened up. "Hurt how? What happened to her?" He saw Jones hesitate and then snapped, "Out with it, man. What's wrong with her?"

"Well, sir, I ain't one to carry tales, but in this case you might ought to know. She was—with a man, and they 'ad some kind of argument, and the man stabbed her."

Brandon stilled. With another man? She hadn't . . . Not since . . . He looked up. "Is it bad?"

"Right bad, so Rez said. Sorry to give you bad news, Master Winslow."

Brandon leaped to his feet and grabbed his cloak and hat. He did not go for his horse but ran down the street. When he got to the tiny house he had purchased for Lupa, he found Rez standing in the middle of the room.

"What is it, Rez? How is she?"

"The doctor's been with her, Brandon."

"What did he say? How did it happen?"

"She was drinking with a pretty bad man, and they had some sort of fight, and he pulled a knife and stabbed her."

"What does the doctor say?"

Rez lowered his head and fumbled at his jerkin. Brandon

could see that he was badly shaken. He grabbed Rez's shoulders. "How is she, Rez?"

"The doctor says she can't live."

The news struck Brandon like a blow, bringing with it a sharp sense of guilt. He had not been here . . . He had been unkind to her . . . "Is she conscious?"

"At times. She just lost too much blood, the doctor said, and she can't make it."

"I should never have left!"

Rez said, "Well, don't hold it against her about the man. She missed you, Brandon, and she needed someone." He suddenly broke down. Brandon flinched.

When he got into the bedroom, he was shocked. Lupa was lying flat on her back. Her face was pale as parchment. He took a deep breath and a few unsteady steps to the side of the bed. He took her hand. "Lupa, can you hear me?" he whispered.

Lupa's eyes opened, but she did not seem to see anything. A shudder went through her. She turned her face to him, and recognition came. "I'm dying, Brandon," she whispered.

"No, you're not dying!"

"Yes, I am."

Brandon wished desperately that his uncle or one of his parents was there to speak to her. "Call on God and confess your sins, Lupa."

"No. There's no mercy for me. I'm going to die. I'm going to hell." She suddenly arched her back and with a surprising show of strength screamed, "I'll be burning—burning—burning!"

She would not stop. Rez came in. He said nothing to Brandon. He leaned over and whispered something to Lupa in Spanish, and she stopped then began to cry.

Brandon kept her hand in his and sat there as miserable as he had ever been in his life.

❧

Brandon heard a church bell chime and knew that he had been sitting there for three hours.

"Brandon . . ." He saw that Lupa was watching him. He leaned over and kissed her and said, "Lupa, don't die."

He saw sheer terror in her eyes. "I—loved you, Brandon. But you never loved me."

And then she took a deep breath and expelled it. And then she was very still.

❧

The funeral was small. Rez and Brandon stood beside the open grave. The coffin was lowered into the earth. Brandon stood numbly watching as the priest said words he was unable to hear.

When the ceremony was over, Rez asked, "What are you going to do, Brandon?"

"I don't know, Rez." A profound sorrow claimed him. Something was tearing at his spirit. "I feel like the heavens have fallen."

"They have," Rez said. He walked away without another word.

Brandon walked in the other direction. He went to his room, gathered what few things he had, stuffed them into a bag, then went to the stable for his horse. He paid the bill, watched as the hostler saddled his mount, and then rode out.

As he left Dover, the snow began to fall again. He rode along the road that led to London for a time. Needing a break, he got off his horse, tied him to a tree and walked over to gaze down upon a wide river covered with ice and snow. Brandon had never felt so utterly devastated in his life. He had been ready to leave Lupa, say good-bye. But knowing he had let her down, had failed to protect her, chafed him. Brandon stood on the river bank, motionless misery flooding him, and he looked up into the sky and cried out, "God, I didn't love her, but you could have allowed me to save her, as she saved me."

There was no answer from the silent heavens, and the falling snow blotted out the heavens themselves.

Brandon felt tears gather in his eyes. He was not a man who cried, but now he began to weep. Not in neat little tears but in great sobs, he cried out, "God—God, where are you? Is she with you now? Have mercy on Lupa, God! Have mercy on her!"

How long he stood by the river he didn't know, but in the midst of the swirling snow, Brandon Winslow realized that God was there. He had never felt God this close before, and it frightened him. He crumpled to his knees. The knowledge of what he was—and the sudden thought of an eternity looming before him—brought him to his feet. He stumbled, then began to run, all the time dimly recognizing that he couldn't run faster than God.

PART THREE

The Rescue

13

The harbor at Southampton blossomed with what seemed to be hundreds of sails. The cold weather had broken, and a hint of spring was in the air. Brandon stood on the deck of the *Cloud,* and for a moment took in the beauty of it before turning to face Lord Fairfax, who had come down to give him funds and last-minute instructions. Fairfax's face was pale, and the March wind ruffled his silver hair. He seemed to be at a loss for words.

Brandon said, "I understand the task before me, Lord Fairfax. I know that I carry your hopes with me, as well as your funds."

"I believe you can do it, my boy. I've heard stories about your courage from your commanding officers and even from Queen Mary herself."

Fairfax produced a bulging leather bag. "Here are more funds for you. I don't know how much you'll need, but this should cover all of it."

Taking the bag in his hands, Brandon seemed to weigh it. For a moment he was silent, then he looked up and asked, "Are you certain that my uncle is safe?"

"For the time being."

"What does that mean?" Brandon saw that Lord Fairfax was nervous, and it troubled him.

"Nobody is really safe in this country unless they swear to abide by Catholic tradition," Lord Fairfax said flatly. "It's bad, and it's going to get worse, but I'll do the best I can for your uncle. I understand your father is very close to the queen. He will appeal to the queen too."

A breeze stirred the harbor, bringing a wave that tilted the *Cloud* to one side. Then the ship settled. Putting the bag into his inner pocket, Brandon said, "It's going to be difficult, but I'll do my best, sir."

"It's going to be more than difficult. You'll be killed by Mendoza if he suspects anything. Here are the documents that prove you are interested in buying fine horses in Spain—in my name, of course. That will lead you to Jaspar Mendoza's business. At least, one of his businesses, I should say, fine horses. This should give you access to him and to my daughter." He pulled out another paper and said, "Here is a letter from Queen Mary to the emperor. She introduces you and asks that he accept you as a friend of Spain."

"How in the world did you get this?"

"Well, the queen has a warm spot in her heart for you. She remembers that you came with the troops when it was in doubt whether she would ever be crowned or not. She's never forgotten that. She's a puzzling woman."

"Yes, she is, and a troublesome one."

"Well, get our daughter back, my boy. Do anything you have to do." Suddenly a thin smile turned the corners of Lord Fairfax's lips upward. "If you have to, court her and make her fall in love with you. Then elope to England to get her safely home."

"I doubt if that would work, but I'll tell her what she's missing over here. As for any other method, I hope it doesn't come to that."

"So do I. God bless your efforts, Brandon. My wife and I will pray for you every day."

ꕥ

The harbor of San Sebastián was not nearly as large as Southampton's. There were ships there, but most of them small. Brandon stood at the rail, desperately racking his brain, as he had for most of the past three days, for some way to extract Eden Fairfax and transform her from Dolores Mendoza into an Englishwoman.

A voice made him turn to see that Captain Bailey had come to stand beside him. Bailey, a short, barrel-shaped individual with frosty blue eyes and a shock of white hair, was studying him carefully.

"Well, it's been an easy voyage, but I tell you, Master Brandon, I'm glad you're getting off the ship."

"Not very considerate of you, Captain. I thought I behaved rather well."

"Other than winning too much money from my passengers."

"I'm sorry. Voyages are boring, and gambling is one way to break it. But I think I did outdo myself."

The two men stood together as the *Cloud* was hauled into the harbor by two long boats, each with twenty sailors at the oars. As the ship nosed its way in, Bailey asked, "What brings you to Spain, Winslow?"

"I'm on a quest to buy horses. But I've heard that Spanish women are quite beautiful too."

"Better be careful. Spanish men are jealous of their women. They'll slit your throat."

"I'll try to avoid that."

"Farewell, Winslow. Have a good visit."

"Thank you, Captain."

The *Cloud* continued to edge forward. When a gangplank was thrown down, Brandon marched down it. He had his bags carried by one of the sailors. When the man put the baggage down on the dock, Brandon gave him a coin, saying, "Thanks for your help."

"Yes, sir. Anytime."

"Do you know anything about getting about in this country?"

The sailor smiled. He had a big gap between his teeth and a scar that ran from the corner of his cheek all the way down to his neck. "It bloody irregular, but easy enough to navigate once you get the way of it they say."

Brandon looked about and made his way to a building that seemed to be an office of some kind. There he found a tall, thin man wearing a white shirt and a red sash around his thin middle.

"I've just arrived in the *Cloud*. How does one get from here to Madrid?" Even as he spoke, he remembered Lupa teaching him Spanish, and, as always, felt a sharp regret for her death.

"With great difficulty, I'm afraid." The clerk shrugged. "There is no regular service. You can hire a carriage or a horse. It's a little dangerous though. The highwaymen have been pretty busy of late."

It was already late in the day, so Brandon knew he would be going nowhere until the next day at the earliest. "Where can a man get a good lodging, a clean place with good food?"

"Try the White Dove Inn down the street there. Just follow the street and you'll see it on your right. Tell them Manuel sent you. The owner is my brother-in-law. He'll give you a good price and good food."

"Thank you very much, Manuel."

Brandon hired two men to carry his luggage. The White Dove proved indeed to be a clean, attractive place. He tipped the men when they had put his luggage in his room and went to stare out the window. He could see the ocean. The March winds were making whitecaps on the teal sea. He went downstairs and ate a good meal of veal and fresh vegetables washed down by a Spanish wine that was surprisingly good. It was too early to go to bed, so he walked the streets of San Sebastián for an hour and then made his way to the harbor and sat on a sea wall watching the ships as daylight faded. Some of the ships had lanterns on their mast that reminded him of fireflies as they bobbed erratically. At length he made his way toward the inn.

He was almost there when a dark shape came out of a side street, and said threateningly, "Give me your money or I'll kill you!"

The man was very close. Brandon stepped to one side, at the same time throwing a hard punch. It caught the man in the face, and he staggered backward. Quickly Brandon was on him and struck two blows that laid him out. He was still. Brandon leaned forward. "I hope I haven't killed him." He could see by the pale silver light of the moon that he was a small pale-faced man. *Looks English,* Brandon thought. He stood up and waited uncertainly, and when his victim finally began to stir, he demanded, "What's your name?"

"I—my name is Smith. Philemon Smith."

"You're a highwayman, are you?"

"I tried to be, but you're the second man I've tried. The first took my pistol away and beat me with it."

Brandon smiled. "I think you've mistaken your vocation. You're English by your speech."

"Yes, sir, I am."

"Why are you here?"

"I was a servant, sir, to Lord Watson. I was afraid I'd be burned if I stayed."

"Burned? For what?"

"Well, I'm not a Catholic, sir. I was a deacon in a small church in Kent. My pastor and two of the leaders of the church were arrested by the queen's forces. They were coming for me, but I got away. I stowed away on the first ship out of England. When the master found out I had no money, he beat me and put me ashore here."

An idea suddenly came to Brandon. He pulled the man up. "You're accustomed to looking out for gentlemen?"

"Oh, yes, sir. I was with Lord Kenneth Watson for eight years."

"Well, come along. Where did you get a name like Philemon?"

"My mother picked it out from the Bible, she did."

"A good place to find a name."

The two walked down the street lit by a pale moon. When they got to the inn, Brandon called the innkeeper over and said, "Bring up some good food and wine to my room for my friend."

"Is he staying with you, sir?"

"Yes, he is."

"Then that will be extra, I'm afraid."

"That is fine. Put it on my bill. And please hurry with the food. Come along, Philemon."

He led the way upstairs. When they got to his room, he looked the man over. Philemon Smith was a slight man of medium height with sandy hair and light-blue eyes. His cheeks were gaunt, probably from hunger, and his cheek and his eye were swelling from Brandon's punches.

"Sit over here."

Philemon obediently did as he was bid. Brandon dipped a cloth into a bowl of water and said, "Put that on your eye to stop it from swelling." He sat down and questioned Philemon carefully. As far as he could determine, the man was telling the truth. His speech was better than that of most servants.

Finally the meal came.

"Are you hungry?"

"I haven't eaten in nearly three days, sir."

"Well, don't gobble too much."

For a time he watched as Philemon ate. Then he said, "Smith, I want you to serve me."

Smith looked up and blinked with surprise. "How can I do that, sir?"

"My name is Brandon Winslow. I'll be in Spain for some time, and I'll need somebody to take care of my clothes and do the things that you probably did for Sir Watson."

"Oh, indeed, sir, I can do that!"

"Very well. You'll sleep in this room. I'll have them rig up some sort of bed. Tomorrow we'll fit you out with new clothes, and we'll see how it works out. I'll pay you well for your time."

"How long will you be here in Spain, Mr. Winslow?"

"That's uncertain. I'm going to Madrid tomorrow. You'll go with me."

"Oh, thank you, sir. I'll serve you well!"

"Why, you look much better, Philemon," Brandon said. He stepped back and looked at his new servant, who had been fitted out with new clothes and had had his hair trimmed. His eye was still swollen, but he looked well in the brown suit that the tailor had provided. "Now, come along. I need to get to Madrid, and the safest way is to buy my own carriage. Can you drive?"

"Not as well as you, I would think, sir."

"Well, you'll do well enough."

The morning was spent finding transportation. Brandon bought two bays, perfectly matched, and a fine carriage. The carriage had belonged to a Spanish don who had lost it gambling. It was just what Brandon needed. He also bought a pistol for Philemon and an extra one for himself. By noon they were ready to go. Philemon loaded the carriage, climbed into the driver's seat, and Brandon said, "Well, we're off to Madrid."

"I thank the good Lord that you found me, Mr. Winslow. Or that I found you."

Brandon shared a smile with him. For a moment, he was tempted to say something about his dangerous mission, but he dared not trust the man. He spoke to the horses, and they started out at an eager trot. "A beautiful team, aren't they?"

"Yes, sir. May I ask, sir, are you a Christian?"

"I was baptized. Why do you ask?"

"Well, things are so bad in England now that if a person is a Christian, he'd better be a Catholic or his life may be forfeit."

"That'll change some day."

"I hope so, sir. I purely hope so!"

❧

The trip from San Sebastián to Madrid took three days of hard driving. Brandon chose to spend the second night at a small inn. He was pleased with Philemon, who cared for him as if he were royal. The man knew how to arrange clothes, how to dress him, and he shaved Brandon as neatly as any barber. Not since his days at Stoneybrook had Brandon been so well cared for.

At midday, Brandon pulled the carriage up in front of an inn in Madrid. "That looks like a good place to stay. I'll see if they have a room."

Philemon took the reins. Brandon found the innkeeper, arranged to have the horses cared for, got a room, and added an extra mattress for Philemon. Then he went outside and said, "Philemon, I want you to do something. There's a man here in Madrid called Jaspar Mendoza. He has a daughter named Dolores. I want you to make some friends here and find out what you can." He pulled some money out of his pocket. "Find some woman that gossips and romance her a little. I wish you spoke Spanish."

"Why, I *do* speak Spanish, sir. I spent two years with my master while he was an ambassador in Madrid. Exactly what did you want to know about this Mendoza?"

"Everything you can find out about his family. Who their friends are. If there's any gossip about the girl. And keep your mouth shut. You understand?"

"Of course, sir. That's understood."

Brandon went at once to the royal palace, an ornate building with many spires. The palace swarmed with crowds of people. He was directed to a gate, where he was halted by six sentries. "I have a letter here for the emperor," he said in Spanish.

"And your name is?"

"Brandon Winslow."

"I will see if the emperor will see you, but it may be a long wait."

"That'll be fine."

"Please sit down over there. I'll have some wine sent if you'd like, sir."

"That would be excellent."

Indeed, it proved to be a long wait, at least two hours. Finally the guard he had spoken with returned and said, "The emperor will see you, but his time is very short."

"I will be very brief."

Brandon followed the guard into the palace, which seemed to be an intricate maze of hallways. Beautiful pictures were on the wall, many of them of the Virgin and of Jesus on the cross. Eventually they came to another guard.

"What is your name, sir?"

"Brandon Winslow. I have a letter for the emperor."

The guard disappeared through an impressive door and was back almost at once. "You may come in."

Brandon was somewhat surprised to find a rather ordinary-looking, aged man in fine clothes—the emperor, the most powerful man in the world—sitting at a desk, just as his father might. His hands were unsteady. He had an aquiline nose and aristocratic features.

"I thank you for seeing me, Your Majesty," Brandon said, stopping ten paces away. "I have a letter here from Queen Mary."

"Ah, very good!" The emperor beckoned him forward, took

the letter, opened it, and scanned it. "It is good to hear from my fellow monarch. She speaks well of you, sir."

"She's been very kind to me and to my family."

"You've known Queen Mary for a long time?"

"Oh, yes, Your Majesty. My father, Stuart Winslow, is one of her favorites."

"Well, I want to hear much more, but I have no time just now, Mr. Winslow." He paused, considering him. "We're having a ball tonight. Please join us and afterward we'll have time to talk."

"Thank you. That's very gracious of you." Brandon saw that he was dismissed.

He made his way back to the inn and sat down for a meal. While he was eating, Philemon Smith came in and said, "Well, sir, I've heard a few things."

"Sit down. Order something." He waited until Smith had ordered his food and said, "Now, what did you find out?"

"Well, I found out that Mendoza is a cutthroat. He was a pirate in his younger days until middle age. Bad reputation, sir. Not a good man to cross."

"What does he do now?"

"He breeds horses, and he does a few other things that are not quite so respectable. He owns three ships, and they have been known to raid others and bring the booty into San Sebastián."

"What about his daughter?"

"Why, the lady I was talking to says she's a beautiful creature. She had a friend who was a maid to Miss Dolores, and this friend of hers said that the lady is unhappy."

"Why is she unhappy?"

"Her father's determined to marry her off to a rich grandee. Someone who can raise Mendoza's status. He's looking for respectability."

"He'd have to give up pirating if he got that."

"I suppose so. But if his son-in-law is powerful enough, he won't have to do such things. Anyway, Miss Dolores's maid said that she was unhappy because she's romantic, and there's not much romance about a marriage in Spain among aristocrats. The family decides, the girl obeys."

"A little like in England, isn't it?"

"Even more so here, sir."

When Philemon finished, Brandon said, "I'll be going to a ball tonight. Find me something suitable to wear."

"Shall I go with you, sir?"

"No. You keep nosing around to see what you can find out."

"Yes, sir. I'll do some more digging."

❧

Dolores Mendoza snapped angrily, "Juanita, you're sticking me with that pin!"

"Oh, my lady, I am sorry! I'm so clumsy."

Dolores looked at herself in the mirror and shook her head. "This is a frightful dress."

"Well, it cost enough. It ought to be pretty."

"Well, it's not. It's hideous."

"Who will be at the ball tonight, lady?"

"The same people that are always there."

"So many men that want to marry you," Juanita clucked in approval as Dolores stood up. "It must be wonderful to have so many men after you."

"They're not after me. They're after my father's money. I'm sick and tired of it, Juanita. Women are kept like prize dogs or horses. One of my father's horses has more freedom than I have."

"Oh, lady, you mustn't say that!"

"Why not? It's true. I wish—" Dolores broke off abruptly as her father entered the room.

"Ah, you look charming, my dear." Mendoza was a strongly

built man with dark coloring and a pair of sharp black eyes. He wore expensive clothing, but it could not hide the lack of grace in him.

"Thank you, Father."

"I have good news. Don Pedro Varga will be at the ball. I want you to show him a great deal of attention."

"Of course, but he's an old man."

"Why, he's not old. He's only fifty-two, and he's one of the most influential men in Spain. The emperor has complete trust in him. He would make you a good husband."

"You have different ideas from I about a husband. I want love! With a young man!"

Mendoza laughed, came over, and touched her cheek. "You're too romantic. Who has filled you with such foolish ideas?" His expression grew more serious, determined. "You must pay much attention to Don Pedro, Dolores. He's a man who can do great things for us."

Dolores listened and she nodded, but she dreaded the idea of spending time at the ball with an old man. Almost at once after Medoza left, her stepmother came in and said, "You need to hurry, Dolores. And do as your father says about Don Pedro."

"Yes, Mama." She used the term solely as a means of paying respect. Her mother was Mendoza's third wife. She was only twenty-six. She was fairly plain, but her father was wealthy, and a huge dowery had come with her.

"What a catch Don Pedro would be! You'd be one of the nobility. Your father wants that."

"He wants to wipe out his early days as a pirate, but that can never be."

"Oh, yes, if you have money enough, anything is forgiven." She looked at Dolores, then shrugged. "I know you're not happy about this man, but I felt the same about your father. We women do what we have to do."

❧

The ballroom was crowded, and Dolores was bored. She had danced with many of the young men and some of the older ones, but she had danced the most with Don Pedro Varga. Her father said he was only in his fifties, but he appeared much older. He was a thin man with care written on his face, and even a dance fatigued him. He finally departed, kissing Dolores's hand and murmuring something about what a pleasure it had been.

Dolores was bored to tears. She had done all this before, but this time she knew her father was in earnest. Suddenly disgust filled her, and she went out into the garden outside the ballroom, coming to stand beside a large fountain. She stood looking into it. Her thoughts were unhappy and even angry. *I can't stand that old man! Maybe Father will change his mind.* But she knew he would not, and a black melancholy filled her at the thought of what it would be like to marry a man she cared nothing for.

"I take it you are bored, señorita."

Dolores turned quickly, taken off guard. She answered sharply, for she hated to be surprised. "You are intruding, sir!"

"Forgive me. May I introduce myself? I'm a visitor to your country, as you might guess. My name is Brandon Winslow."

Dolores hesitated. She studied the man carefully, impressed by his good looks. He was easily identifiable as English. He was perfectly dressed. He had a wedge-shaped face with a wide mouth and a pair of the lightest blue eyes she had ever seen. His hair was auburn with a tint of gold in it. There was an assurance in him that challenged her. "Do you often force yourself on young ladies, sir?"

"How might I apologize enough? I still say you look bored."

"What is that to you?"

"You are quite right. It is none of my business, we being strangers and all." He looked up at the sky. She admired, despite herself, the lean, muscular length of his body. The suit fit him to perfection. He had broad shoulders and a narrow waist, and there was an air of strength about him. "I came out to look at the stars." He looked back at her. "They are beautiful, aren't they?" But as he said these last words, he was staring into her eyes.

"I—I suppose so."

"They always remind me of love."

"The stars? Why would they remind you of love?"

"Because lovers are like the stars. They burn brilliantly for a time, but then they fade."

"I don't believe all stars fade. Some burn brightly for hundreds of years." Dolores was intrigued. The man had a brashness that challenged her. "I suppose you have written many poems to your lovers back in England."

"No, I'm not a poet. I do have one that I like, though. Would you like to hear it?"

"Yes, I would."

"It is a very old poem about a man and a woman in love. It goes like this:

Gather ye rosebuds while ye may,
Old Time is still a-flying:
And this same flower that smiles today
Tomorrow will be dying.

The glorious lamp of heaven, the sun,
The higher he's a-getting,
The sooner will his race be run,
And nearer he's to setting.

That age is best which is the first,
When youth and blood are warmer;
But being spent, the worse, and worst
Times still succeed the former.

Then be not coy, but use your time,
And while ye may, go marry:
For having lost but once your prime,
You may forever tarry.

Dolores stared at the man. He had a musical voice. She said, "I don't understand it. What does it mean?"

"Why, lady, it means that men and women are to love while they are young, for that is the time of love."

"It must have been written by an Englishman. We Spanish are more moral than the English."

"Ah, but that's what the poet warns against. He says you must smell the rose while it is young, for soon it will be dry and withered. And women and men must use their youth for love, for the time will come when love will not be possible." Moving closer, Brandon whispered, "Don't let the time for love pass you by. Do not hide behind morality. That's what the poem means."

"I'm not interested in your talk about love! You Englishmen are too forward. You have no manners. We have not even been properly introduced."

"May I know your name, señorita?"

"I am Dolores Mendoza. My father is Jaspar Mendoza."

"And I am Brandon Winslow. I am happy to meet you."

Dolores asked, "What are you doing in Spain?"

"I came to buy horses to take back to England."

"My father's horses are the best."

"So I understand. I'd like to see them."

"Well, they are for sale." She paused and then said, "Are you married, Señor Winslow?"

"No."

"Why not?"

"God has not given me a helpmate as he did for Adam. But he will give me a wife some day."

Dolores was intrigued. "How will you know her? Will she be beautiful?"

"Inwardly yes, for inner beauty is what a man should seek."

"I've never heard a man say that before."

"Well, consider it, señorita. A woman can lose her outer beauty through the pox, or an accident can scar her face. Even if that doesn't happen, she will age and lose the beauty of her youth."

"I suppose that is true."

"If a pleasing form or a beautiful face is what a man falls in love with, love will leave. But suppose a man sees something inside the woman, something that age will not change? This inward grace draws a man, and he will love her when she loses her beauty. When she grows old and has white hair and wrinkles, he will still love her."

Dolores found herself wondering about this tall Englishman. "You have strong ideas about love."

"I suppose I do, but every man has the dream of his perfect mate, and sometimes he is fortunate enough to find her." She turned suddenly to see her father, who had appeared and come out to stand beside her.

"What is this? Who are you, sir? Why are you out here with my daughter?"

"I am Brandon Winslow, sir. I stepped out into the garden and found your daughter here. We were discussing poetry."

"Poetry?" Mendoza was stern. "Our women here are not lax like the English. They will not see a man without a duenna present."

"I apologize, Señor Mendoza. I was unaware of the custom."

"Father, he's come from England to buy horses."

Mendoza instantly settled down and grew more friendly. "Now, that is interesting. I have some fine horses."

"So your daughter was telling me. Might I come and see them, sir?"

"Certainly. Come on the morrow. I will gladly show you the finest horses in Spain."

"I will certainly do that. I apologize again, señorita," he said, with a small bow. He turned and gave another to her father. "Señor Mendoza." He left them, and when he was gone from sight, Dolores felt sorry indeed.

14

Philemon bent over the iron skillet and inhaled deeply. He smiled with pleasure, and pulling the knife from his belt, he tentatively probed the beefsteak. "Tender as a baby's bottom," he breathed. He impaled the steak on the point of a knife, transferred it to a wooden trencher, and placed it on a tray. He looked at the steaming potatoes and the tender carrots, then put a small vase containing a bell-shaped flower of a violet hue on the tray. He added a flagon of ale, then quickly put a snow-white cloth over the lunch. He lifted it up, put it flat on his palm, and held it just over his head in an accomplished fashion. He moved away from the table, and as he passed a sturdily-built woman with coarse, coal-black hair, he pinched her bottom.

"You must not do that!" the woman said, but she was smiling, and there was a light in her brown eyes. "I'm a respectable woman."

"You certainly are, Rosa, and a beautiful one, too."

Rosa pouted and shook her head. "You are bad, Señor Smith! You are a danger to the women of this place."

"Oh, I'm as innocent as a child, Rosa. After you get off tonight, suppose we take a little walk down by the river. I've found a beautiful place where we could sit and talk."

"I know what your talk means. You probably have a wife back in your own country. You should be faithful to her."

Philemon Smith shrugged and shook his head. A look of sadness crossed his features. "I've had two wives, but both of them went to heaven before me."

"They're probably looking down right now, seeing how you treat a poor Spanish woman."

"Oh, they were very understanding." He squeezed her arm gently. "We'll leave about the time the moon gives way to the sun."

"You are bad! I will have nothing to do with you." She hesitated, then said, "What about your master? What's he doing?"

"Oh, he came to buy horses, but I think he's more interested in a woman."

"You mean Señorita Dolores Mendoza? Well, he can forget her."

"Why should he do that?"

"Because her father is an old pirate, a greedy one. He raised her up for one purpose, to marry her off to a rich man. Now he's found one."

"Who is that?"

"His name is Don Pedro Varga. He's old, but he's rich."

"Well, my master's rich, and he's not old, and he's fine-looking."

"He may be all of that, but he's a foreigner. He can do nothing to lift Jaspar Mendoza up to the nobility."

"I suppose the girl is obedient and will do as her father says."

"She has little choice, has she? This world is run by men."

"Well, I'm a romantic fellow. I think my master will steal her heart away."

"Go on away with you. I have work to do."

He lifted her face. "As soon as it gets dark, we'll go down and watch the moon come up over the river. I will be gentle, and I will say a poem to you."

Rosa giggled and shook her head. "If my father found us, he would cut both our throats."

"We must not let him find us, then. As soon as it's dark, I'll see you." He winked and, still balancing the tray, took the stairway up to the second floor.

"Time for your breakfast, sir. I've obtained for you one of the most tender steaks in all of Spain and some good fresh vegetables."

Brandon had been lying in bed, his hands locked behind his head. He wore only a pair of the smallclothes he used for sleeping, and as he came to a sitting position, the muscles in his stomach tightened and his eyes lit up at the sight of food. "I'm starved to death. That smells wonderful."

"Here. You start on this, sir."

Philemon began to select the clothes that Brandon would wear that day. "Are you going out to the Mendozas' villa today?"

"Yes, I am. This is great steak. You'd make some man a good cook."

"I did, once. One of the maids downstairs says that Mendoza is determined to marry his daughter off to a rich old man."

"That's so. These carrots are tender. How do you make them that way?"

"Skill, sir. Nothing but skill. What about your progress with Mendoza?"

"Well, I keep looking at horses, but we haven't made any deal yet."

Philemon picked out a pair of doeskin hose and put them on the bed. They were tight-fitting in the Spanish style with silver discs down the side. "I think this will suit." He put them down and said, "You know, sir, I have a feeling that you're not as interested in horses as much as you are in Mendoza's daughter."

"How can you think that?"

"You talk in your sleep, sir. You cry out for Dolores."

"Well, there are many women named Dolores here in Madrid."

"I'm sure there are. Rosa says this girl isn't happy. She doesn't want to marry an old man."

"How would she know that? She's a servant."

"Well, she has a friend who is maid to Señorita Dolores Mendoza. She told me everything. Said the señorita is a romantic and is very unhappy to be forced to marry a man old enough to be her father." Philemon came over and watched as Brandon ate heartily. "It's plain to see that you've got the woman in your sights."

"Don't be a fool, Smith."

"Well, that's what you'd be if you tried to marry that girl. Her father's an old pirate anyway. He'd have your throat slit or run you out of the country."

Brandon chewed thoughtfully on the tender steak. He raised one eyebrow and a smile turned the corners of his lips upward. "I admit, it began as a plan to extricate her. But now . . . I'm intrigued by her. What do you suggest, Philemon?"

"Forget her. Women are pretty much alike. You can find another one just as good-looking. But I don't suppose you will pay any heed to my advice."

"Do you expect me to?"

"No, I don't. A wise man will attain wisdom, but stripes are for the back of a fool. I suspect you've got your stripes chasing after women, sir."

"I suspect you know too much."

"Yes, sir. Well, finish your meal. I'll dress you, and then you can make a fool of yourself over this Dolores Mendoza. I wish you'd give me enough money for a passage home. I'll need it after they cut your gizzard out."

15

Brandon dismounted from the sleek black horse and spoke to the guards who came to greet him.

"Good morning, Bartola, and you, José." Both were tough-looking men armed with swords and pistols and looked like a pair of highwaymen—which they probably were. "I need to see your master about the horses."

"He's not here, señor," Bartola said. "He's gone to Avila."

"To look at horses?"

The two men laughed, and the shorter of the two said, "No, he has a woman there. He won't be back for a day or two."

"Well, maybe I can speak to someone else about the horses. Just to look at them, don't you see. I'm deciding today between two different stallions."

"You know where the stables are. Ask for Mateo. He knows all about the horses."

"Thank you." Brandon nodded pleasantly and entered the compound. It was surrounded by an eight-foot wall with carved wooden spikes studded along the top. There were only two entrances, and both of them were kept well guarded. As Brandon moved around, he studied the situation from a military standpoint. *I think I can forget about a plan to kidnap Eden Fairfax. It would be difficult even if I had a troop of soldiers. Too many armed men, and then I'd still have to travel all the way to the coast with a screaming woman.*

The thought discouraged him, but he went on to the stables, where he found Mateo, the Mendozas' horse master.

"I'd like to try out that stallion I was looking at the other day. The bay."

"His name is Capitán, señor. A fine horse."

"He looks like he's big enough to carry my weight."

"He is one of the prizes of Señor Mendoza's herd. I don't know if you would be willing to pay the price he is asking."

"If he's the horse I want, I'll pay it. I'll come back a little later."

"I'll have him saddled, señor."

"Thank you, Mateo."

For the next fifteen minutes, Brandon moved around the compound. He was somewhat discouraged, for he could not think of a way he could break into the house, obtain Eden, then get her all the way to the coast. If he did get her out of the compound, there would be an alarm, and a troop of these ruffians working for Mendoza would be on his trail, all mounted on the fastest horses he'd ever seen.

He stopped at a beautifully arranged garden and admired the flowers. They made a colorful display in the bright morning sun. He had hoped to see Dolores Mendoza, and he was pleasantly surprised a few moments later to see her come out of one of the large oak doors. A servant bowed as she passed through. Brandon saw at a glance that she was wearing a riding outfit. He pulled his hat off and approached her.

"Good morning, señorita. A fine day, is it not?"

"Are you here again to look at horses, Señor Winslow?"

"Yes. I thought I might. I'm going to take one called Capitán out for a ride." A quick thought came to him and he said, "I wish we could ride together, but as I learned from our first meeting, you can't accompany a man without a duenna."

"I think you're a man who doesn't pay much attention to rules."

"Why, señorita, you wound me! I always keep to the rules—unless I want to break them."

"I sometimes feel the same way, Señor Winslow."

"You do not know a man's confinement."

"No," Dolores said, tossing her head as a rebellious light came to eyes, "I know worse. You are a man, and you have no idea how a woman is bound by a thousand rules. I think sometimes I'm in a prison."

"What would you do if you were not bound by rules?"

"I'd do what you and all men do—I'd be free."

Brandon studied the woman. Her face was a mirror that changed often. He had seen her laugh a few times and knew that she had a great deal of pride. That much was obvious. Yet sometimes a sadness seemed to touch her like a cloud. Impulsively he said, "Ride with me, señorita. Break one of the rules."

"It is up to you," she said with a shrug. "If my father catches us, he may have you whipped."

"It's worth the risk."

Mateo saddled both animals. Hers was a mare. She gave Brandon a slight smile but did not speak. Brandon followed her to the big stallion, who bucked a couple of times, then settled down to accept his saddle.

As soon as they were outside the gate and away from the walls of the compound, Dolores smiled at him. "Would you like to race? I always like a race. You see that big tree out there? It's about half a mile from here. Are you ready?"

"Any time you're—"

Brandon blinked as Dolores touched the mare with her spurs and gave a sharp cry. The mare shot ahead as if propelled from a cannon, while his big stallion, startled by the action, bucked and turned sideways. Quickly Brandon got him under control, but by that time, Dolores was fifty yards ahead. He kicked the sides of the big horse, and the animals sped over the terrain. It was impossible to catch her, and when he reached the tree, she watched him approach with a triumphant smile.

"You are slow, señor."

"I think you have the better animal."

"Yes. She's the fastest horse on the place. She's won many races. Come along."

She did not say where they were going. She led him down a well-worn path and then they climbed a gently rising slope that grew sharper as it rose. When they reached the crest, Brandon saw a beautiful valley on the other side, with a clear stream running through it.

"That's the prettiest thing I've seen in Spain."

"Do they have nice scenes like this in your country?"

"Oh, yes. Many of them. But this is beautiful." A thought came to him, and he asked, "What was your life like—as a child, I mean?"

Dolores didn't answer at once; the question seemed to trouble her. Finally she said, "I never knew my real parents."

"Señor Mendoza isn't your father?"

"No. He saved me from a wreck at sea. He took me as his daughter."

"Do you remember anything about your real parents?"

"I—sometimes dream of them." Dolores turned her eyes on him, and he saw a longing and a sadness there. "Of course, I can't really remember what they look like, but I wish I could have known them."

"Forgive me. It must be very hard." *If I can take her back to her parents, it will benefit her as much as Uncle Quentin. She's miserable here, and she'll be even worse off if she's forced to marry an old man.* "Shall we go on?" he asked.

She didn't answer but led him down a path. When they got to the river, she let the horses drink. She did not speak for a time. Then she lifted the mare's head and walked her slowly along the river. When they came to a grove of trees, she dismounted and tied the mare to a tree. Brandon tied his horse and followed her into the trees. The shade of the trees made the air cool. She sat down on a fallen tree.

"I come here to fish sometimes."

"Do you catch any?"

"Oh, yes. The river's full of fish. I let most of them go." She turned to him and asked, "Tell me about your life in your country."

Brandon cast about for something appropriate to tell her. "Well, I was a soldier for quite a while."

Her eyes lit up. "That's what I would be if I were a man. A soldier. Tell me about it. The battles and the adventure."

Her eyes were wide open, and she seemed to be hungry for something—what? "Well, it's not as romantic as most people think. As a matter of fact, I had rather romantic notions when I joined the army. Mostly it's days of tedious boredom broken by short periods of sheer terror." Brandon laughed and said, "That's not very romantic, is it?"

"Tell me, were you truly afraid in battle?"

"There's hardly time for it, at least for me, but I found out I was afraid after the action stopped. Once we had a terrible battle with some Irishmen. There were dead people all around, and I had a couple of wounds myself. I didn't even think about dying or getting hurt while it was going on. There was no time for it. But when it was over and everything grew quiet, I started to walk away." He shook his head at the memory. "My knees suddenly got weak as water, and I had to lie down flat on the ground."

"What were you afraid of, Brandon Winslow?"

"I realized I could have died and I would be in no condition to meet God in judgment. It frightened me."

"I never heard of such a thing as that. Tell me some more about the battles."

As the cool breeze touched his face, Brandon told some stories of battles, but finally he shook his head. "War is a terrible thing."

"What about your family?"

"Oh, you would like them, Dolores." He forgot to add *señorita,* but she seemed not to notice. "They've been married for years and years, and they love each other like a pair of youngsters falling in love for the first time."

"Really?"

"Yes. My mother is miserable when Father's gone, and he's miserable when he's away from her."

"Do they ever argue?"

"Oh, yes, they argue. They make each other laugh, and they make each other cry."

"Why should you cry if you love someone?"

"My father says to love is to put yourself into the hands of another person. Sooner or later they'll fail you."

"Your mother cries sometimes?"

"Not very often. Father's very careful. He brings her flowers and he tells her how beautiful she is. But once he paid a little too much attention to a pretty woman, and Mother got jealous. She cried then. I was just a child, but I asked her why she was crying, and she couldn't tell me. But then when Father came in he saw her crying. He ran over and fell down and held her, and they made things right. I was just a child, but I saw that there was magic in my parents' relationship."

There was silence for a moment. Brandon listened to the sibilant murmur of the river as it flowed by. He was trying to figure out what she was thinking.

"Do you know any more poems like the one you quoted for me the other day?"

"Well, I know one that's been a favorite of mine for a long time."

"Would you tell it to me?"

"All right. I'll tell you some of it. It's about a man and a woman who are in love, and the first thing she says is, 'Let him kiss me with the kisses of his mouth: for our love is better than wine.'"

"I'm not sure this is appropriate."

"Oh, it's a good poem. They love each other dearly. She describes him. She says, 'A bundle of myrrh is my wellbeloved unto me. He shall lie all night betwixt my breasts.' And he says, 'Behold thou art fair, my love; behold thou art fair; thou hast doves' eyes.'"

He continued to quote the poem and said, "I told you that lovers cry. That's in the poem too. They had a quarrel. The man came one night when the woman was asleep. He whispered, 'Open to me, my love, my dove, my undefiled.' But she would not. She said, 'I have put off my coat. How shall I put it on? I have washed my feet. How shall I defile them?'"

"What did he say?"

"He didn't say anything, but when she left her bed and she saw he was gone, she said, 'My beloved has withdrawn himself. My soul failed when he spoke.' And then she began looking for him, and she couldn't find him."

Dolores said, "This isn't a fit poem for a man to say to a woman."

"Why, Dolores, it's from the Bible."

"That can't be!"

"But it is. It's called the Song of Solomon and it is in the Bible. You can read it yourself."

"I've never read the Bible. I never thought such a thing would be in it."

"Well, señorita, as a matter of fact, it's about the only part of the Bible I know well enough to speak of. I thought like you the first time I read it. I couldn't believe such a passage was in the Bible."

"I've never even seen a Bible. The priests tell us what it says."

Suddenly Brandon laughed. "I bet they don't talk about this poem too often, but it's a beautiful love story. They love each other so much that he says, 'O, prince's daughter, the joints of your thighs are like jewels, the work of the hands of a cunning workman. Thy navel is like a round goblet, which wanteth not liquor. Thy belly is like a heap of wheat set about with lilies. Thy two breasts are like two young roes that are twins. Thy neck is as a tower of ivory, thine eyes like the fishpools in Heshbon. How fair and how pleasant art thou, O love, for delights.'"

"That—that can't be in the Bible!"

"Well, my uncle is a preacher, and he has studied the Bible a lot. He says that it's probably a true story about Solomon and his lover, but it's also a story of Christ and the church. Jesus is the bridegroom and we are the bride, and we are to love each other. We are to love Christ as a woman loves her husband." He smiled. "My Uncle Quentin said someday I would quote those verses for some reason other than seducing women."

"Is that what you're doing?" she said, lifting a hand to her breast. "Seducing me?"

"God help me, I don't intend to do that. Not that you aren't quite beautiful and tempting. No, today I think I spoke those verses to you because you should know there is something so wonderful within the Scriptures. My uncle would be happy I told them to you."

Dolores suddenly stood up, and when he joined her, he saw that she had tears in her eyes. "Don't be sad," he said in confusion. "It's a beautiful poem. It tells how God loves his people and how we're supposed to love him, but it's also about a man and a woman. Someday, Señorita Dolores, you'll find a man who can make you laugh and cry."

She looked up at him, and faint color stained her cheeks. For a moment they stood like that, something whirling rashly between them, swaying both of them in violent compulsions that neither of them really understood. He sensed her vulnerability and suddenly he realized there was more to this woman than he had thought. She was still, waiting, staring up at him, beckoning, so sweet. . . . He put his arms around her and felt her lips come up to meet his, quick and eager. It was like falling into layer after layer of softness. There was never any completion to the kiss. Never the full giving of those things in him and never the whole receiving from her. Never enough. She caught her breath, and he knew that she had felt the power of their connection as much as he. He held her loosely, stirred by the fragrance rising from her hair, and it was then that he knew that this was a woman that he could truly love. How cruel! She would hate him once she knew his goal had always been to steal her away, not win her heart.

Dolores stepped back and stared at him. Her cheeks were flushed and she was angry. "How dare you take such a liberty!"

"Dolores," he said in surprise. "Forgive me for offending you." His heart beat quickly. Had he destroyed everything? She seemed truly furious.

"I'm angry with myself for being so easy." She turned and walked away quickly to her horse, mounted, and rode away at a fast clip. Brandon stood looking after her. *I can't steal her, but I might make her fall in love with me. She's the kind of woman who would run away to England with a man she loves.*

Shame came on him as he thought of how he would have to use deceit, but his mind responded with justification. She was not happy here. She'd have a good home with the Fairfaxes, everything she wanted. And she could find a man to love truly before she married. He went to his horse and slowly led the animal along the river, thinking, thinking.

Why had her kiss so shaken him?

16

Morning clouds had gathered and poured a cooling rain over the terrain, then had passed away in the late afternoon. The sun had come out, and as Dolores sat looking out the window, she was conscious once more of the beauty of the countryside during the month of April. The grass as the sun struck it looked like diamonds flickering and glittering. But as her seventeen-year-old maid Juanita brushed her hair, she was aware that she was unhappy. There was something in her, a discontent, for which she could not account.

Juanita was chattering on about her usual subject, a young man named Antonio.

"Are you two engaged to be married, Juanita?"

"Oh, not yet, but I'm sure we will be soon."

"Is he acceptable to your family? A proper young man?"

"Well, they are a little disappointed that I don't aim to marry higher, but I love Antonio."

Juanita was a pretty little thing with dark eyes and thick, dark hair. Her eyes glowed as she began to speak of her suitor.

"He is so handsome, lady! Very handsome indeed."

"Does he ever kiss you?"

"Oh, yes. Many times."

"That would not be permitted for a woman of my station."

"Well, there is some advantage in being only a poor girl. We don't have to have a duenna watching us like a hawk."

"That must make Antonio very happy."

"Oh, he's very persistent." Juanita flushed and said, "He is sometimes impertinent, señorita."

"Oh, he does more than kiss you?"

"Well, he tries."

"I trust you have discouraged such behavior." Dolores saw the confusion in the girl's face and asked, "I suppose he wants to make love to you."

Juanita looked even more flustered. "Yes. He says we're going to be married anyway so we can love each other—in every way."

"And what do you think about that?"

"I don't know. When he puts his arms around me and holds me and kisses me, I feel so helpless, and I—" She broke off and looked down at the floor. "I must confess. I would like for him to make love to me." The girl looked up and said, "Is that wrong?"

"You know it is wrong, Juanita."

"Have—have you ever felt like that about a man, señorita?"

The simple question stirred something within Dolores. She had felt the same stirring when Brandon held her. She could not admit this to a servant, however. "You must be very careful. Men are selfish, Juanita. They will take what a woman has, then walk away and leave her after they've had their way."

"Oh, Antonio would never do that."

"He's a man, and men are greedy. A woman has to guard herself."

Juanita blinked and then blurted out. "Were you ever in love as I am?"

"No," Dolores snapped, "and we don't need to be talking like this. I just warn you that you need to be careful with Antonio."

Juanita had no chance to respond, for the door opened and Dolores saw that her father was there, accompanied by Don Pedro Varga.

"Ah, we need to speak to you, my daughter. I have good news."

"Yes, Father?" Dolores stood up and waited with some trepidation. What was welcome news to her father might not be good news to her.

"It is the best of news. I rejoice that my good friend Don Pedro Varga," he said, sliding an arm around the man's shoulders, "has asked for your hand in marriage. Is that not wonderful?"

It took everything in her not to scream and run away. She straightened, smoothed her bodice, and said, "Don Pedro, you do me great honor with your offer."

Vargas stepped forward. He was a small man, not as tall as Dolores herself. His voice was that of an old man. "It will be my honor, señorita. I will do my best to make you happy." When Don Pedro reached forward for her hand, Dolores gave it, and when he kissed it, she had to suppress a shudder. His lips were dry. She had a moment's dreadful thought of what it would be like to have such a man for a husband. She knew little enough about the intimate side of marriage, but the idea of this man touching her and kissing her was abhorrent to her.

She managed to carry on a conversation until her father said, "I wanted to give you the good news. Come, Don Pedro, we will draw up the papers for the marriage."

As soon as the two men left the room, Dolores walked to the window and stared out but could not see anything. Emotions raged through her. She had tried to let her father know that she was not interested in Don Pedro Varga, but Jaspar Mendoza was accustomed to having his own way, certainly with his own daughter. She put her hands on the window and leaned out. She could think of nothing but the need to keep this thing from happening. A sharp fear filled her heart. She saw herself married to this old man. He would die one day, but until then he would be her master and would use her as he saw fit.

She paced the floor, her mind going from one solution to another, all of them impossible. She came back to the window and, looking down, she saw Brandon Winslow speaking to Bernado, one of the grooms. Desperate, she knew she had to get out of the house. She swept out of the room, and her mother called to her as she passed. "Where are you going, Dolores?"

"Oh, I'm going to—to confession."

"Yes. That will be good."

"And afterward I'm going to spend the night with Damita."

"She's a good girl. You come back early tomorrow."

"Yes, Mother."

Leaving the house, she walked until she saw Brandon. His eyes lit up when he saw her. It made her feel good to know that despite her great trouble this man seemed to care for her.

"Good morning, señorita. You out for a walk?"

"I am going to church to confession."

"Perhaps I can escort you."

"That would be very nice."

The church was only a short distance away. They stopped beside a fountain, and Dolores said, "I love this fountain. It's beautiful, isn't it?"

"Yes, it is. I've not seen a finer one."

Dolores looked up at the church ahead of them. "Are you a Catholic, Englishman?"

"I'm afraid I'm not either Catholic or Protestant, Señorita Dolores."

"You never go to confession?"

Brandon smiled. He had a charming smile. His teeth were white and quite even. "I do go to confession in a way."

"But if you're not a Catholic who is your priest?"

"Jesus is my priest—or he will be one day. At least, that's what my uncle tells me."

"What does it mean, to have Jesus as your priest?"

"My father's favorite book in the Bible is called Hebrews, and he made me memorize much of it as a child. It says that when Jesus came to earth he fulfilled the law, and all the religion of the Jews, so there was no need to sacrifice lambs anymore, because Jesus, the Bible says, was the Lamb of God. When he died, he was the true Lamb of God. And he also said that Jesus is our high priest. Let's see if I can quote it." He paused for a moment and tried to think. "It says something like, 'Seeing then that we have a high priest which has passed into the heavens, Jesus the Son of God, let us come boldly to the throne of grace that we may attain mercy and grace to help in times of need.'"

"That's very beautiful, but is it true?"

"It's true if the Bible is true. At least, my family says so. Now, you understand my uncle tells me these things. He says that one day I'll be able to go to Jesus with my sins, but not until I find God."

"Do you think you ever will?"

"I don't know, señorita. I certainly need to. I have good parents and a good uncle, and I have seen true believers. But I don't have that spirit within me. I don't know God even though I've seen him in others."

They walked on until she reached the church. Dolores said, "I must go to confession."

"I'll wait here. Perhaps we could walk some more."

That pleased her greatly. She went to confession and made a quick enough business of it.

When she came out, it was growing dark. Brandon came to join her. "Let me escort you home."

"I'm not going home. I'm going to my friend Damita."

"Well, let me take you there."

"Very well. You may walk with me."

When they passed the fountain, it was growing darker. Dolores's attention was caught by a movement over to her left. She saw a young man and a young woman embracing. Glancing at Brandon's face, she saw that he was smiling.

"They must be in love, kissing like that," he said.

"My maid was asking about love. She has a young suitor named Antonio. He urges her to—well, to let him love her before they're married. She asked me what to do."

"What did you tell her, Señorita Dolores?"

"I told her it would be wrong. Don't you think so?"

"I'm not the man to answer that question."

Suddenly they were not far from Damita's house. Dolores stopped and said, "Have you had many women?"

"Too many." He shook his head. "I have not been a good man."

The confession struck Dolores. She felt it was honest. Suddenly she blurted out, "My father came to see me just before I left the house. He brought Don Pedro Varga with him. He—he told me that Don Pedro has asked for my hand."

Her voice was strained. Brandon leaned down to look more closely at her. "That doesn't make you happy, does it?"

"No. I don't love that man."

"Can't you refuse?"

"You don't know my father." Overwhelmed by the thought of her bleak future, Dolores started to walk away. Brandon caught her arm and turned her around. She saw that there was compassion in his face. "I wish I could help you," he said.

"No one can help me."

The tears ran down Dolores's face, and she cried out bitterly, "I wish I were an orphan. I wish Mendoza had left me where I was. I'd be happier in a one-room house than in our grand villa, if I could be free."

A spasm of crying shook her, and Brandon felt pity for her. He put his arms around her, whispering, "Maybe I can help." He held her as she cried and clung to him.

She stepped back and, pulling a handkerchief from her pocket, she wiped her face.

"If you would like to get away from here, Dolores, where would you go?"

"I don't know. Some place where I'd be free."

Brandon knew this was the time for him to speak, and he knew it was dangerous. She might be terrified and even tell Jaspar Mendoza, but he knew he had to take the chance. "I'll help you get away, if that's what you want, Dolores."

She looked up with astonishment, for none of her possible solutions included running away. "Get away? Where would I go?"

"To England."

"Run away to England with you?"

"Yes."

"But—I don't know anybody there. What would I do? How would I live?"

"You'd be free, but here's what you'd do. You would stay with my parents. Or there's a wealthy man and his wife," he added, "a couple named Fairfax. They would take you in. They lost a child, and they've always been lonely."

Dolores was still trembling, but she put her hand on his chest and whispered, "Can I trust you, Brandon?"

"You must think about it, Dolores. I'll get you to England if you choose to go." He lifted her hand from his chest and kissed it. "I can see the dread in your eyes, Dolores. I don't want you to have a miserable life with a man you don't love. If I could get you away, you could have the freedom you long for."

"How could that be?"

"It would be as I have told you. Lord Fairfax and his wife would love to take you in. Or even my parents—they are the most loving people in the world. They would take you in and you'd be part of our family." Brandon wanted to tell her that the Fairfaxes were her real parents, but decided later would be better.

Dolores looked up into Brandon's face, and asked again. "Can I trust you, Brandon?"

"I'll never harm you, Dolores, and I'll help you find a new life."

Brandon felt her hands gripping his and knew that she was

vulnerable. *I've got to convince her that she can have a good life in England!* He spoke more of how she would find happiness in England.

Finally she looked up at him and asked, "Do you love me then, Brandon?"

He had to struggle not to pull himself away from her in surprise. Knowing she was terrified and that he had to assure her, he leaned forward and kissed her gently, then told the lie he knew was necessary. "Yes. I love you, Dolores."

Brandon saw hope ease into her eyes. She clung to him and whispered, "I'll—I'll go with you. I'll do as you say."

Relief came to Brandon but also guilt. *She doesn't love me. When she gets to England, she'll realize it was desperation that made her think of love.* To cover his confusion and his guilt, he said quickly, "This will take some careful planning. I'll have to get us to the coast safely. Are you certain you want to do this, Dolores?"

"Yes! But now I must go," Dolores said, then whispered, "Please don't be false with me, Brandon. Keep your word that you'll take care of me. I'm putting all my hope in you."

Brandon lifted her hand and kissed it. "I promise to not harm you, and I will do my best to get you to England and find you some place where you will be free and happy."

She reached up and touched his cheek, then said again, "I must go." She left then, and he watched her all the way to the end of the street.

Dolores thought about what it would mean to leave her father's house, the only home she had really known. She thought of little other than the feeling she had for Brandon and the desire she had to escape a marriage she did not want. She spoke to no one.

The next day her father came to her and said, "Don Pedro is ready to marry you. He wants to be married within a week."

"That's too soon!"

"No, it's not."

"Please, Father. I need more time," she begged, but Jaspar Mendoza could only see an easy life ahead, once he was allied with the house of Don Pedro.

"I'll make all the arrangements. Do not fret, Daughter. I'll see that you have a beautiful wedding dress in time." Dolores knew nothing would change his mind, and she knew that only Brandon Winslow could save her.

She saw him later that day, and they had a moment's privacy. She reached out, and he took her hand. "My father says I must be married in a week."

Brandon whispered, "Do you still want me to take you to England?"

"I can't marry that man."

"I'll help you escape, Dolores."

"I have only you to trust, Brandon. Please don't fail me!"

Brandon guiltily took her in his arms, kissed her, and said, "We'll get away from here. You'll be happy in England. I promise you."

"And we'll be married then?"

Brandon could not answer. He had not once thought that she would assume his profession of love meant he would marry her. *How can I promise her we'll be married? She won't come with me unless I do.* Instantly he knew he had to make a promise that he knew he would never keep. But he truly believed that when she was safe with her real parents, she would see that he'd done the right thing.

"Yes, Dolores, we'll be married," he said.

Dolores clung to him and whispered, "I thank God for sending you to save me, Brandon. I—I feel that I've come out of a terrible storm into a safe harbor."

Brandon could not say a word, but as he again took her in his arms, he knew that at some point, he would pay a steep price for his deception.

17

Brandon ran his fingers through his hair in a gesture of total distraction. He had paced the floor for over an hour, and now he glanced over at Philemon and said, "I don't think there is any way that I can make this work."

"There's always a way, sir. If I knew what it was that you were trying to do, perhaps I could help."

For an instant Brandon hesitated. He had grown quite fond of Philemon. He had learned that the man had a keen brain beneath his plain features. Almost in desperation, he told Philemon the whole story. He ended by saying, "So that's the problem, you see. I must get the woman out of there to a ship and then to England. It will be like robbing the Tower of the crown jewels to get her away. Her home is guarded like a prison. She will be missed within the hour."

Philemon leaned back in his chair and drummed his fingers on the table for a moment, then said, "Well, sir, I would agree that is a difficult problem. Have you thought of praying for an answer?"

"Prayer? My father and uncle would say the same thing, but God's surely not listening to me at the moment."

"Well, my father was a man of prayer, Master Winslow, and he taught me a few things. Why don't you let me see if I can get God's mind on the matter?"

"Go ahead, but I'd be shocked if God were interested in my little problems."

Brandon mounted his horse and rode to the Mendoza estate. He had arranged to meet Dolores at the small river where she often went for a ride. She was there when he arrived. No sooner had he dismounted and tied his horse than she was beside him with a smile on her face and a happy tone in her voice. She extended her hands, and when he took them, she cried, "Brandon, I was afraid you wouldn't come."

"Why, you needn't fear that. I've only been trying to think of some way we could get you out of here."

"Come. Sit down with me." Dolores pulled him over to a log beside the river, and they sat down. She took his left hand with one of hers and held it tightly. "I dreamed about you last night, Brandon."

"Not a nightmare, I trust."

"No, it was a very good dream. I can't tell you all of it, for it's somewhat . . . private. Perhaps after we are married."

Brandon felt another sharp pang of guilt. He could think of nothing to say. "It's going to be a difficult thing, Dolores, but I'm going to get you out of this place one way or another. It will be dangerous, though."

"I don't care. I have you now, Brandon, and if I had to die, I could face that. What I couldn't face is staying here and getting married to a man I don't love." She suddenly dropped his hand and pressed herself against him. Her face was glowing. She had a way of smiling and laughing that was extremely attractive, her chin tilting up and her lips curving in pretty lines. A small dimple appeared to the left of her mouth, and a light danced in her eyes. She made a provocative challenge, and Brandon knew that somewhere this woman had a rich, racy current of vitality within her. He knew she wanted him to speak the language of love, but he could not force himself to do it.

"I must see your father and talk about horses. If I don't continue to pursue the purchase, he'll be suspicious. And I'll lose my reason for calling at the villa."

"You are abandoning your quest to secure horses to take back to England?"

Brandon cleared his throat. "I have you. There is nothing else I need."

They got to their feet. Dolores put her arms around his neck, pulled his head down, and kissed him.

"I love you, Brandon," she whispered.

Brandon swallowed hard and said, "You're such a lovely woman. Any man would be proud to have you, Dolores." He shook his head and said, "I must go now. If we are seen meeting like this, it will destroy everything."

Philemon stood up as soon as Brandon stepped in the room, saying, "Sir, I think I have a word from the Lord."

Brandon stopped abruptly. "I've always been suspicious of those who said God talks to them."

"Well, the Lord does talk to us. I don't hear a voice, but I just asked the Lord to give me some kind of a plan to get the young woman to England."

"And you think you have one?"

"Yes, sir. Sit down and let me explain it to you."

The two men sat down at the plain table they used for writing and for meals, and Philemon said with excitement, "The problem, sir, is that Mendoza knows the country. He knows that you landed at San Sebastián, and if he chased you, he would probably head for there. What has to happen is we get the woman, tear our way to the harbor, and as soon as we get there, board a ship that leaves immediately."

"How can I find a ship like that?"

"First you buy the horses from Mendoza. It'll take twenty of them."

"Why twenty?"

"Because we're not taking the horses all the way to the ship. Here's the plan. We'll station these horses at intervals, two of them at each place. Then you'll get Miss Dolores at midnight. That will give you most of the night to travel, and hopefully she won't be missed until nearly noon. So you ride twenty miles, change to fresh horses, do another twenty, and so forth all the way to the sea. In other words, you'll make the journey non-stop."

"Well, that just leaves two problems. One, how do we know a ship will be leaving just at that moment?"

"As I say, sir, you buy the horses, and we'll leave with them. We'll make the trip to San Sebastián, leaving the horses at different places along the way, and when we get there, we'll find a ship. You will have to pay the captain whatever he wants in order to wait for us. As soon as that's settled, you return to retrieve Miss Dolores, while I wait at the harbor to be sure the captain keeps his promises. Don't you see? You get the lady out, then you and she ride those horses as fast as possible. You get to the coast, jump on the ship, and where is Mendoza then? Miles and miles behind you."

Brandon stared at Philemon in wonder. "You think this comes from God, this crazy idea?"

"Why, it's not crazy at all, sir. You'll have fresh horses all the way. You can travel all the way there, and even if Mendoza figures out that you've taken the girl, it'll be too late. You'll be safe aboard a ship."

"Yes, if there is a ship."

"Why, the Lord Jesus had to say more than once to his disciples. 'Where is your faith?'" Philemon smiled. "You'll see, sir. This is too clever for me to think of. It has to be of the Lord."

"Well, it'll probably get us both killed, but I don't have any better plan. I'll deal with Mendoza for the horses, and we'll depart tomorrow for San Sebastián."

❧

Brandon rode directly to the Mendoza villa. He asked to see Mendoza, who fortunately was home. "I have decided on the horses I want, Señor Mendoza. I'll take twenty of them."

"Excellent! They are the finest horses in Spain." Mendoza's eyes gleamed. "When will you leave?"

"As soon as I can. I'm anxious to get home."

"Come along. You can show me which horses you want, and then we'll settle up."

❧

Brandon had examined the horses more than once, and he had a good eye for horseflesh. He picked out twenty of the finest that Mendoza had and haggled with him over the price. They arrived at something that was close to being fair, and Mendoza said, "Will you need help getting them to the ship?"

"No, my man and I can take care of that. We'll go slowly. I think I'll look them over a little more if you don't mind."

"Of course. They're your horses now."

As soon as Mendoza left, Brandon went back to the corral. As he suspected, Dolores knew he was there and slipped out to meet him. It was not long before she came out. She came to stand beside. He whispered, "Dolores, we must leave at once."

"You mean today?"

"No, not today. You know that old dead tree that you can see from your bedroom window?"

"Yes, of course. We pass it every time we go to the river."

"I'll be leaving with the horses, but I'll be back for you as soon as I make arrangements. Here's what you do. Every day you look at that tree. One day you'll see a piece of white cloth tied to a small branch. When you do, that's the signal that I'm back, and we'll get you away from here."

"But how can we do it, Brandon?"

"When you see the flag, tell your parents you need to go see that friend of yours, Damita. Pretend to spend the night with her. You've done it often enough. That night, after everyone is asleep, you slip out. I'll be waiting near the outside gate."

"What about the guards?"

"I'll take care of that. I'll be there waiting for you."

"Oh, it's going to be wonderful, Brandon!" Dolores reached out, then quickly drew back her hand and nervously glanced around. "Just think. Soon we will be out of here and we'll be free to marry."

Brandon managed a smile, but that was all he could do. "Remember. Watch for that flag. I must go now." He turned and left quickly.

Philemon was waiting for him. "Will the girl be ready?"

"She'll be ready. Now, let's get these horses out of here. The quicker we get to the sea and find a ship, the better I'll feel about it."

Obtaining the horses took little time. Brandon had them roped together nine to a group. The plan was he would lead half the horses, and Philemon the other half. They were getting ready to leave when Mendoza came out.

"Leaving so soon, señor?"

"Yes, Señor Mendoza. I'm very proud of these horses and eager to get them home to England."

"It will be quite a way to San Sebastián."

"We plan to leave from Corunna."

"Well, they have a fine harbor there. You come back any time you need some fine horses."

"I'll do that, señor. Farewell."

Brandon took the lead rope of one group of horses and led them out of the compound. Philemon did the same, and as soon as they were clear, they picked up the pace. They rode hard all day, and by dark they had reached Brihuega. Brandon had no trouble in finding someone to board two of the horses for a few days. Then he found a room for himself and Philemon. They ate and then went to bed at once.

As he lay there on his pad, Brandon was gloomy. "I don't think this is going to work. It's too complicated."

"You just wait and see, sir," Philemon assured him. "God never fails. His ways always come to pass."

"Well, there it is," Philemon said, "San Sebastián."

They were down to the last two horses now, for the rest had all been stabled along the way. Finding proper places had been troublesome, and it was a complicated plan. If just one thing went wrong, all would be lost. Brandon nodded in a gesture at the harbor. "I'm going down to see if there's a ship. You find a place to stay."

There were several ships in the harbor, but none of them was bound for England. He spent all morning and part of the afternoon trying to find a ship. He even offered to pay a captain to go back to England, but the captain was adamantly opposed.

That night Brandon was disgusted. "This plan won't ever work. We'll have to take the herd to some other harbor."

"Don't give up too quickly," Philemon said. "Get a good night's sleep. Tomorrow is a new day."

Brandon was so discouraged and filled with tension that he slept very little until the early hours of morning. He woke up when Philemon came in and said, "Sir, a ship came in today. It's a Dutch ship, the *Flower,* and I've talked to one of the sailors going back to Holland. They have to pass right by England.

Brandon dressed quickly and went down to the harbor. Sure enough, there was a three-masted ship. He went aboard at once and asked one of the sailors, "Is the captain here?"

"That's him on the quarterdeck there."

Brandon made his way to the quarterdeck. "My name is Brandon Winslow. You are the captain, sir?"

The sailor was a short and rather bulky individual. He looked Dutch: guileless blue eyes, blond hair, and a florid complexion. "My name is Jan Kirkegard. What may I do for you?"

"I have a rather unusual request, Captain."

"Well, let's hear it."

"Where are you headed?"

"We are headed for Portugal. We unloaded all our goods here, and now we're going south to pick up cargo destined for Holland."

Brandon hesitated. "This may sound mad, but I'd like to persuade you to take me and my two companions to England."

"With what cargo?"

"None, and we'd be the only passengers."

"I can't afford a trip with only three passengers. I have to have a cargo."

"What sum would you need to be able to take us there?"

"Including making up for my losses if I don't import Portuguese goods?"

"Yes."

Kirkegard stared hard at him. "Are these criminals you're talking about? I won't have anything to do with that."

"No. It's my manservant and a young woman. We have to get away from Spain." He hesitated and then said, "We're hoping to steal away to be married, Captain. Her father is an important man, so the young lady and I need to get as far away from him as we can."

The captain's stern face broke into a sly smile. "What's his name—the father, I mean?"

Reluctantly Brandon said, "His name is Jaspar Mendoza."

"Jaspar Mendoza? He was a pirate in his younger days. He raided a ship that my father was on. Killed most of the crew. Is he still a pirate?"

"From what I can gather, he's interested primarily in landlocked opportunities of late. What do you say? Can you wait until I get the young lady and then leave as soon as we get back? I'll pay your price."

"You must be a rich man."

"If it is fair, I will pay it."

"All right. Let's go down to my cabin, and you can tell me more about this plan."

Brandon knew after a moment that his one chance was to tell the absolute truth. Captain Kirkegard had penetrating blue eyes and a look of experience. He was likely to see through lies. Brandon decided to lay the whole truth before him, and he did so. He ended by saying, "So we'll have fresh mounts all the way to the end, and as soon as we get here, you'll cast off and take us to England."

"That would take a miracle, sir."

"I suppose it will, but I must try."

Kirkegard leaned back in his chair and looked up at the ceiling, deep in thought. Finally he gazed at Brandon and said, "Well, sir, I am a young man, and on behalf of all those men who forfeited their lives in his attacks, I would like the opportunity to rob a pirate of his stolen booty. Get your sweetheart."

18

As soon as Dolores looked out the window in the late afternoon, her heart seemed to leap. "There it is!" she whispered. "The white banner! Brandon's come to take me away!"

At once she packed a small bag with clothes suitable for travel. Going downstairs she said, "Mother, I'm going to spend the night with Damita, if that will be all right."

"I thought we were going to finish our plans for the wedding. It will soon be upon us."

"We can do that later. Damita's going to help me make tiny nosegays out of dried flowers for the guests."

Her stepmother wavered, considering. "All right. Come back in the morning, though."

"Yes, I will, Mother."

Leaving the house, Dolores went at once to the home of her friend Damita, and Damita's mother, Señora Ricardo, met her with a smile. "Damita's not here, but she'll be in later. Come in, and make yourself at home."

"May I have the same room I had the last time?"

"Why, of course. Go and put your things there. Damita shouldn't be too long."

The time seemed to pass very slowly for Dolores. She was nervous, but by the time Damita returned, she had made herself calm. The two girls spent the rest of the day making nosegays, which Dolores knew would never be used. *Perhaps Damita can use them when she marries.* The work kept her hands and mind occupied as she waited for nightfall.

"Are you excited about your wedding?" Damita asked.

"Oh, I suppose every woman is excited about her own wedding," Dolores said, looking away.

Damita hesitated. "But he's such a dry stick of an old man." She immediately looked guilty. "I'm sorry. I didn't mean to speak in such a fashion."

"It's all right. Don't even think about it."

The evening passed slowly. Then Dolores went to her bedroom. She paced the floor for two hours until the house was still. Quickly she changed into the riding clothes she had stuffed into her bag.

She opened the door very carefully; when it squeaked rather loudly, her heart gave a lurch. She remained perfectly still, however, and heard nothing. She scurried down the stairs to the front door. It was bolted with a steel bolt that grated when she undid it, and again she paused, but no one came. She edged the door open, being as quiet as she could, and stepped outside.

A dark shadow suddenly appeared. "Dolores? Over here!"

"Brandon, you're here!"

"Yes. Come now, we must get away quickly, Dolores."

"What about the guards at the gate?"

"We don't have to worry about that. There was only one, and he won't bother us."

"Did you—did you kill him?"

"No. I just got him drunk. He won't wake up for hours. Come along."

Dolores held tightly to Brandon's hand as they made their way across the compound. A dog barked at Brandon's reproof but then was silent. They reached the gate, and by the light of the moon she could see the guard, slumped with his back against the wall, unconscious. It was good that Brandon had come for her here—at home there would have been three more guards. They passed through the gate, and he led her to a clump of trees.

"It's going to be a hard ride, Dolores. We're going straight through, if we can, all the way to San Sebastián."

"We can do it, Brandon." Excitement came to her then, and she turned to him and said, "Tell me you love me!"

"What man could keep from loving you?" Brandon said. "Come now, there will be time for talk later." Dolores was disappointed. This was the most dramatic and romantic thing that had ever had happen to her. But she knew that they had to hurry. Her father would be after them soon enough. The two of them walked their horses until they were past Damita's house. As soon as they were clear, they mounted and he said, "Ride as hard and as long as you can."

"I will. I'm riding to freedom and love!"

Brandon said, "That's true enough. Come along."

As they sped down the road illuminated by a full silvery moon, Dolores was happy.

She did not glance back as the town disappeared in the distant shadows.

Captain Kirkegard had become rather fond of Philemon. Both of them were Christians, and every day they talked about doctrine. Kirkegard had wormed out of Philemon most of the details about Brandon.

They were sitting on deck at high noon when Philemon jumped to his feet. "Look. There they come! Master Winslow and the young woman!"

Kirkegard raced down the gangplank, closely following Philemon.

The man and the woman dismounted. Kirkegard noted that the horses were lathered and the young woman looked strained and tired.

Philemon said at once in English, the one language they all shared, "Captain Kirkegard, may I present Miss Dolores Mendoza."

"I'm very pleased to know you, ma'am."

"Captain, it's good to see you." Kirkegard saw that she had a good smile. She asked, "Are you going to take us to England soon?"

"As soon as you can get aboard."

"You mean we can leave now?"

Kirkegard pulled off his hat and scratched his head. "Well, we can try. Please notice, there is almost no wind. If God smiles, it will pick up. Come aboard now."

Kirkegard led the way, and Philemon came forward with a smile. "Well, Master Winslow, we've got a miracle."

"Not yet. Come, let's do what we can to be ready," Brandon said abruptly. He escorted Dolores on board, and Captain Kirkegard shouted orders for men to board the two horses, then loose the sails. He paused to say, "Philemon, show this lady her cabin."

"Certainly, Captain, I'll do that." Philemon led the way below and stopped at a door. "This will be yours, ma'am. We'll bunk together in that one right there, Master Winslow."

Dolores's cabin was small; it contained only a bed and a table. "It's not very luxurious, but that's fine." She looked at Brandon. He was too large for the cramped passageway. "Let's go up and watch as we leave the harbor. I'll be nervous as a cat with a dog on the prowl if I stay down here."

"All right." Brandon helped her up the stairs and onto the deck. They took a position at the rail. Suddenly something changed in Dolores's face.

"Look. You see that ship?"

"That one over there? The *Mirenda?*"

"Yes. That's my father's ship." They could both clearly see

the cannon lined up along the deck as well as in gun ports along the side.

"It looks like a fighting ship."

"He still owns it. Sometimes he goes away in it and comes back with a lot of money."

"Still dabbles in piracy, then?"

"I suppose that's true," she said, chastising herself inwardly for so foolishly believing him when he said he'd left all that behind.

Slowly the sails unfurled and were filled slowly by a light breeze. There was just enough to move the *Flower* out of the dock. Brandon shook his head. "That wind had better pick up or it'll take forever to get out of this port, let alone make it to England."

They were willing the sails to crack open and billow with wind. The captain came to stand beside them. He glanced up to the sails. He shrugged. "I have hope."

"So do I," Dolores said. "God hasn't brought us this far for nothing."

❦

Mendoza was mad with rage. When he had discovered his daughter was gone, he had every one of his men out searching for sign of her around Damita's home. It was obvious that whoever had taken her had chosen the cover of darkness, and no one had seen anything.

Finally César Lopez, Mendoza's most trusted man, came in. He was smiling. "Good news, sir."

"It had better be. What is it?"

"The guard who was drunk at his post said the man who gave him the liquor was an Englishman."

"An Englishman? Winslow! He's stolen my daughter!" Rage suffused Mendoza's face, and his eyes glittered with fury. "I will kill him slowly! He said he was heading northeast, but that was to throw us off."

"He came from San Sebastián."

"And that's where he's headed. Get the best horses we have and all the men you can round up. We may still catch them."

"What's the date, I wonder? I've lost count," Dolores said.

"It's April 16. My uncle's birthday. I wish we were there with him."

They were standing on the deck, looking down at the water. The ship was still moving very slowly, struggling forward on the feeble breeze. Suddenly Dolores clutched Brandon's arm. "I'm so happy, Brandon. Are you? How do you feel about what's happening?"

"It's exciting," Brandon said. He was very much aware of the beauty of this young woman and her soft form pressed against his side. She clung to him. He knew that sooner or later he would have to tell her the truth.

"Tell me about your parents. Will they like me, Brandon?"

"Of course. They will love you."

"When will we be married? Soon, I hope."

Brandon looked out across the sea, trying desperately to think of something to say. "You know, Dolores, you'll have many suitors—a beautiful young woman like you. You may fall in love with a very rich man. Not a poor fellow like me."

"No. God sent you to bring me out of slavery, and you've saved me. I love you, Brandon." She pressed herself against him, she laid her head on his shoulder, and Brandon Winslow had never felt such impotence in all his life. The worst of the trial was over, but as she held onto him, he smelled the fragrance of her hair and felt the strong presence of her personality and with a start realized that this was a woman that any man could love—including himself.

He was in misery, thinking about the future. *Well, at least my uncle is saved.* That thought gave him at least a bit of comfort. But not much.

❧

Two days later, Philemon was questioning Brandon about Dolores. They were up in the bow of the ship. Dolores had gone below.

Philemon said, "She's quite a young woman, sir."

"Yes, she is."

"Don't know as I ever saw a prettier one."

"Very beautiful."

Philemon turned to face Brandon. "She's in love with you, isn't she, Mr. Winslow?"

Brandon was startled, and grimly felt the heat of shame rise up his neck to his face. "I never wanted that. All I wanted to do was get her out of Spain and into England. I wouldn't want her to be hurt."

"No, you wouldn't want that, but what about now? You saved her from a pretty bad life, and she's leaning on you with everything she's got. Why, her eyes follow you whenever you're in sight, and she has a certain smile every time she sees you. What are you going to do about that?"

"I don't know, and I wish you'd keep your own counsel!" Brandon stalked angrily away. Philemon wisely didn't follow.

Captain Kirkegard was standing beside the wheel, staring at the horizon. "Well, the wind is picking up. That's the good news."

"That is good," Brandon said. "I hope it picks up still more."

"We have a shadow."

"A shadow?"

"You can barely see it there, but take my glass." He took a brass telescope from his pocket and handed it to Brandon, who followed his directions and swept the horizon.

"She's a long way off."

"But she's fast, Winslow, and she's making straight for us."

"Well, aren't there ships going and coming all the time?"

"I'll know more in a few hours," Kirkegard said, taking back his telescope. "I'm putting on more sail. To my way of thinking, we'll need all the speed we can get."

Brandon picked at his food. Sitting beside him, Dolores tried to get him to speak more of England. Brandon saw the love in her eyes, and he wanted more than anything to blurt out the truth. But he did not know how to say it without making her absolutely miserable. He couldn't simply tell her of the Fairfaxes, her lost family. He could plainly see that he had become very important to her, her only hope.

They heard a shout from topside and Dolores said, "What was that?"

"That was Captain Kirkegard. Let's see what it is."

They went to stand beside Kirkegard, who gave them a rather serious look. "Well, she's coming for us, and she's armed much heavier than we are. I think it's a pirate vessel."

"May I see?" Dolores took his telescope and looked at the ship. At once she drew a sharp breath. "That's the *Mirenda*, my father's ship from San Sebastián." She handed the telescope back to Kirkegard.

"Can we outrun her?" Brandon asked.

"No chance," Kirkegard said. "We're built to carry cargo, and she's built to skim across the water. She'll be up with us in four hours."

"Can we defeat them in a battle?" Brandon asked.

"It would take a miracle. Her crew is likely trained to fight. My men can fire guns fairly well, but they're mere sailors."

Nobody left the deck. All eyes were on the ship that seemed to be eating up the seas between them. "Her guns are run out," Kirkegard said, peering through his telescope.

Dolores said, "May I see?" With trembling hands she took the telescope again and peered through it. "That's my father," she said faintly. "He's aboard that ship. He'll kill all of you and take me back to Spain." She glanced up at Brandon with fear-filled eyes.

He said quickly, "No, it's not over yet. God can bring us through this." But even as he spoke, he was aware that he was merely parroting the faithful. For what reason should God answer his prayers now? He put his arm around Dolores and felt a sudden fear not for himself but for her. He could think of nothing else to say, but his depth of concern for her rattled him.

An hour later the *Mirenda* had come just aft of the *Flower*. Captain Kirkegard had armed his men with pistols and swords. Brandon stood beside him. "What will they do, Captain?" he asked.

"They'll board us. We'll keep them off with the big guns as long as we can, but those men are practiced in boarding other vessels. And if they get aboard, my poor fellows can't handle them."

A memory suddenly seemed to explode in Brandon's mind. He said to Kirkegard, "You know, Captain, once when I was in the army, we were about to be overrun by a heavier force. About the same situation that we have here."

"What happened?"

"I decided we'd have to surprise them, so instead of waiting for them to charge us, I told the men we would beat them to it, and we made a charge. I thought I was a dead man. But they were taken off guard. They retreated, and we won the battle."

Kirkegard stared at him. "I think I hear you saying that we need to take advantage when they come alongside."

"Yes. Our marksmen will knock down as many as they can, but as soon as they touch, we'll throw ourselves down on them."

"And we'll surprise them."

"They can't retreat. The battle will be immediate and soon decided. Let me lead the charge, Captain."

Kirkegard bit his lip. "All right," he said. "You want to talk to the men?"

"Yes."

Kirkegard spoke to the first mate, who blew his whistle. The men gathered, and Kirkegard said, "Mr. Winslow is an experienced soldier, and we are soon to be under attack. He has a plan to tell you about."

Brandon said, "We've got some heavy odds here, men, but I think we can win." He went on to describe his plan. He said, "I'll be the first one across, and I'll lead you. Will you come with me?"

There was little hesitation. The first mate said, "It's the only chance we got. I say let's go with the soldier."

A cheer went up. Captain Kirkegard said, "Everyone to his station. Lash additional ropes now, so we're ready!"

The two ships moved closer together. Men with muskets were firing. One of the men on the *Mirenda* fell, but four men on the *Flower* went down and lay still.

"They're not firing their big guns."

"It's Dolores. Her father wants her returned unharmed," Brandon said.

Captain Kirkegard said, "I've given orders. We should hear a charge any minute now."

The ships drew closer together. When they were even, the guns below deck went off. The *Flower* shuddered.

"Those guns were filled with pieces of old iron. Look, it took some of their fellows out."

"They're still coming on, though," Winslow said. "I'm going, Captain."

"God be with you, Winslow!"

The two ships slipped closer together. Brandon scuttled down the leeward deck beside the rail, hoping that all his men on deck were fairly hidden from view. "As soon as they're close enough, we get them. All right, fellows?"

A yell met his cry. Brandon waited. All seemed quiet except for the waves slipping by and the groaning ship timbers. Peeking over the rail, Brandon could see the fierce faces of Mendoza's men. He glanced at the quarterdeck of the *Mirenda*—and there was Jaspar Mendoza.

Mendoza saw him and let out a wild cry. "I'll kill you, Englishman!"

At that moment the ships closed the gap. The crew of the *Mirenda* was ready to board, but Brandon screamed, "Come on, boys, let's get them!" He took a leap, cleared the space of blue water, and landed on the deck of Mendoza's ship. He had his sword in his right hand and his pistol in his left. Lying on his back, he fired the gun and blew a hole in the breast of a man who was coming at him with a pike. He scrambled to his feet, aware of the sound of battle all around. Men screamed with rage and pain and fear. He crossed swords with a huge, bare-chested sailor with one eye and a fierce leer who was strong but fortunately not talented. Brandon parried his thrust and swiftly cut his throat with one sweep of his sword. The man fell, and instantly two more leaped into his place.

Brandon fought his way along a deck already slippery with blood. He fought until his arm grew weary and suffered one cut along his side. Suddenly he saw Mendoza, who was steadily making his way toward him. His face was twisted with fury and he screamed something unintelligible. Moving to meet him, Brandon raised his sword, but Mendoza raised his pistol and pulled the trigger. Something struck Brandon in the thigh, driving him to the deck. He watched as Mendoza started screaming with his sword lifted high. Brandon had lost his own sword and struggled to get to his feet, but he saw that he would never make it.

As Mendoza closed in, Brandon Winslow cried out, "Oh, God, be with me and help me in this hour!" And even as he prayed, he saw a small black hole appear over Mendoza's left eyebrow. The last thing he saw was Philemon lowering his pistol, and smiling in his direction.

Captain Kirkegard had tied the two ships together. The surviving members of the pirate crew had been put below in the brig, and the fighting crew of the *Flower* were coming back on board, many of them wounded. Dolores saw Brandon, his arm looped over Philemon's shoulders, his clothing soaked with blood, his face pale. She ran to help Philemon with him.

"He took a musket ball in his leg, but it ain't bad," Philemon said. "He's got to have that musket ball out. Come along, sir."

Captain Kirkegard called for the member of the crew in charge of wounds, who ripped away Brandon's clothing. "This won't be much fun," he said. He pulled what looked like a pair of pliers from his pocket and probed for the ball. Dolores was hanging onto Brandon's hand and watched as he clenched his teeth and bared his lips but uttered no sound.

"There. That wasn't hard at all. He'll be right as rain." The sailor grinned. Sweat ran down in rivulets from Brandon's forehead.

Kirkegard had come to watch. "Another miracle, eh, Philemon?"

"I'd say so, Captain."

Dolores held Brandon's hand. "What about my father?"

Brandon was weak, but he managed to whisper. "He'll never trouble you again."

"Did—did *you* kill him?"

"No, I didn't."

Dolores kissed his hand. It was bloody, but she paid no heed. "I'm glad. He was not a good man, but it would have been something between us." She kissed his cheek, and Brandon's eyes closed as he fainted.

19

Philemon was carefully changing the bandage on Brandon's wound. He had proved himself to be quite efficient in such matters as this. Now he looked up and saw that Brandon was smiling at him. "You feeling better, are you, sir?"

"Much better." Brandon hesitated then reached out his hand. For a moment Philemon stared at it, then he grasped the hand. Brandon said, "You saved my life, Philemon."

"Oh, probably not. You would have recovered in time to have fought that man off."

"No, I was helpless. If you hadn't been there and put a ball right in his brain, he would surely have killed me. What can I do to reward you?"

Philemon said, "Why, let me serve you, sir. That's all I ask."

Brandon studied the faithful little man and smiled. He said, "That's no reward."

"Well, perhaps it is. We can help each other, sir. I can be your servant and your friend at the same time."

"I would like that very much. Now I think I'll go up on deck."

"Are you sure? Do you feel up to it, sir?"

"Oh, yes. I feel very well."

"Well, let me dress you." Philemon scurried about, trying to find his master proper dress; they had had to leave their clothing in Spain. He'd been forced to buy clothing from crew members. "When we get back to England, sir, it'll be an enjoyment to dress you again as a gentleman should be dressed."

Moving rather slowly and cautiously, Brandon made his way up the steps. The wound he had taken was not serious, but loss of blood had weakened him. As soon as he got to the deck, he saw Dolores speaking with Captain Kirkegard. For a moment he stood and studied her. She was looking at the captain and did not see him. The wind was stronger now. It ruffled the wealth of dark golden hair that framed her face, and he noticed the touch of red in it. She was serene one moment, laughing the next, and it came to him that he thought she was altogether quite charming. She turned as he approached, and he saw her whole expression light up. "Brandon," she said, coming to him. "You shouldn't be up."

"I'm fine. The air will do me good. The wound really wasn't all that bad."

"Well, the Lord was with us," Captain Kirkegard said with a smile. "I'm always happy to be a part of one of God's miracles."

"You really think it was a miracle, Captain?" Brandon asked curiously.

"What else could it be? We were lost, I tell you. My men would have been defeated had we allowed those villains to get on our ship. They would have cut us all down. We'd all be dead by now. Don't be short with God, Winslow. When he does something, praise him for it."

Brandon dropped his eyes and shook his head. "That's what my uncle would say too."

"You need to get right with God, young man. You could have been killed and would have gone directly to the pit. Aren't you afraid of that?"

"I—I try not to think about it too much." He glanced at Dolores, who was watching the conversation unfold with great interest.

"Oh, that's foolishness." Kirkegard shook his head impatiently. He put his hand on Brandon's good shoulder and squeezed it. "Give your heart to God, man! Give your heart to God! It's the only way to live. Well, I'll leave you two alone. I have a ship to run. We'll be in England tomorrow, God willing, and then you two will no doubt get married and as in all the romantic tales live happily ever after."

Brandon glanced quickly at Dolores and saw her eyes light up and a smile touch her lips. Quickly he said, "Thank you for your offer, Captain, but I want to be strong when I take a wife."

"He's a wonderful man, isn't he, Brandon?"

"Yes, he is. I like him a great deal."

"He's very outspoken about his religion. I don't have that kind of faith."

Brandon turned to face her. "Are you satisfied with your Catholic faith?"

"To tell the truth, Brandon, I never gave it much thought. I just did what I was told to do by the priests and by my father. I went through the routine, but I never felt like Captain Kirkegard does, that God is present inside you and directing you. And Philemon—he feels the same."

"Some people seem predisposed to it. My family is."

"I'd like to be like that too. Maybe when I meet your uncle, since he's a preacher, he could help me."

"I'm sure he'd be happy to. Come along. Let's walk around the deck. I need to build my strength up."

The *Flower* plowed through the whitecaps that were tossed up by the brisk speed of the ship. Night had fallen. Already the stars overhead were flickering. Brandon looked up and said, "My uncle told me once that there are billions of stars and God knows the name of every one of them."

"I think that's wonderful. I don't know the name of any of them."

"Well, I don't know many of them." He leaned on the rail. She stood beside him. She took his hand; it had become her habit. He noticed that she seemed to need to touch him constantly—almost as if to reassure herself that he was there for her.

"I'm so happy," Dolores whispered. "You saved me from a lifetime of misery, and we're going to have a beautiful life together, aren't we?"

At that moment Brandon was torn internally by two opposing forces. The first was a deep sadness and grief for what he was doing to this young woman. He knew she had fallen in love with him and for him to tell her the truth would be a terrible thing. The other, which disturbed his mind, was that he found himself drawn to her as a man is drawn to a woman he loves. He stood silently leaning on the rail and listening to her speak of the wonderful life they would have, and suddenly he knew that the time had arrived. They would be arriving in England tomorrow, and she would find out then, anyway. He had to tell her the truth.

He said, "I'm—I'm not the man you think I am."

"Why do you say that?"

Haltingly Brandon said, "Well, sometimes a man does a wrong thing to—to do right."

"I don't understand that."

"I have to tell you something, Dolores, and I want you to listen carefully."

"You're frightening me, Brandon. Is there something wrong?"

"I'm afraid you'll think so."

"What is it?" She leaned against him, and he felt the warmth of her body and smelled the fragrance of her hair. But this was not the time for that. He cleared his throat and spoke slowly, halting at times.

"I have to tell you what's happening in England. Queen Mary was raised a Catholic by her mother, Catherine of Aragon, who came from Spain. She was a godly woman, and she instilled Catholicism strongly into her daughter. When Mary became queen, she was kind and wanted to please everybody, but her mother's teachings had stronger roots than she thought, Dolores, and she began to insist that people accept the Catholic religion and give up the new faith that had come under the reign of her father, King Henry."

"I have heard some talk of this. But what does it have to do with us?"

"Some time after she came to power, she began demanding that people become Catholics, and when they refused, she had them punished."

"Punished how?"

"Some of them she put in prison, some of them she had burned at the stake."

"How awful! That happened in Spain too. It's called an *auto-da-fé*. My father wanted me to go, but I could never stand the thought of people being burned alive. I couldn't understand why God would demand such a thing."

"Queen Mary has become a fanatic, and since she married Philip, the two of them have caused hundreds to be put to death." He hesitated and then said, "My uncle, Quentin Winslow, was on a list of people to be arrested. I found out about it when a man named Lord John Fairfax came to talk to me." Brandon studied Dolores, waiting to see if she recognized the name. But she remained still and waiting. "As a matter of fact, Lord Fairfax is a member of Queen Mary's Privy Council, the highest body in the realm, and he told me that any person on that list who refused to recant would be burned at the stake."

"How terrible!" She lifted a hand to her chest. "Your own dear uncle!"

"Lord Fairfax is not a vicious man. He did not want anyone to die, and he knew my father slightly, so he came to me with a proposition. He told me that he could save my uncle, or at least stave off his arrest. He said he could do this, but only if I would do him a service."

"What did he want?"

Brandon could not face her for a moment. He looked down at the deck. Then he forced himself to meet her eyes. "He told me that he and his wife had only one child, a girl. She was on a ship with her governess, and pirates attacked the ship. Everyone on the ship reportedly died. Lord Fairfax and his wife were crushed."

"That must have been terrible." She knitted her brows in confusion, and he could almost see what she was thinking: *Why is he telling me all this?*

"Yes. It was many years ago, but the pain and grief are still with Lord Fairfax. I could see it in his eyes." He hesitated slightly then said, "A short time ago a man came to see him. He was a Spaniard. He had been a sailor. He told Lord Fairfax that the child did not die. She was taken captive by the captain of the pirate vessel. He took her to Spain with him and adopted her."

The wind whispered. The sails flapped in the breeze. Brandon watched Dolores and waited. Even by moonlight he could see she was pale.

She finally whispered, "Are you telling me, Brandon, that I was that little girl?"

"Yes. The pirate's name was Jaspar Mendoza, but you're not his daughter. You've always known that." Brandon knew she was frightened by his words, but he knew the story must be told. "You are the daughter of John Fairfax and his wife Barbara. Your real name is Eden Fairfax. Your parents are two of the finest people in England, and they love you dearly. They've never forgotten you. They asked me to bring you back to them."

"I can't believe it. But it must be true if you tell me." And then she said, "And you found a way to get me to accompany you. You fell in love with me."

"I—I couldn't think of any other way to get you free of Mendoza's power. I had to do something."

"But you did fall in love with me?"

"I wish I could—"

Seeing his expression, she cried, "You—you don't love me!" She backed away from him, shaking her head. "It was all a lie. Just a trick to get me away to take me to England!"

"It—it was the only way I could devise in the short time I had." Brandon saw that she was trembling and he reached out to seize her arm. He wanted to embrace her, but she struck him in the chest with her fists.

"Don't you ever touch me! You lied to me, you deceived me! I never want to see you again!" She turned and fled down the deck.

Brandon felt absolutely drained. He saw that his hands were trembling. "I never thought anything could do that to me," he whispered. Absolute misery seized him. Perhaps the hardest of all to bear was that only in the last few days had he realized that he felt for her things he had never felt for any other woman he had known. Was it love? He didn't know.

One thing was certain, Brandon decided, as he leaned against the rail and shut his eyes. He was the most miserable man on board.

PART FOUR

Eden

20

"You know, my dear, in a way this is your birthday."

Eden gave her mother a startled glance. "Why, Mother, my birthday is in January."

"I know, but it's exactly two years ago today that you came back to us. I'll never forget that day as long as I live." She put her arm around Eden and hugged her. Ever since Eden had come home, there had been love flowing from John and Barbara Fairfax almost like a river. Eden could not enter a room, it seemed, without one or other of them giving her a slight touch, an arm around her shoulder, something to reassure them that their daughter returning to them was not a dream.

Eden kissed her mother on the cheek. "You and Father have made life so wonderful for me."

As if on cue, the door opened, and John Fairfax walked in. He came over to Eden at once. "Is that another new dress?" he exclaimed with feigned surprise. "I don't remember being with you when you chose that fabric."

"I chose it all by myself, Father." Eden had developed a wonderfully close relationship with her parents, and as she saw the love in their eyes, she felt a profound sense of gratitude.

"I have a surprise for you, Daughter."

"Oh, good. I like surprises. What is it?"

"We're going to visit Queen Mary."

"Really, John? You never told me that," Barbara said.

"Why, I only found out today. Of late time spent at court has been more of a burden than a joy, but I do believe you two will enjoy this visit. And you'll find lots of young men there," John said to Eden. "What about your suitors? Which one has the lead in the race for your hand now?"

"I don't think much of any of them," Eden said with a gentle smile. "They are all rather boring."

"You're far too exacting, but you're too beautiful not to find a husband."

"Most of them are only after your money, Father." She shrugged. "If I were a poor girl, the line would be considerably shorter."

"Not so! Not so! Well, I'll be telling you more about our visit to the palace later. Now I must go." He kissed Eden and then his wife. "Two beautiful women in my house—how could I be so fortunate?"

As the door closed behind him, Eden said, "He's such a good man, Mother."

"The best I know." Barbara's brow furrowed as a thought came to her. "I am a bit concerned about your future. You must marry at some point, Eden."

"I am not at all sure about that."

"Well, what a thing to say! What else is a woman to do but marry and have children?" Barbara stood close to Eden, looking into her eyes. She was not as tall a woman as her daughter, but she still retained traces of early beauty. "Sometimes I think that you judge men rather harshly. Is that because of your time in Spain, because of what you endured there, darling?"

Eden lowered her head, and when she lifted it, her teeth were clenched. "I've told you how Brandon Winslow deceived me."

"But, Eden, that was two years ago!"

"It doesn't seem like it to me. He made me believe that he loved me, and I—I believed that I loved him. He deceived me, Mother!"

"But, dear, not all men are like that. Look at your father. Besides, he did what he had to do to get you away from that awful place. Don't you feel some gratitude to him for that?"

Eden shook her head. "He tricked me into loving him. I'll never trust a man again, Mother, as long as I live!"

On the last day of May, a messenger brought a disturbing message to Brandon's lodging in Dover. A small, swarthy man in his late forties appeared at his door and said in a rumbling bass voice, "Lord Fairfax wishes to see you right away Mr. Winslow."

"Do you know why?"

"No, sir. He simply asks you to make your way to him as swiftly as possible. I'll ride back with you, if you like."

"Oh, that won't be necessary. I can find my way." Brandon pulled a coin from his pocket and handed it to the servant. "Thank you," he said, then turned away, ignoring the man's speech of gratitude. He had found himself extremely restless of late. He led an easy enough life, making plenty of money at the gambling tables, but an emptiness left him dissatisfied.

He left at once, riding hard. Still, the shadows were growing long when he brought his steed to a halt before the Fairfax mansion in Rochester. He said to the groom "Rub him down and see that he's grained."

"Yes, sir." The groom led the horse away, and Brandon ran up the steps. He had no idea what Sir John wanted. He had not seen him since bringing Eden home from her captivity. Sir John had sent him money twice, urging him to accept his reward, but he had returned it.

His nerves were tense. Eden was in this house. Would he see her? Speak to her? He had thought about her almost every day of the two years since he had reunited her with her family. England had buzzed with the story of how she had been rescued from captivity in Spain, and over and over, he was asked to tell the story, making it impossible for him to forget her. The country's distrust of Spaniards made Eden Fairfax into something of a national heroine.

A servant came to the door.

"I am Brandon Winslow. Lord Fairfax sent for me."

"Yes, sir. He's in his study."

Brandon followed the servant down an ornately decorated hall, glancing at the pictures of Fairfax men—all prominent, all wealthy—and felt oppressed.

Brandon found Lord Fairfax standing beside a tall window. "I came as quickly as I could, sir."

"I'm glad you made such good time, Brandon," Fairfax said, a troubled expression on his face. "I have rather bad news, I'm afraid."

"What is it, my Lord?"

"I'm afraid I can no longer keep your uncle from danger. You must speak to him at once!"

"What has transpired?"

"Nothing new. I simply cannot hold back the tide." Fairfax's eyes grew stormy, and he said, "The queen is getting worse. More and more people are being sent to the stake, even women and young people, because they don't fall in with her Catholic doctrine."

"What about you and Lady Barbara? Will you be safe?"

"Well, we are cowardly people, I suppose. We adopt the Catholic line, but it's a matter of form with us. But you must get your uncle out of the country."

"My father would be the one to do that. And believe me, we've tried to talk him into it before."

"I know, Master Stuart Winslow has told me that his brother

won't listen to him. Go to your uncle, Brandon. I realize he is stubborn, but he must leave the country." Fairfax paused and then put his hand on Brandon's shoulder. "I have such kindly feelings for you, my boy, as does my dear wife. You saved my daughter in order to spare your uncle, and I can never forget that. I'll do everything I can, but the Tudors are stubborn and they can be cruel. I thought Mary would be different after growing up with the cruelty of her father, but she is not. You must do what you can."

"Yes, sir. I'll try."

Fairfax hesitated and seemed to hold back words that were in his heart. "May I have a more . . . personal word with you, my boy?"

"Why, of course, Lord Fairfax."

"Your parents are wonderful people. Your father is one of the most honorable men I've ever met, and your mother is such a gracious woman."

"You need not say it," Brandon smiled bitterly. "I am well aware, sir, that I am the black sheep in the family."

"But you don't have to be, my boy. You can have a better life. I hear stories of your gambling and your dissipation, and it hurts me. I would do anything at all to help you be the son your parents can be proud of."

Brandon lowered his head, unable to meet the eyes of the older man. "I've thought about it often, sir. I hope you'll keep me in your prayers. I don't know why I behave so badly. It's almost like I'm a bad seed."

"Nonsense! God loves you as he loves all sinners. Find God, Brandon, and be the man that God made you to be."

"Yes, sir. I'll try."

"You'll stay for the night?"

"If I may. It's too late to find my uncle now."

"I'll have a servant show you to your room."

"Thank you sir. I'll leave very early, so we won't see each other—but I'm grateful for your concern for our family."

❦

The morning sun was making a thin line of light in the east when Brandon left his room and descended the stairs. A movement to his right caught his eye. He saw that it was Eden and stopped abruptly.

Her eyes widened, and she exclaimed, "What are you doing here?"

"Your father asked to see me."

Eden's face was flushed. "Are you here to extort more money from him for saving me from the Spaniards?"

Brandon did not answer. A shock ran along his nerves, for the sight of her stirred up feelings that he had long kept buried. Although he knew that she hated him, excitement ran through him. "You're looking well, Eden." When he saw that she did not mean to answer, he added, "I hope you're happy in your new life."

"Oh, I'm certain that is a concern for you." Bitterness flared in Eden's eyes, and her voice was cold as she said, "I had hoped never to see you again!"

"I know you despise me."

"Why shouldn't I? You betrayed me. I'm surprised you didn't complete your conquest and bed me."

"I couldn't find another way to get you free, Eden."

"Liar! You must have enjoyed making a fool out of me!" Suddenly she struck him a ringing slap on his cheek. "Be gone! Never come here again!" she cried. She whirled and ran away.

Brandon touched his cheek, staring after her. He was more shaken by the encounter than by any battle he'd fought. He was startled when a thought came to him. *Did I really feel something for her two years ago?* He could not answer the question, but neither could he get Eden out of his mind. Bitterness took him as he thought of his life and what John Fairfax had said about becoming a better man. He knew it was useless for him to see his uncle, but he was also grimly aware that he must try.

Eden had looked forward to the ball and seeing Nonsuch Palace. The occasion was interesting enough. She met the young ladies of the court, and one of them said, "Miss Fairfax, if you'd care to be one of us, I am sure that Her Majesty would be glad to have you as one of her maids." The offer held no attraction at all for Eden, for life at court, at least what she had heard of it, was rife with immorality and seemed somewhat like what she had endured in Spain.

Now, as she entered the banquet hall, she saw that it was crowded. Her parents were already there, seated at one end of a long table, and when they smiled at her, she returned their smile.

She heard her name called, and turned to see a couple moving toward her. The resemblance of the man to Brandon was striking. He was an older edition, very handsome, but with a much sweeter expression than she had ever seen on Brandon's face.

He said, "Pardon me for introducing myself, Miss Fairfax. I'm Stuart Winslow, and this is my wife, Heather."

Eden made her curtsy and tried vainly to think of something to say. "I am happy to meet you."

"Brandon has told us so much about you," Heather said. "We're so happy that you were delivered from the kidnapper."

"Yes," Stuart put in. "Your parents are as happy as I've ever seen them."

Eden managed to carry on a conversation with them, although her knees trembled from being so near Brandon's parents. She remembered clearly that Brandon had told her that his parents were more in love than any people he had ever seen. He had said, *They're like a young couple on a perpetual honeymoon. I've never seen love so true, so strong.* She believed it when she saw Heather look at Stuart with obvious affection.

After Eden had made the usual remarks, she heard herself asking, "I wonder about your son, Brandon." She saw that they were reluctant to speak of him and said, "I hope he's well."

"No, he is not well, Miss Fairfax," Stuart said. "He's living an ungodly life."

"But we believe," Heather said quickly, "that God is going to put his hand on him. That he'll find himself and be the man God wants him to be."

Eden did not know how to speak to this pair. At length, they wished her well and moved away, and Eden went to sit beside her father.

"I've just met Brandon Winslow's parents."

"They are wonderful people, Daughter. There is not a more honorable man in England than Stuart Winslow, and his wife is what a woman should be."

"They're very unhappy about their son."

"Yes. He's a gambler. Very good at it, but a gambler all the same." Fairfax shook his head, adding sadly, "He's breaking his parents' hearts."

"Why would such a bad man come to Spain to save me? I suppose you paid him a great deal of money."

"What? Not a bit of it, Eden," her father said in surprise. "He did it to save the life of his uncle, Quentin Winslow. Reverend Winslow, I should say." He remembered himself and where he was, lowered his voice, and whispered in her ear, "I went to him and told him that if he would get you free, I would save his uncle from being burned at the stake—at least for a while."

"He didn't ask for money?"

"No, he didn't. As a matter of fact, I've sent money to him twice, but he's sent it back each time with a rather sharp note saying that he didn't do what he did for gain." He looked about to make sure no one was listening. "I fear for Reverend Winslow. It would be a shame to lose him. He's a fine preacher and as good a man as his brother."

Eden asked no more questions, but she was deep in thought. This side of Brandon Winslow she had not known.

Eden's meeting with Queen Mary was brief. She was brought to her room, and as she curtsied, she was shocked by how old and sickly the monarch looked. Mary's complexion was almost the color of stale biscuits, and lines of pain showed around her eyes and on her forehead. Her voice was deeper than Eden expected. She spoke for a time about how glad she was that Eden had been brought back and reunited with her parents.

"Would you like to come to court as one of my ladies?" Queen Mary asked.

"It is a grand and gracious offer, Your Majesty. But I missed so many years with my parents that I feel I must spend all my time with them."

Mary nodded. "That is a good thing. Your father is an excellent man. I respect and trust him utterly. Are you a good Catholic?" she asked abruptly.

"I grew up in the faith," Eden said. She could have added that it had been nothing more than a formality for her, but she knew that would be a dangerous statement.

"Well, that it is good. England must return to the old religion."

Later Eden's father told her how pleased he and his wife were that she had chosen to stay with them instead of going to court.

"It was no sacrifice, Father." Eden shook her head. "The queen is sickly, isn't she? She's not what I thought."

"Yes. She's sick physically and I fear in other ways." Fairfax shook his head and said bitterly, "She has brought much misery to England. And only God knows how many more must suffer!"

21

Eden and her mother were walking along one of the spacious hallways inside Hampton Court. The very size and ornate furnishings of the structure were astonishing to Eden.

"I never saw such a house, Mother. It's enormous!"

"Yes. Cardinal Wolsey built it. More than twenty-five hundred men were employed to build it."

"It has so many rooms!"

"Yes. A thousand rooms, so they say. Of course, Wolsey didn't keep it long. King Henry confiscated it in 1529. It is a little ostentatious, don't you think?"

"Quite. Who would want to live in a place like this?"

"Not me, I'm sure. Big is not better, is it?" Lady Barbara paused for a moment, and when Eden turned to face her, she said with some urgency. "Your father and I have been wondering what you think about Sir Ralph's offer of marriage."

"I don't think of it at all." Sir Ralph Spencer had everything that a man should have who would court a woman of Eden's stature and social standing. He was fairly handsome, though rather short. He was wealthy, but had little wit about him. "He bores me to death, Mother. All he can talk about are his dogs."

"Well, he has a lot to recommend him, but he is rather

boring. But Eden, you haven't looked with favor on any suitors." Lady Barbara hesitated and then said, "You're not still grieved over the way Brandon Winslow treated you, are you?"

Eden did not answer for a time, and then she shook her head. "I can't forget one thing, Mother. As badly as he treated me for that brief period of time, I loved him, and I thought he loved me. It was like nothing I had ever known before. If I can't have that kind of feeling for a man, I'm not interested in marriage."

They strolled on in silence until someone called out, "Lady Barbara!"

They saw that the Princess Elizabeth was approaching them. Elizabeth came up to them with a smile and said, "I must have your opinion on some things, Miss Fairfax. Oh, and I believe your husband is looking for you, Lady Barbara. I trust you can find him in this huge pile of bricks."

Lady Barbara laughed, for she liked the Princess Elizabeth immensely. "I'll find him. I have to keep him away from these beautiful young ladies of the court."

"I don't think you have anything to worry about there when he's married to one of the loveliest ladies in England." Elizabeth gave Lady Barbara a flashing smile, then took Eden's arm, saying, "Come along with me. As I said, I have need of your opinion." Eden was flattered. She had met Elizabeth twice before and liked her. "All right, if truth be told," Elizabeth said in a conspiratorial manner, "I just wanted to get you away from your mother and hear the story of your rescue from that pirate in Spain. I've heard rumors, but I'd like to hear all the romantic details from you."

Eden was embarrassed, but she said, "Well, it was quite a daring thing. I was more or less a prisoner, although the man who called himself my father wouldn't say that. When Mr. Winslow came, I had no idea that he had come for me."

"And did you fall in love with Brandon? He is so very handsome, don't you think?"

Eden was taken aback, but she knew that Elizabeth was very outspoken, so she said reluctantly, "I'm afraid so, and—and I thought he was in love with me." She went on to relate that Brandon Winslow had made her fall in love with him and then had used great ingenuity to get her to run away. Then she spoke of the time on the ship when she discovered the truth. "When I found out that he really didn't love me, Princess Elizabeth, I felt like the biggest fool the world has ever known."

"Why, if this were a romance," Elizabeth smiled, "the daring hero would have fallen in love with you, and you would have married him. Weren't you tempted?"

"Yes. I was tempted, but when I found out that he had lied, I hated him."

"I've been thinking a lot about Stuart Winslow and his wife Heather," Princess Elizabeth said. "I've noticed that he often takes her hand simply for the pleasure of it. Not many men have the courage to show that kind of affection in public. I know nothing of a loving couple's marriage." She did not mention that her own father had been a cruel tyrant, but Eden of course knew her history.

"I know of what you speak. Brandon told me that they're still deeply in love after all the years of marriage, but there aren't many marriages like that, are there?"

"I'm afraid not." Elizabeth grew serious and lowered her voice. "I'm concerned about his uncle, Reverend Quentin Winslow."

"Is he really in danger, Princess?"

"He's a fine man, but I think he has survived this long only because of your father's efforts. But every day of his life he's in danger."

"I hate these burnings of people! I expected it to be different in this country."

Elizabeth turned to face her. The sunlight caught the gold tints in her reddish hair. She had the fairest skin of any woman in England. She liked to laugh, but just now she was deadly serious. Her eyes slid back and forth before she spoke in a hushed voice. "If I were queen, Eden, it would be different. I would never have people put to death because they differed with me because of their religious beliefs." Suddenly she remembered herself and laughed with some embarrassment. "Please don't mention what I said. They might put me in the Tower."

"Oh, that could never happen."

"It did happen, Eden. I was taken to the Tower when I was a very young woman, and for a while it seemed that I would lose my head, as my mother did."

"Were you very frightened?"

"Facing death every day? Of course I was! But God brought me through it. I was afraid for my life, and that's not a pleasant thing. You must talk to your father and get him to do all he can for Quentin Winslow, although I'm sure he already has. Despite how my sister sees it, the Winslows have always been very loyal to the Crown. Well, I will let you go now. Can you find your way?"

"I doubt it. This is too big for me."

"It's too big for anyone. It's a big pile of vanity!"

After her conversation with Princess Elizabeth, Eden thought more and more about Brandon Winslow, and her thoughts went from him to Quentin. She had heard that he was preaching at Eastbourne, and decided rather abruptly that she would go to hear him preach. As a Catholic she had not heard many sermons, although she had gone to Mass many times. A stay in Eastbourne was not difficult to arrange, for a distant relative of her mother and close friend of the family lived there. Eden made up her mind. *I'll visit Mrs. Benson, and I'll hear Quentin Winslow preach. I need to know what kind of a man he is.*

It was easy enough to persuade her mother to let her go for a visit to Eastbourne. She took simple clothing rather than the ornate gowns that were her usual attire. All the way to Eastbourne she was thinking about Brandon and his family. The bitter feelings she'd had for Brandon had been mitigated, and now she was anxious to meet the uncle for whom Brandon had risked his life.

❦

Most of the churches that Eden had grown up in were large and imposing. She had attended services at a large cathedral in Spain, and after coming to England, her parents had taken her to a very large church in Dover. She had been aware of the small churches, of course, but she had never attended one, so when she entered the church in Eastbourne where Reverend Winslow preached, she was slightly shocked by the stark simplicity of the interior. Accustomed as she was to ornate statues and fine windows and all the trappings that went with the high church style, she was stunned by the simplicity of the church. The people matched the church; they ranged from the very poor to the middle class. She saw few signs of wealth among them. Most of them were working people, and although she had selected a simple, inexpensive gown, still her attire and her appearance drew the eyes of many and made her slightly embarrassed. She took a seat in the middle of the church, where she could more or less hide herself from the eyes of the preacher.

She had sat there for only a brief time when a man came to stand in the pulpit; she knew instantly that this was Brandon's uncle. He had the Winslow look about him: auburn hair, a wedge-shaped face, wide mouth, and light-blue eyes that were very piercing. Just a glimpse of him brought back her memories of Brandon, the bittersweet memory of the love that she had felt for him, and then, of course, the painful memory of how she had been deceived.

The service continued. It was unlike Catholic services. Everything in this church was in English, not Latin.

When the singing was over, Quentin Winslow stood before the congregation. He had a pleasant look on his face. His voice was clear and carried well in the small building. He welcomed the congregation and then said, "My sermon this morning, if I had a title for it, would be something along the lines of 'Three Women Who Met Jesus.' Nowhere in the world are women honored as in Christian countries. If you were to go to most foreign countries where paganism rules, you would find women treated worse than animals. So it is in Africa and in most parts of the world. When Jesus came, he did more than any other man to lift women from a lowly status to a place of honor. And this morning I want you to think about three women who had their lives changed by Jesus Christ. First we will read the story of the woman described in Luke 8:43." He began to read, and Eden, who had never read the Bible and knew only the remarks on scripture made by the priest, to which she often paid little attention, suddenly began to unfold like a drama as Winslow began to read.

"And a woman having an issue of blood twelve years, which had spent all her living upon physicians, neither could be healed of any, came behind him and touched the border of his garment: and immediately her issue of blood stanched. And Jesus said, 'Who touched me?' When all denied, Peter and they that were with him said, 'Master, the multitude throng thee and press thee and sayest thou, Who touched me?' And Jesus said, 'Somebody hath touched me: for I perceive that virtue is gone out of me.' And when the woman saw that she was not hid, she came trembling, and falling down before him, she declared unto him before all the people for what cause she had touched him, and how she was healed immediately. And he said unto her, 'Daughter, be of good comfort: thy faith hath made thee whole; go in peace.'"

"Isn't that a wonderful story!" Quentin Winslow exclaimed. "This poor woman who was unclean, for according to Jewish law, any woman with an issue of blood was as unclean as a dead person. No one could touch her without becoming himself unclean. And for years she had sought to be healed and spent all her money on physicians but was no better."

He went on to describe the woman so well that Eden seemed to see with her eyes, and she was so caught up in the drama that her heart beat faster.

"This poor woman, who had been failed by man on every hand, thought, *If I could just touch the hem of the garment of Jesus of Nazareth, I will be healed.* Ah now, there is faith, my friends, there is faith! And you have heard how she did touch just the hem of the garment of the Lord Jesus, and instantly she was healed. Bless the Lord, oh my soul! That's what happens when people come to Jesus. They are healed.

"Now let's move on to the second woman that I would speak of. In John's Gospel, chapter four, there is a marvelous story. I will not read it all. It is rather lengthy. The Bible says that on one of his journeys Jesus grew weary, and he came to a city of Samaria and he sat down on the side of a well. There cometh a woman of Samaria to draw water. Jesus saith unto her, 'Give me to drink,' for his disciples were gone away into the city to buy meat. Then saith the woman of Samaria to him, 'How is it that thou, being a Jew, asketh drink of me, which am a woman of Samaria? For the Jews have no dealings with the Samaritans.' Jesus answered and said unto her, 'If thou knewest the gift of God, and who it is that saith to thee, Give me to drink, thou wouldest have asked of him, and he would have given thee living water.'"

Looking up from his Bible, Winslow said, "Let me pause here and inform you that there was great bitterness between the Jews and the Samaritans. There were two different races completely, it seems, and they despised one another, much as we have had altercations with other nations such as the French and the Spanish and have hated them and have fought wars with them. So this woman was shocked that a Jew would even speak to her, first of all because she was a woman, second because she was a hated Samaritan. So Jesus said he would give her something to drink called living water.

"The woman saith unto him, 'Sir, thou has nothing to draw with, and the well is deep: from whence then hast thou that living water?' And then Jesus had a conversation with her. And he said this: 'Whosoever drinketh of the water that I shall give him shall never thirst; but the water that I shall give him shall be in him a well of water springing up into everlasting life.'

"And then, bless the Lord, the woman's heart was touched! 'Give me this water,' she said, 'that I thirst not.' Jesus said, 'Go, call thy husband.' She said, 'I have no husband,' and Jesus answered, 'Thou hast well said for thou hast had five husbands; and he whom thou now hast is not thy husband.'"

Quentin continued the story. "And finally Jesus said, 'The hour cometh, and now is, when the true worshippers shall worship the Father in spirit and in truth: for the Father seeketh such to worship him. God is a spirit: and they that worship him must worship him in spirit and in truth.' And the woman said, 'I know Messiah is coming.'

"And Jesus said in verse twenty-six, 'I that speak unto thee am he.'

"That's the story. The woman ran back to her village and told everyone, 'Come, see a man who told me all the things that ever I did,' and she brought others to him.

"So this second woman that we are looking at had nothing to recommend her to God but she found the love of God in Jesus. Isn't that a wonderful story? Now, let's move on quickly to number three. You'll find this also in John's Gospel, the eighth chapter."

Quentin looked out over his audience, and his eyes met

those of Eden. She squirmed, for he seemed to be looking deep down into her soul, and for that one moment she knew that this was a man of honor and truth.

"In the eighth chapter of the Gospel of John we find this third woman. The scribes and the Pharisees brought unto him a woman taken in adultery; and they had said to him, 'Master, this woman was taken into adultery, in the very act. Now Moses in the law commanded us that such should be stoned. But what sayest thou?'

"The law, indeed, was clear that adulterers should be stoned. But Jesus did a very strange thing. He 'stooped down and with his finger wrote on the ground as though he heard them not.' And finally he looked up, and he said words that I have treasured and have very carefully kept. Jesus said, 'He that is without sin among you let him cast a stone at her.' The Bible says that they were convicted by their own conscience and went out one by one, beginning at the eldest even unto the last. And Jesus was left alone, and the woman standing in the midst.

"The Bible doesn't say this, but I like to think this dear woman who was a sinner but yet a loved sinner came to Jesus and bowed down and held to his feet. We do know what Jesus said. He said, 'Woman, where are those thine accusers? Hath no man condemned thee?' And she said, 'No man, Lord.' And Jesus said unto her, 'Neither do I condemn thee: go, and sin no more.'

"Three women. This morning I would like us to think of ourselves in relation to what happened. All three women needed God desperately, and all three found him by making a desperate attempt to reach out to Jesus Christ."

The sermon went on for some time, and Eden listened intently. She found that her heart was beating hard, and then suddenly for no reason that she could understand she found herself weeping. She had never heard the Gospel in English, and Jesus to her was a distant statue on an altar, but this was a living

Christ that Quentin Winslow spoke of! She sat there, unable to control her tears. She knew that the service was over, but she found herself too weak to rise. Finally the place grew quiet as the crowd left, and then a voice said, "Are you troubled, my lady?"

Eden looked up swiftly and saw Quentin Winslow standing beside her. She did not know what to say, but finally she whispered, "I don't know what's wrong with me, sir, but I never heard of anyone speak of Jesus as you did in your sermon."

"Come and take a walk with me. It's a fine day."

It was not something that Eden would usually have done, but she found herself unable to refuse. She rose, and the two left the church.

Quentin led her along a paved walk behind the church to a cemetery with ancient, moss-covered stones, and then paused under the shade of a spreading oak tree. "If you could tell me your problem, I would be glad to pray with you."

Suddenly Eden burst out, "I am Eden Fairfax. I am the woman your nephew delivered from Spain and brought home to my family."

Winslow's eyes opened in surprise. His voice was warm as he said, "I've heard the story, but we've never met. I'm so happy that you have been restored to your parents. I hear good things about how they've made a home for you. How is it, lady, with you and God? You seemed troubled in church."

"I don't know God." The words burst forth from Eden. "I don't know how to find him. Those stories you read, I've never heard them before. I've never read the Bible. We weren't permitted to read it in Spain."

"Miss Fairfax, the one fact that you must understand is that Jesus loves you just as he did those three women. He's alive, and his desire is to live in your heart."

"But how can that be?"

"It's a miracle of God's grace."

"I would like that," Eden whispered, "but I don't know how."

"You are just three steps away from God, as we all are."

"Three steps? What are they?"

"Repentance is the first step. That means you must confess any sin you've done and you must not hate anyone."

Eden knew that Quentin had seen her face suddenly tighten. He said quietly, "I see that you do have harsh feelings."

"Yes, Reverend Winslow, I do." She told him how she felt when she learned that Brandon had deceived her. Finally, her voice unsteady, she said, "I—I don't know how to stop hating him."

"You spend time in the company of Jesus. After all, he forgave those who were nailing him to a cross. That's the first step, and you must make it, and no one can make it for you. And you must forgive Brandon. He's in Dover now, and he needs Jesus just as you do."

"I—I don't know if I can forgive him."

"You must."

"What is the second step?"

"Faith, my lady. Simple faith that Jesus is the Christ. And the third step is very simple. After you've repented and you've come to a position of faith in Jesus, you simply call on him, and ask God in the name of Jesus to forgive your sins." He smiled. "You can do that right now, my lady."

"No, I can't! I cannot."

"Well, then, what you are feeling will stay with you. I feel that God is on your trail, so to speak. I have a copy of the Bible in English that I want to give you. As you read the Word of God, you will hear God speaking to you. And at some point you must call on him and ask him for forgiveness. You can do this in your bed. You can do it while you are out walking. The time and the place are not important. Repentance, faith, and calling on God—that's all it takes to be in God's family."

"Thank you, sir. I will think about it. But I must ask you, do you know the danger you are in? You could be beheaded for your preaching."

"Oh, yes, I'm well aware of that. But"—there was a joy in his eyes—"Jesus loved me enough to die for me, and if he wants me to die for him, I must do it."

Eden felt she must get away. She said, "Thank you for talking with me."

"Farewell, lady. Know that I'll be praying for you. But come and let me give you the Bible I spoke of."

Weak and almost unable to walk, her mind in a turmoil, Eden returned to the front of the church, where she waited until Winslow emerged and placed a book in her hands, saying, "Let me pray for you now—and be certain that I'll be praying for you and Brandon every day."

He bowed his head, and Eden felt for the first time in her life that God was real and very near. She knew suddenly that she must seek God. There was no other way.

22

After her visit to Quentin Winslow, Eden found herself spending much time alone. She often spent the entire day reading the Bible that he had given her. At times she felt she understood nothing, but at other times the words would almost leap off the page, causing her to see truth about her life and her spirit. Her behavior obviously puzzled her parents. Both had approached her at different times asking what was troubling her, but she put them off with a feeble excuse.

Finally a thought came to her that shocked her at first, but it came repeatedly. *I must see Brandon! I must settle things between us or I shall go mad.* She was aware that some of the affection she'd felt for him was still in her heart, but she could not be certain how he felt about her.

She knew that Brandon was in Dover. She had a close friend named Helen Montrose who lived there. The two young women had visited each other several times, for Helen lived with her parents in a townhouse in the town. Eden made the arrangements with her parents and sent Helen a letter, which was answered at once:

Come as soon as you can, Eden. We'll have a lovely time.

ꕥ

For three days Eden spent most of her time with Helen Montrose. They went out every day and saw most of the sights of Dover. She didn't have the courage to face Brandon, and she reasoned that she didn't know where he was anyway.

Then on Thursday night at a small gathering at the home of one of Helen's friends, she heard a man say, "You know, I lost a lot of money to that Winslow fellow. I think he cheats, but I can't catch him at it."

"I'd like to try him," another man spoke up. "Where does he play?"

"Oh, at the Anchor and Albatross, but you'd better stay away from him. He can read the backs of those cards. I would have called him out, but I couldn't catch him at it."

Eden turned away and filed the name of the inn in her mind.

The next day she spoke to a servant named Giles, a small, thin man with light-green eyes. "Giles, I want you to do something for me. I'll pay you well for it, but you must keep quiet."

"I'm a living tomb, Lady Fairfax. What do you need?"

"There's a man called Brandon Winslow. He gambles at the Anchor and Albatross. I want you to find out where he lives."

"Right! I'll let you know as soon as I find something."

Eden was prepared to wait, but late that afternoon, Giles came back. "I found him, lady. He lives in a green house right across from the smithy. You know where that is?"

"Yes, I've seen it." Eden reached into her pouch and fished out a coin. "Remember, you must keep quiet about this."

"Quiet as the tomb, lady! Quiet as the tomb!"

Eden told Helen that she needed to look for a few items. For a long while she wandered the streets of Dover, and her courage almost failed her. But she prayed silently, *Lord, help me to do this thing. I need to make this right with Brandon.*

She finally came to stand in the front of the smithy and

looked at the green house across from it. It was just as Giles had said, but now that the time had come to meet Brandon, she felt weak and terrified. *What will I say to him?* The thought seemed to claw at her nerves, and she almost turned and went back to Helen's house. But she had come for a reason. She straightened up, and her mouth drew into a tight line. She walked up to the door and knocked. There was a long silence, and she knocked again. The door opened and Brandon stood before her. He was unshaved and looked rough, but his voice was eager as he said, "Eden, I can't believe you're here!"

Eden had never felt so weak. She managed to whisper, "I—I need to talk to you, Brandon."

Brandon gave her a long look then said, "Come, Eden, Let's get some air and go for a stroll." But once they began their walk, he seemed so taken by surprise that he could not think of a word to say. Neither of them could find a way to break the silence. They reached the brink of the white cliffs of Dover. It was a beautiful, spectacular sight, the cliffs falling away sheer to the sea. The waves below curled, and the whitecaps battered the shore for miles, it seemed. Eden could not think of a single way to explain what she was doing there that did not sound half mad.

"What's the trouble, Eden?"

She saw that he was looking at her with compassion. She was embarrassed. "I went to hear your uncle preach."

"Did you, now? What did you think?"

"I had never heard preaching before. I sometimes heard a sermon in Latin, which I don't understand, but I've never heard anything like your uncle's sermon in my life."

"What was the sermon about?"

Eden went over the sermon slowly and thoughtfully. She saw that Brandon was watching her carefully. From far off came the boom of the surf, and overhead sea birds were calling in raucous cries, but he paid more attention to her than any of these. He stared at her intently as she concluded.

"Did you decide anything?" he asked.

"Your uncle told me that you can't be a real Christian unless you forgive your enemies."

"That's true enough. It's set forth in the Bible very clearly."

"He told me I would have to forgive you."

Brandon blinked in surprise. "He said that?"

"Yes, he did."

"And are you able to do that?"

"Oh, Brandon, I don't know! I've hated you for two years now. You deceived me. You made me think you loved me, and I believed you. I was such a silly fool!" Tears gathered in Eden's eyes. Brandon's face was blurred, but she felt him take her hand in both of his and hold it tightly. His touch was soothing and made what she had come to say easier.

"I can't blame you for hating me, Eden. It was the only way I could think of to get you out of that place. But let me say this." He suddenly lifted her hand and kissed the back of it. "At first I wanted to get you free in order to save my uncle, but by the time we were on the ship, and as we made our voyage, I realized that my feelings for you had changed."

"Changed how?" Eden whispered. She was very aware of the warmth of his hand and the strength of it.

"I realized that I had been a fool for years and had never known what real affection was. When I found out what I felt for you—affection that I'd never felt for a woman—it was too late."

"You truly had feelings for me?"

Brandon seemed to think deeply for a moment, then he spoke, and his voice was soft. "Every man has some sort of ideal of a woman in his head, some sort of picture. The kind of woman he wants. But usually it's a picture built up of more than one woman, not just one."

"That's not very fair, is it, Brandon? How could a man ever get that in one woman?"

Brandon put his free hand on her shoulder and pulled her

closer. She saw in his eyes a softness, a gentleness, and yet a hunger that she recognized echoed her own.

"When a man finally gets his woman, he finds all those things in her that he wants to see."

As he spoke, Eden found herself asking, *How much do I care about this man?* And the answer came. Love to a woman meant a heart that was full, as she had felt it in those early days for Brandon. It was a wild, strange, and ever-changing feeling, and nothing else was like it. She had always thought of love as something that came upon a woman like the striking of a bell, with a clarity that she had never heard. She thought of it as an understanding that passed from man to woman. She knew that this was happening to her again, and it both frightened her and gave her hope.

She caught his glance and held it. She knew she was beautiful. He was a man like all other men, she knew, with all the primal impulses. He put his arms around her, and she was glad that she had the power to stir him to the deepest of hungers. She longed to ease the sense of loneliness that resounded from him. He brought her to him with a quick sweep of his arm, and as he kissed her, she felt a thrill race through her. When she pulled her head back, she brushed his lips with her fingertips and swayed until she was against him again.

She was shaken and said, "Can we walk?"

"Yes, of course." They walked along the edge of the cliff, both lost in thought.

Finally she stopped and turned to him. "It makes a big difference, Brandon, knowing that you truly had some feeling for me. That it wasn't all a lie. I can forgive you."

He held her with his glance and said almost bitterly, "I have been a lost soul since the time you cast me off, Eden. I'm not a good man, I wish I were, but I'm not. But I'm glad you talked to my uncle. I hope you find God. It seems you already have."

"I know the path there, anyway. And I hope the same thing for you, Brandon. You're breaking your parents' hearts."

"I know. That's the worst of it."

They looked out on the sea. The path was empty. It was this that gave Eden courage to speak. Finally she said with a strange intensity, "Brandon, I know so little about God. You've heard about Jesus all your life." She spoke in a broken voice and tears were in her eyes, blurring her sight of him. "Can't we find God together? Your uncle told me that anyone who wants salvation has to do three things. I've been going over and over those things ever since I spoke with him. I suppose you know what those things are."

Brandon stilled. "I think he probably told you that when anyone sins they must come to God and repent of their sins and they have to believe that Jesus is the Savior."

"That's what he said. And he said that if I want to find peace with God, I have to call on God to save me by the blood of Jesus."

"That's the Gospel, Eden. As you said, I've heard it all my life." A bitter expression twisted his face. "I know how to find God, but I've never been able to do it."

Eden's heart beat very fast, and as she looked intently into Brandon's face, she saw that he was deeply troubled. A thought came clearly to her: *If you don't call on God now, you may never have another chance.* She had a fullness in her throat and could only whisper, "Brandon, isn't it a decision? There is no mystery to solve. To accept him as Savior is just that, acceptance. Couldn't we call on God right now?"

Brandon didn't answer. His eyes brimmed with tears. She knew he wasn't a man who wept a great deal, but the sight of his face gave her courage to say, "Do you believe in Jesus?"

"Yes! I always have. But I've sinned so greatly. I don't see how God could forgive me."

"But Jesus forgave the adulteress. Your uncle told me that Jesus would forgive every sin. I need only ask."

A silence seemed to surround them and Eden felt so weak that she could barely stand. She cried out, "Brandon, we need God, both of us!"

It was then Brandon Winslow knew that he could not run from God any longer. He felt trapped, but along with that he felt a breath-stealing presence that could only be God. He said in a broken tone, "I need Christ in my life. I've needed him for so long. Let's kneel down right here and ask God to forgive us and to save us."

Eden fell to her knees with Brandon beside her, Brandon cried out to God and waited for Eden to do the same through her tears.

Afterward, neither of them could say how long they prayed, but there came a time of peace for Brandon. Looking into Eden's face, he felt a great joy. "We've found our way with God, haven't we, Eden?"

"Yes, we have." He pulled her to her feet and with a great gentleness whispered, "I'll never forget this moment, Eden. If I ever have doubts about my salvation, I'll come back to this very spot and I'll tell God that this is where I gave my heart to him. Alongside you. I'll treasure the memory forever."

"What will we do now?" Eden asked weakly, but her face was awash in joy. "I know you must tell your family, and they'll be so glad for you."

"Yes, I must go to them. And I think you should tell your family as well."

They walked along the edge of the cliff, and finally Eden asked, "What about us, Brandon?"

"We must move slowly, dear," Brandon said. "I'd like to claim you right now, but I know that I must prove myself. Walk awhile in these new boots. It will take some time, but I ask you to be patient. When the right time comes, God will tell us what to do with our lives." He smiled then and took her in his arms. "I love you, Eden, and I believe that God will guide us toward each other."

And then Eden Fairfax laughed, "I can wait, Brandon! I know you care for me and I know that God has touched me. Farewell for now, beloved. Go to your family; it will be the happiest day of their lives when you share it with them. When God speaks to you about us, come to me. I'll be waiting."

Stuart and Heather were sitting beside the fire. She was reading. Stuart was merely staring into the fire, thinking long thoughts. They had been there for over an hour without saying a word. Suddenly a maid entered to say, "Sir, there's somebody at the door for you."

Even as she spoke, they heard the door slam. Stuart got to his feet. Abruptly the doorway was filled with the form of Brandon. Heather cried out, "Brandon!" Leaping to her feet, she ran to him, and he opened his arms. He was stiff with cold, but she held on to him and cried, "What is it, Brandon? What's happened?"

Brandon could not speak for a moment, and when he did, his voice was husky. He reached out his free hand, and his father took it. "Father, you and mother have prayed for me all my life, and I thought your prayers were wasted, but they weren't." He struggled, tears came to his eyes, his voice broke. "I found the Lord. I'm going to serve him the rest of my life."

And there in that room with the fire crackling and snapping and roaring up the chimney, Stuart and Heather clung to their son, crying out their thanks to the God who had brought the prodigal home.

23

Betsy Price looked down at the child she was nursing, and lines of care appeared in her face. She held the child tightly and tried to ignore the dark fears for the future that rose in her.

"Betsy, girl, I don't know what we're going to do." John Price was lying on a bed, his leg bound to a splint. He had been trampled by a horse. The break was bad enough to lay him low for weeks, perhaps months. The doctor had said he would walk again but he would always have a stiff leg.

"We'll be all right, John."

"I don't know how." John Price's voice was weak. He looked around the rough room at his two small children playing in a corner and then at the cupboard that he knew was nearly bare. "I won't be able to work. What will we do, Wife?"

"We'll make out fine. I'll raise a garden, and you'll get well and be able to do your work again."

"The doctor said I never would be able to handle horses again. I'll never ride again, he said."

Betsy was silent, for she was taking counsel of her own fears, but she tried her best to smile and said, "We've never starved, and we never will. God will take care of us."

The two were silent then. They knew each other so well, and now they felt the pressure of poverty crushing them.

Suddenly a knock came at the door. Betsy looked up. "Who could that be, I wonder?" She got up and went to the door. When she opened it, she exclaimed, "Mr. Winslow!"

"It's me, Betsy. I came by to see how you and John were doing and your little ones."

"Well, sir, he's been in considerable pain, and—" She broke off, unable to state the naked truth that they were facing a most bitter future. "Will you come in, sir?"

"Yes. I want to have a word with you and John." Betsy stood back as the tall man entered the room, pulled up a chair, and sat down beside her husband's bed. His voice was cheerful as he spoke. "Well, John, how is it with you today?"

"The pain's not as bad, I don't think, sir."

"Well, that's good. We'll just have to take good care of you, won't we, Betsy?"

"Yes, sir. I'm doin' the best I can."

"How are your fine children doing?"

"They are—they are doing fine, Master Winslow. Just a little—" She would not say "hungry"; that would sound like begging. She saw Winslow's eyes go to the children in the corner, who were watching him, and then to the infant in her arms.

He said quickly, "Well, I've decided that it's time for Christmas to come a little early. Let me step outside. I've brought something." He disappeared.

As soon as he was gone, Betsy whispered, "What is he doing, John?"

"I don't know. He seems a changed man!"

When Winslow came in, his arms were full of a huge ham and several bags. A short, grinning servant was behind him, also loaded with food.

"Here, we've got some good things for you. A big, fat ham and some fresh fish. Two gallons of milk from the finest cows in

England and plenty of fresh-baked bread. Put the stuff right over there on that table, Philemon."

"Yes, sir." The servant loaded the table, and Brandon added his own burdens to it until it was stacked high. "Bring the rest of it in and just put it anywhere."

"Oh, sir," John said, tears welling up in his eyes. "How kind it is of you to think of us."

"Well, why wouldn't I think of you? After all, John, you were always kind to me when I was a lad just learning to ride. I remember all the lessons you gave me."

John Price spoke huskily. "It's a godsend, sir, I must say. I've been fretting a bit."

"Fretting about what?"

"The doctor said I won't be able to do the things I used to do."

"Well, that comes to all of us. Sometimes it's just age. I've found out I can't do the things I could do when I was eighteen. But you're going to be all right, John."

"No, sir, I'm afraid not." Price lifted his eyes, and the misery showed in them. "I don't know what I'll do, sir."

Brandon Winslow seemed to fill the small room, his voice full and reassuring. He smiled, and his blue eyes seemed to light up his face. "Well, I'll tell you what you'll do, John. You'll go on working for the Winslows as you have for most of your life. Maybe you can't do your old job at Stoneybrook so well, but there's plenty of work to do around here. I'll see to it that you have a good place as long as you want it. I've always thought well of you and Betsy and your fine children." He got to his feet and said sternly, but with a good smile, "Now, I don't want you worrying. If you need the doctor or if you need anything, send word to me. I'll have Philemon, here, check on you too." He put his hand out and took John's thin one in his. "God's going to take care of you, my dear friend. Don't worry." Turning, he put his hand out to Betsy. She felt the strength of his grip and lifted her eyes to his.

"You take good care of this man and of these children. All right?"

"Yes, sir. God bless you, sir."

"I'll be seeing you then."

As soon as the door was closed, Betsy began to cry. "He's not the same man."

"No, he's not. Ever since he's come back home again he's been different. Everybody's talkin' about him. Been six months now, and he's not the same at all. He never cared much for people except for himself."

"I was talking to Lady Heather. She was telling me," Betsy said, "how he serves God now with all his heart."

"Well, I believe in miracles, and our miracle is Mr. Brandon Winslow. We're going to be all right, girl."

"Didn't I tell you God would take care of us?"

Stuart looked out the window and saw Brandon speaking with some of the servants who worked with the horses and in the fields. "It's a miracle, isn't it, Heather?"

Heather came over to stand beside him. They looked down as their son spoke to each man, clapped some of them on the shoulder, and then led them off. "It really is a miracle, isn't it?"

"Indeed," she said.

"All those prayers for all those long years. There were times, I must admit, I didn't know if God was listening or not."

"He brought our son back to us, but he's not the old Brandon. He's got a heart in him now, hasn't he? God is so real in his life."

"Yes. Quentin is ecstatic over the change. He's noticed that Brandon hasn't missed a Sunday in church and that he's filled with the spirit of God. We've got a lot to be thankful for, Wife."

"Yes. We have. This our son was lost and now is found. I think there's a scripture like that." Both of them stood giving thanks to God for the new son that God had sent them.

24

Queen Mary had always been a headstrong woman, but now she was almost fanatical, and the cause of it was clearly Philip. Philip of Spain had married Mary—most understood except Mary herself—in a marriage of convenience. Philip cared nothing for Mary. He was interested only in making England part of the Spanish empire. He had succeeded beyond his dreams. Mary had never admitted to herself that Philip did not love her. She was infatuated with the man. Now in the middle of 1558 she was ill, and Philip had gone back to Spain. Rumor had it that he had given up on producing an heir. But before he left, he persuaded Mary to declare war on France. The struggle that was going on between Spain and France at that time was equal, but Philip had convinced Mary that England's weight would give the advantage to Spain.

Sir John Fairfax had grown to dread his visits to the queen. Now as he entered the room, he found Mary seated in a chair. He was shocked to see how ill she was and even more startled to see that she was wearing armor. Her bosom and waist were covered with burnished steel. Sir John was at a loss for words. He thought, *This is madness. What can the woman be thinking?*

Mary's voice was deep as any man's. No matter how ill she became, always her voice was powerful and strong. "You're surprised at this armor, are you not?" She tapped the steel with her fingertip. "I do it to protect myself. There are assassins who would kill me, and I must take every precaution."

"Certainly, Your Majesty," Fairfax murmured. "I think that's very wise indeed, and I'm sure that you have increased the guard."

"Yes. I'm guarded at all times." Mary's face was the texture of old parchment, sallow and mottled. The shadows under her eyes were deep, her thin lips were drawn tightly together, and her eyes were dull. She fastened them now on him and said, "I have bad news for you, for all of us, John."

"What is that, my queen?"

"We have lost Calais."

"Yes, it is a great loss, Your Majesty."

"Yes. She's been our possession for many, many years, and always we have taken great pride in this. But she has fallen now to the French."

"I grieved to hear it, Your Majesty."

Mary whispered, "Heaven has deserted us." Then she fastened her eyes on John and whispered huskily, "When I die, when they open my body, they will find Calais written on my heart."

"We must withdraw our troops. It is a futile battle."

Mary nodded wearily. "So all of my counselors say, and it shall be done."

"Your Majesty, may I speak plainly?"

Mary's eyes suddenly grew wary. "As always, I'm willing to listen to you, John."

"I would like to persuade you to mitigate the executions of those who are not of the Catholic persuasion."

"I will never do that! God has put me on the throne of England to bring this nation back to the true faith, and I will do it as long as I live."

"But Your Majesty, some of those who are executed are very young. And some are old and infirm and really do not know their own mind."

Mary seemed not to hear his words. "I will bring this nation back to the true faith! Those who will not submit to the pope and to the Catholic religion must pay for their heresy."

John Fairfax argued for a time, but he saw how hopeless his argument was.

As soon as he could take his leave, he took a deep breath. *The woman has lost her power of thinking. She's besotted with Philip, who cares nothing about her. Why is it she can't see this?* Depression gripped him as he thought of those who were already in the Tower and would soon die and those who would soon be arrested, as many were every day.

❧

Eden walked among the roses, stopping from time to time to inhale the fragrance. She bent over and peered at a toad seated underneath a large plant. "Well, how are you today, Master Toad? Caught lots of flies, have you?" The toad croaked and hopped away. As she straightened up, she thought of how her life had changed. Ever since she had knelt with Brandon and called on God, her entire world had been different. She had heard her father say once, "A fellow bends over to pick up something, and when he straightens up, the whole world is different."

She had not understood at the time; now she did. "So it's been with me," Eden whispered. Her life in Spain had never been happy, and the bitterness she'd felt about Brandon had made her life miserable since coming to England. But now she was filled with peace and joy. She had told her parents about finding God but had told them little about Brandon. She knew that at some point she would have to tell them of their love, but she felt it was too soon.

Time had passed slowly, but she and Brandon had written to each other over the long months since they parted. He had said, "I long to come to you, dearest, but our time isn't yet. God is doing a work in my life, and in yours also, from what you say.

Let's rejoice in that and have faith that soon we'll be ready for the next step that God has for us." He had signed the letter, "With all my love," and for Eden that was enough. She knew in the depths of her soul that she and Brandon would find God's way and that they would share their lives.

Leaving the garden, Eden passed her father's study. The door was open; she knew he had a visitor. She stopped short when she heard the name Winslow mentioned. She drew closer and listened to the voices of the two men. "It's come to that at last, I'm afraid, Lord Fairfax."

"There's no question about it?"

"No, sir. Not any. The order has been given. Queen Mary has signed it, and Quentin Winslow is one of those who will be taken to the Tower."

"When will this happen?"

"Almost at once, sir. I know you fought for this man, but he is doomed, it seems."

Eden waited until the messenger left, then went at once to her father. "I overheard what Lord Humphrey had to say, Father."

"It's terrible news, Daughter. I've done all I can, but it has not been enough."

Eden made an instant decision and said, "Father, I must go to the Winslows. I can't do anything, but perhaps I can comfort them in some small way."

"Of course, Eden. We must do all we can. I'll have Jensen drive you in the carriage. But you'd better inform your mother."

Eden found her mother at once. She said, "Mother, I feel I must go to the Winslows for a time." She told her mother about the danger to Quentin, and her mother said at once, "I think you might be of some comfort. Of course you must go."

Eden packed a few things and within the hour she was in the carriage, headed for Stoneybrook. She wondered at herself taking such an action, but she knew Brandon and his family had to know about the dangers that awaited Quentin Winslow. And her heart pounded as she thought of seeing Brandon again at long last.

❧

A servant had told Brandon that a carriage was coming, and from his window he had seen it was Lord Fairfax's. When he reached her, she put out her hands, and he took them.

"Eden, my love. I cannot tell you how happy I am to see you again. But your face is plainly troubled. What is it?

"I'm afraid so. It's about your Uncle Quentin."

"What is it?"

"An order for his arrest has gone out. One of Father's friends told him about it."

"It's what we've most feared, Eden. Thank you so much for coming. Please come in."

He took her to a small parlor and ordered refreshments brought.

"Now tell me all about it." She repeated what she could remember of the conversation, and he shook his head. "It's come at last. I've been afraid of it for a long time."

"Isn't there something someone can do, Brandon?"

"I'm afraid it's out of human hands now. Only God can help."

"Do you think much about the time in Dover when we called on God?"

"Every day," he said instantly. He studied her and then asked, "Do you ever get impatient? About us, I mean."

"At times—but then I pray and God gives me peace. I trust him and you, Brandon."

He took her hands, kissed them, and said, "There'll be a time for us, Eden. You and I, together."

"Yes, God has promised us this, hasn't he?"

25

Quentin Winslow was arrested and charged with treason on October 13, 1558. He was taken to the Tower, where he joined others who were awaiting a judgment. Quentin made no protest, and the soldiers who took him were amazed at his calm demeanor.

He spoke to one of them on the way to the Tower, asking him if his heart was right with God, and the soldier answered roughly, "Mind your own business!" But after Quentin was delivered to the Tower, the soldier shook his head. "He's got enough problems, hasn't he, without worrying about my bloody soul."

The prison was a foul place. Even the three privies that served all the prisoners in the block in which Quentin was kept did not meet the need. By noon each day the close stools were overflowing with excrement, and the smell was as bad as a midden. It invaded everything and threatened to shrivel the very lungs.

Quentin spent his days in prayer and comforting the other prisoners. He had become a pastor of sorts to all his fellow prisoners. He was the first to greet newcomers with a comforting word and the last to speak a word of comfort to those taken out to be burned at the stake. His heart was pained by the cruelty of the punishment as men, women, and children, even the blind and the lame and the simple, were hauled past him. Some women were with child, and the child, of course, was burned with them.

"The sacrifice of innocence, Lord!" he cried out in prayer, weeping. "Only you could know such pain!" Some were seen to be moving after four hours in the flames. One of the guards who had a cruel streak recounted the details with great relish to those who would yet face the fire. His words reverberated in Quentin's mind. *Spare us, Father. Spare us!*

With the aid of Lord Fairfax, Eden and Brandon had managed to get permission to visit Quentin. The stone walls were cold and seemed to have soaked up the misery of years. Eden trembled as she thought of all who had suffered in this place. They were shown into a large room in which were some twenty male prisoners, and the stark agony in the faces of some of them wrenched Eden's heart.

"Look," Brandon said. "There's Quentin." They made their way across the cold stone floor, and Quentin, who had been sitting on the floor with his back against the wall, dozing, awoke when Brandon called his name. He came awake instantly and stood on his feet. His clothing was filthy, and his silver hair was unkempt. He was not as large a man as Brandon or as strong or as active, but there was peace in his eyes.

"Brandon," he said, "And you, Miss Fairfax, how good to see you both!"

The two men embraced. Then Eden stepped forward. Quentin said, "It's good to see you again, lady."

"It grieves me to find you in such a place."

Quentin shook his head. "Do not grieve. All will be well. You know, there's a verse in the Bible that says all things work together for good to all that love the Lord."

"How could this be good?" Eden exclaimed.

"I don't know that, lady. It's not for me to know the ways of God, but as he speaks, I obey."

"We tried to bring food, but they kept it down below. I hope it gets to you."

"I hope so. The food here is not good, and some are very sick and weak."

A guard came for them then, cutting their visit short, and Eden said as Quentin took her hand, "How can you bear it, Reverend Winslow? Aren't you afraid of death? What if the Lord doesn't choose to save you?"

Quentin's smile was gentle. "Then one moment I'll likely be in terrible pain, but the next I'll be in eternal bliss with him that I love with all my heart." He squeezed Brandon's and Eden's hands, and they could see the warm light of assurance in his eyes. "I can't tell you how greatly I rejoice that you have given your hearts to Jesus. When my brother brought me word that you had both been saved, I shouted for joy—and I could still shout!"

"You never gave up on me, Uncle," Brandon whispered.

Eden's eyes misted over, and the tears rolled down her cheeks. She turned away, unable to speak, while Brandon said his farewell to his uncle. As they left, Quentin called out, "Be of good cheer, Nephew, and you, lady, trust in the Lord, for his mercy endureth forever!"

When they were out in the open, Eden turned to Brandon. "I can't bear to think of it! He's such a good man!"

"He is—and I believe that God is going to deliver him."

"How can you believe when everything is so dark?"

"That's what faith is, Eden. It's believing God when all seems hopeless."

The two walked on, and when they reached the carriage, Brandon helped her in and then joined her. He did not pick up the reins however, but turned to her and said, "Eden, this is a terrible time, but I must tell you that I love you with all my heart and I always will."

Brandon's hands closed upon hers, he leaned forward and kissed her, and she gave herself to his caress. His arm went around her, and he held her tight. Eden knew that whatever terrible thing might happen, there was one true man who loved her with all his heart.

"I love you too, Brandon," she whispered.

"We'll love each other, and we'll see what God can do with all those he loves."

❧

The date for Quentin's execution was set for November 18. Time seemed to fly for Eden, for she had found a great love in her heart for Quentin Winslow. She thought often of how his words had led her to seek Jesus Christ and prayed for his release with a fierce intensity. She had opened her heart with her father and mother, telling them of her love for Brandon, and they had accepted him. They had always been grateful to him for returning Eden from her captivity and putting her back into their arms again, and now they both agreed that the young man's life was changed.

Eden stayed at home for a few days, but then she couldn't bear it. A restlessness troubled her, and she knew she had to be with the Winslow family. She asked her parents if she could spend some time with the Winslows, accompanied by Mrs. Taylor, and they readily gave their permission. She went to Stoneybrook that very day, only a day's journey, and both Heather and Stuart welcomed her as, of course, did Brandon. "I had to come," she told Heather. "I can't do anything, but I need to be with you."

"Why, you are family now, Eden," Heather said warmly. "I'm glad that you've come."

"Do you really believe that Quentin will live?"

"It looks so dark, and in the natural way of things it's impossible—but with God all things are possible."

"I know that, but sometimes I become so frightened. Terrible doubts come to me, and I can't believe with my whole heart."

"I think all God's people go through that, my dear. When you read the book of Psalms, you can see that David, a man after God's own heart, was often tormented with doubts and fears. He was God's favorite, but at times he had to walk through the dark valley of doubt. He even cried out many times, 'God, where are you? Have you forsaken me?'"

"It seems wrong. I feel that I'm doubting God."

"We have an enemy, the Devil, who can put thoughts into our minds. I found many years ago that some of my thoughts were not mine but thoughts put there by Satan."

"That frightens me, Heather," Eden said. "Is there any way I can avoid such thoughts?"

"Perhaps it's impossible to block such thoughts, but there is a way to avoid letting fears and doubts harm you." Heather took Eden's hand and her eyes were glowing. "When fear comes into your heart, speak to the Devil! Give him the Word of God. When this happens to me, I say, 'Satan, the Scripture says, "God has not given us the spirit of fear!" In the name of Jesus, leave me alone!'"

"I've never heard of such a thing!"

"It's what the Lord Jesus did, dear. When he was alone in the desert and Satan came to tempt him, Jesus simply quoted Scripture to him. When Satan urged him to turn stones into bread, Jesus said, 'It is written, man shall not live by bread alone, but by every word that proceedeth out of the mouth of God'. And the Devil had to flee.'"

"I don't know enough of the Bible to do that."

"You have a good memory, Eden, so we'll find some scriptures that teach us that God is to be trusted. You can memorize them, and when the Devil brings doubts and fears into your mind, you can rebuke him with the Word of God."

From that moment, Eden began memorizing scripture with Heather's help. She discovered two things. She had a gift for memorization, and she discovered to her great joy that when she grew fearful or troubled with doubt, speaking the promises of God aloud brought relief. More and more she gave herself to prayer and to the Word of God.

❧

On the morning of November 17, Princess Elizabeth was sitting on a bench under an old oak tree outside her country house at Hatfield, reading the Bible in Greek. It was cold, and more than once her ladies had tried to get her to come in, but she had ignored them all. A message had come the night before:

The queen's health is failing. She cannot last the night.

Elizabeth heard the sound of horsemen approaching. Trembling, she stood up. Four horsemen drew rein some twenty-five yards away. She recognized several of the members of the Privy Council. Sir Nicholas Throckmorton separated himself from the rest. Elizabeth waited. When Throckmorton knelt before her as did the others and held out his hand, she saw Mary's ring in his palm.

"Will you, Your Majesty, please to accept the throne and rule of England?" Throckmorton said loudly.

Elizabeth took the ring and knelt down in front of Throckmorton. "Now God be thanked!" she cried. "For this is the Lord's doing, and it is marvelous in our eyes!"

She rose to her feet and went to those who knelt as she came. One of those was John Fairfax. When she paused before him, he looked up and said, "Your Majesty, I beg you to show mercy on those who are awaiting death in the Tower."

"You speak of Quentin Winslow, do you not, John?"

"He is most on my heart, but the others deserve mercy too."

"And I will grant it," Elizabeth said. She said, "Go to him, John, and give the jailers your queen's command that Quentin Winslow is to be released at once into your keeping."

The Winslows had stayed up all night in a small room, praying for Quentin. Eden was sitting beside Brandon, holding his hand. She felt exhausted. It was a new experience for her to seek God in this fashion with all of her heart. She said to Brandon, "I am so tired, but my spirit isn't tired. It's only the flesh."

"I know. I am the same."

Heather had fallen asleep in Stuart's arms. He held her gently and tenderly, looking down into her face.

Eden glanced across the room, where Stuart and Heather sat on a couch. They were both asleep, but she noted that Stuart held her in a close embrace. "They love each other so much."

"They always have."

The two held onto each other, and finally, fifteen minutes later, they heard the sound of voices in the hall. Stuart and Heather woke and came to their feet. "Who can that be?" Stuart said.

Brandon cried with a loud voice, "Quentin!"

It was indeed Quentin! He was wearing the same filthy clothes he'd worn in prison, but his eyes were alight. He took in the four of them with one quick glance and cried with a loud voice, "Thanks be unto God for his delivering power!"

Stuart and Heather stumbled to him, and he caught them in his arms. They were joined by Brandon and Eden. Everyone was weeping for joy.

Finally Stuart managed to ask, "How did you get free, Brother?"

Quentin said, "The queen is dead. Long live Queen Elizabeth. She set me free." He took Eden's hand. "Your father asked the queen to have me released at once, and she granted his request."

They all then joined together. Quentin was hugged and kissed and squeezed and touched until finally Heather said, "We're going to smother him. Come and tell us how it all happened."

"It was a miracle," Quentin said, "but there are precedents. I am rejoicing over the others that are going to be released." For a moment sadness came to him, and he said quietly, "I grieve for Queen Mary and I trust that she has the peace now that she never had on this earth."

"Will all the prisoners be released?" Brandon asked.

"Yes. Queen Elizabeth has given her word that there will be no one punished for their faith."

Brandon said, "It's a marvel how God has used Providence to save you, Uncle Quentin. If Eden had not been captured, I wouldn't have rescued her and her father would not have known me and would never have begged the queen for your life."

"When she realized she was queen, Elizabeth said, 'This is the lord's doing; it is marvelous in our eyes.' That's the one hundred and eighteenth psalm," Quentin said, "and I believe it."

"So say we all," Stuart Winslow said. "Now God be thanked for his tender mercies."

26

England received its new ruler with great joy. Noisy crowds thronged the streets of London when Queen Elizabeth made her first appearance. Peal upon peal of church bells scored the air, and beacons blazed, sending the news of the accession from hilltop to hilltop all across the land. Servants were breaking out firkins and hogsheads of liquor, and cheering revelers were breaking the bright, clear air with shouts of praise. One song Elizabeth heard clearly:

When these poor souls were put to death
We prayed for our Elizabeth,
When all these souls were done to death,
God sent us our Elizabeth.

When Christmas came, there were the usual celebrations with a new feeling of joy. There were masques and mumming, with colors so bright that they were almost painful to the eye. Music was stirring throughout the land, and everyone seemed to be singing. That Christmas and the coronation of Queen Elizabeth would never be forgotten by those who experienced it.

On the day of her coronation, January 15, 1559, Elizabeth paraded to Westminster, then to the palace, then to the old abbey where her father and her father's father had been buried. Then past Saint Paul's, down Ludgate Hill. The roar of the crowd and caroling choirs and bells calling from every steeple and cannon thundering like the crack of doom all filled the air wherever she went.

Elizabeth was carried high for all the people to see. She wore a gown of gold and silver and was drawn in a golden coach under a rich canopy of gold—and sat on a rich nest of white satin. Almost a thousand horses followed in the parade. The people cried out her name for hours.

"Long life and joy! Joy to good Queen Elizabeth!"

And Elizabeth called back, "Bless you all. You may have rulers that will rule you more wisely, but you will never have a ruler who loves you more!"

"What would you like for a Christmas gift, Philemon? Now, have faith! Ask for something big. I'm in the mood for giving."

"Well, sir, since you asked," Philemon responded, "I'd like to have a new suit of clothes. Not a servant's suit, but one like you wear. Lots of gold lace on the doublet and gold thread everywhere. And a fur hat like the one you wear. And a fancy pair of shoes with pointed toes, real leather ones."

"You shall have them!" Brandon said heartily. "But why this sudden interest in fine clothing? You never cared about dress before."

"Ah, sir, but I'm going courting." Philemon nodded, his eyes gleaming. "Courting the Widow Maddox, don't you see? She'll make a fine wife for a deacon, sir. All broke in, so to speak."

"Broke in? What do you mean by that?"

"Why she's been wife, and her late husband, bless his soul, gave her good training. He was strict on that verse that says, 'Wives be obedient to your husbands.' And she took to the training fine, sir."

"How do you know that?" Brandon asked, amused at the turn his man's life was taking.

"Why, I investigated, Mr. Winslow."

"You engaged in some sort of intrigue to find out about her life?"

"Not on your life, sir! No, I listened to the gossip at church. Wonderful place to find out about people. Some of it is a bit malicious, but on the whole, if you sort it all out, you can get the real truth. Oh, she's a fine woman, sir, got a pot of money her husband left her, and she's fond of me."

"You shall have the suit, Philemon. And may God bless your union with the Widow Maddox."

"Thank you, sir. And may God prosper your own self with a good wife."

Winslow was well aware that Philemon was aware of almost every aspect of his private life. He gave him a suspicious look, but the bland features of Philemon revealed nothing. "You're a scoundrel, Philemon!"

"No doubt, sir!"

Eden had rejoiced in the accession of Elizabeth to the throne, but something had come into her life that disturbed her. She had spent the Christmas season partly with her own parents but the latter part with the Winslows. She and Brandon had walked together through the snow. They had ridden in a sleigh. They had laughed. They had feasted. They had exchanged gifts.

But Brandon had said not a word about marriage.

Eden had expected marriage to come at once, and she could not but feel that something was standing between her and the man she loved. She could not ask him, and she tried not to show it, but that was difficult. She loved all the Winslows and entered into the festivities, but on December 25, after almost everyone had gone to bed, when she was sitting in front of the fireplace in the lesser hall, she heard her name called and turned to see Brandon.

"All alone? Why, that won't do." He sat down beside her and put his arm around her. "It's been a wonderful time. A new queen and a good Christmas here with the woman I love."

He pulled her around, and Eden saw that his smile faded as he studied her. "My girl seems sad tonight."

"No, I'm not sad at all. It's been a wonderful Christmas."

"But something's not right. I can see it in your eyes, sweetheart, and in your lips. I can read you better than I can read a book. You're not happy. Something is missing. Tell me what it is."

"There's nothing missing," Eden protested. But her voice was unsteady, and she wondered why he was holding himself away from her.

"Well, I have a Christmas gift for you."

"You've already given me a gift, more than one, Brandon."

"But nothing like this one."

Eden saw that he was smiling then and felt his hand on her hair. She had always loved that. "You're going to like this gift, I hope."

"Well, what is it?" She tried to summon enthusiasm for what? A bracelet? Or a jewelled pin? But Brandon gave her a mischievous grin.

He pulled her to her feet and held her tightly in his arms. "Eden, I offer you this Christmas"—he knelt before her, holding her hands in his—"I offer you my undying love. I wish I had a better gift, but if you'll have me, you can make a better man of me. Please, will you do me the honor of marrying me?"

Eden felt a sudden rush of joy. He rose to kiss her. She felt secure, and she put her arms around his neck and held him close. "I accept your gift, Brandon Winslow." She put her head back, put her hands on his chest, and tried to push him away, but he held her tightly. "I accept your gift on two conditions."

"And what are they?"

"One, that you love me as much as your father loves your mother."

"That's asking a lot, woman! Those two love each other more than any human beings I've ever seen. All I can say is that I'll do my best to love you as Father loves Mother. Now, what's the other condition?"

"The other condition is that every day of our married life you will tell me that you love me."

"Even when I'm attracted to other women?" he teased.

Eden laughed. Joy was filling her. "I know how to keep you at home." She pulled his head down, kissed him again. "I won't let you stray far."

"That's right. You won't, and I never shall."

They stood lost in their love, and then Eden whispered, "We'll marry next week. The first day of 1559. Then you can never forget our anniversary."

"I will forget my own name before I forget that day."

The two stood there, and Brandon held her tightly. "I've got the whole world in my arms," he said.

"And you are my whole world, Brandon Winslow," Eden replied.

The next Gilbert Morris novel in
The Winslow Breed Series will be

The Winds of God

to be published in 2011.

We have included an excerpt from the
upcoming book for a sneak peek into
The Winds of God.

May 15, 1581

Dr. Regis Perry, physician, and head of the College of Physicians, the most powerful medical organization in England, resembled a butcher much more than he did a doctor. He was a thickset man with a square head set on a neck so short he did not seem to have one. His arms were bulging with muscle, and in farmer's clothing he could easily pass for one of that group. Perry had a bulldog face with a lantern jaw, and small eyes set rather close together. They were a muddy brown, but when he grew angry they glowed as with a subterranean heat. His eyes at the moment were able to hide that anger, for he was unable to release it because his visitor was powerful with influence and dangerous to antagonize.

William Farley, the Right Honorable Viscount Withington, was not a large man, at least when he stood next to Perry. He had a tall, slender frame, dark hair and penetrating gray eyes, and there was something imposing about his attitude. He was a man of great discernment, and he could tell in a glance that Dr. Perry was angry. He glanced over at the third man in the room, Dr. John Chadbourn, the head of Oxford University. Chadburn was a small man with mild, delicate features, and he was at all times anxious to avoid confrontation. He seemed caught between the upper and the nether millstone, for the two powerful men who flanked him were both dangerous and influential, and not men to antagonize.

"I think, Lord Withington, you will have to understand that disease is not at any doctor's beck and call." Perry's voice was harsh and had a gravel-like quality to it. He ran his thumb over his thick, choppy lips and attempted to make himself look as amiable as possible, for like Dr. Chadburn he understood that Lord Withington was not a man to be trifled with. "I understand your anxiety for your son, but you must learn to be patient, sir."

Lord Withington put his steady gaze upon Perry and said in a voice that was somehow ominous even though the tone was pleasant enough, "Dr. Perry, I have brought my son, Leslie, to you because he was ill. He has been here now for three weeks and he has grown progressively worse. I am not a doctor, sir, but I do know my son, and I fear for him. He is a sick young man."

"I am sure Dr. Perry is doing his best," Chadburn said quickly. "Disease is a deceitful thing. If you would just be patient—"

"I *have* been patient, Dr. Chadburn. The treatments have not been effective. I have met with your chief physicians more than once, and it is obvious that they have not the foggiest idea what is wrong with Leslie, therefore I intend to take a step I feel is important."

Alarm ran across Dr. Perry's blunt features. "What do you mean, my lord? We have the finest physicians in England."

"That may well be, but my son is not getting any better. I have a nephew, the only son of my brother, and he became very ill, and all the medical attention my brother got for him was useless. He grew worse and was at the point of death. At that time my brother took the boy to Dr. Phineas Teague. I believe you know the man."

Instantly Dr. Perry's face grew red. "I know him, my lord, but I could not recommend him."

"And why is that, Dr. Perry?"

"He has no respect for the forerunners and founders of the medical profession."

"That may well be, as I have said I am not an expert at this, but as soon as my nephew came under Dr. Teague's care along with his young associate, Mr. Colin Winslow, they almost at once brought him back to health." A smile touched Withington's face. "It was a miracle, sir, a notable miracle! I thank the Lord for it. I also thank the Lord that Dr. Teague and Mr. Winslow were used as his instrument for the healing process."

Instantly Perry snarled, "Winslow is not a physician, my lord!"

"I am not aware of the different categories you have set up. All I know is that my nephew was restored to health, while you have not been able to do the same for my son. Therefore, I am going to take Leslie to these two men."

"Colin Winslow is a worse rebel than his mentor, Dr. Teague! He could kill your son!"

"I am not interested in a piece of paper that speaks of a man's qualifications," Lord Withington said. His voice had a thread of steel running through it." I have talked to some of my friends who have had the same symptoms as my son, and several of them have gone to Dr. Teague and his associate. They all say Mr. Winslow, as young as he is, was successful at treating his patients."

"It is very dangerous, I must warn you! Your son could suffer dreadfully if you put him in the hands of these two men! They have no respect for the great physicians of history. Why, they both had the gall to say Galen, the greatest of all physicians in history, was wrong on many counts!"

"Who is Galen? Is he practicing now?"

"Why, no, sir, he is not. He has been dead for many years. But his treatments are used by every reputable physician in the world."

Lord Withington said disdainfully, "Yes, the physicians that treated my nephew followed this authority, and the poor boy nearly died. It was only after Dr. Teague and Mr. Winslow treated him that he lived. My mind is made up. I thank you for your help and I will pay your fees, but I intend to see that my son sees Dr. Teague and his associate."

As soon as the door closed behind Lord Withington, Regis Perry unloosed a string of oaths such as John Chadburn had never heard. He waited until Perry had run down, then said, "If I were you, Dr. Perry, I would not take on Lord Withington as an enemy. He is a powerful man, so you should tread very carefully."

Perry's face grew as red as a furnace, but he clapped his meaty lips together, for he well knew that Chadburn was right. He filed the incident in his mind and made a vow that moment that he would do whatever was needed to bring about the downfall of Dr. Phineas Teague and his associate Colin Winslow no matter what the cost!

"Not a bad old pile of bricks is it, Colin?"

Colin had arrived with Teague at Withington, the home of Lord Withington. They had been driving for what seemed like hours through lands that belonged to Withington, and now the driver halted the carriage in front of the imposing structure.

"It is more than a pile of bricks isn't it, Dr. Teague?"

Indeed Withington was most impressive. Colin stared at it, fascinated by the size. He studied the immense front lawn, which was decorated with fountains, as well as hedges carved into fantastic states. Great gargoyles crowned the structure, which was composed of white towers that seemed to rise to the sky. "It's a huge place, Doctor."

"I never look at these places without thinking that they are nothing more than monuments to man's pride. Who would want a house with fifty bedrooms? Come, boy, let's see what Lord Withington wants. I pray we can give it to him! He is a good man to have on one's side."

Colin leaped to the ground and waited as his companion came down slowly. They stood in a huge courtyard, a place of perfect symmetry, with delicate carvings everywhere. It seemed the stone leaves in the stone trees came to life.

"Shut your mouth, boy, before you swallow a bug," Phineas

Teague grunted. "It's just a house, bigger than most, but when Lord Withington, dies, he will leave it here, just as a peasant will leave his thatched roof behind. Come along now."

The two moved forward and climbed the steps, and as they reached the top, a massive door swung open. A tall servant in livery stood before them, saying, "May I help you, sirs?"

"I am Dr. Teague and this is Mr. Winslow. Lord Withington has asked us to call."

"Of course, sir. He mentioned that you would be coming. Would you step inside please?'

The two went inside and were led down a wide hallway and then entered a massive room with a high ceiling and large windows, which allowed the summer sunbeams to illuminate the place. Carpets were everywhere, so thick they seemed to reach to Colin's ankles, and beautiful paintings adorned the walls.

Rich velvet curtains were pulled back from the windows, revealing beautiful, exquisitely carved furniture. Colin was still looking around when a man entered from the right. Colin turned to face him and saw that Lord Withington was a tall, somewhat imposing man. There was an aura of power about him, an attitude of an expectation of total obedience that Colin had noticed in other men of influence.

"Dr. Teague, I believe."

"Yes, and this is my associate, Mr. Colin Winslow."

"You gentlemen are welcome to my home. I am glad you could come so quickly."

"We came as soon as we got your message. I assumed it was important. Do you have a problem we can help you with?"

"Indeed I do. Gentlemen, would you sit down?" Lord Withington turned to the servant, saying, "Wilkins, bring the gentlemen something to drink." He added, "We can have a meal later, but I can have something brought now if you like."

"Not at all, my lord. We are anxious to be of what help we can." Teague answered.

"Good." Withington waited until the two were seated and the servant had left before he said, "I have one son, gentlemen.

Leslie is nineteen years old, and he has been ill for more than a month. I fear he's growing steadily worse."

"What has been done, my lord?"

"I have had him examined by five physicians, but none of them seem to be able to help him." Worry lines appeared between Withington's eyes, and he seemed less assured. "No physician has been able to find what is the cause or the cure for my boy. I have a brother, Sir Winfred Farley. I believe you know him, Dr. Teague."

"I do indeed, sir. I attended his son in his sickness."

"That is what my brother tells me. He spoke so highly of you and Mr. Winslow that I sent for you at once. I fear I have wasted time with other physicians. They talk a great deal, saying things that no man could understand unless they have studied medicine for a lifetime!" Withington said with frustration.

"I fear my profession hides behind difficult sentences and obscurities in language," Dr. Teague agreed. "I assure you I will tell you nothing but the simplest truth."

"That is what I have been told by my brother."

"What are your son's symptoms, my lord?"

The three men talked about the young man's symptoms and finally Lord Withington said, "I am anxious for you to see my boy. It seems almost hopeless. Day by day he loses strength and weight. My wife and I are terribly afraid."

"That is natural, sir," Teague said gently. He could be a harsh man at times, but toward those who were suffering from illness or had a family member in danger he could be a totally different man. He voice became softer as he said, "I think it might be best that we see the young man before we make any decisions."

"Would you like for me to write down what I have told you, Dr. Teague?"

"Oh, no. My assistant here has a memory that is phenomenal. He can remember anything and quote you back word for word everything that you have said."

Lord Withington set his gaze on Colin, who felt the power of it. "That is a very fine and unique gift for a physician."

"I trust that we will be able to help your son," Colin said

quickly. He felt an instant liking for the man. He had known other powerful men of influence who were arrogant, but he saw little of that in this man. "We will do the very best we can, sir," he added quietly.

"Leslie is probably asleep at the moment, but I would like for you to meet the rest of my family."

Lord Withington spoke to the servant, saying, "Ask my wife and daughter to come in, Wilkins."

Colin was studying the face of Sir Withington and he saw there pain, fear, and helplessness. His thought was that no matter how powerful a man is, when death faces him he is the same as the poorest peasant in England. He and Teague rose as two women entered the room.

"This is my wife, Lady Withington, and this is my daughter, Lady Benton. This is Dr. Teague and his associate, Mr. Winslow."

Lady Withington was in her early forties. She was an attractive woman with a wealth of brown hair and warm brown eyes. At the moment you could see the fear, but Colin saw an attractive, gentle spirit. "I welcome you, gentlemen, and I hope you will be able to help my son."

Lady Benton was a young woman who Colin saw was no more than twenty-five. There was much of her father in her, and little of her mother. She stepped forward and extended her hand. Dr. Teague took it at once, bending over it with a polite kiss.

"I am so happy you are here, Dr. Teague. We are very worried about Leslie."

Colin did not expect her to speak to him since he was a mere assistant, but Lady Benton came at once and extended her hand. Colin followed Dr. Teague's example. He bent over it awkwardly and touched the back of her hand with his lips. When he straightened up he saw that she was watching him in a strange manner. There was something different about this woman. Her eyes were dark, and her skin was flawless. There was an exotic richness in her lips that most women did not have. Her figure was clearly discernible in the orchid-colored dress she wore. "We welcome both of you, and I pray you will be able to help my poor brother."

At that moment refreshments were brought in, and they all sat down while a serving maid passed small drinks and sandwiches around. "I thought you would be hungry after your long journey," Lady Withington said

Colin did not join in the talk, but he listened avidly. Lord Withington said, "I must warn you, I have had a difference of opinion with men that may give you some problems."

"I am used to that." Teague smiled. "No doubt it was with Dr. Perry."

"Yes, you were expecting it then?"

"We have crossed swords before. Our methods differ completely."

"Well, I am glad to hear that, because their methods were absolutely no help! But I would not want to run you into danger in your professional life."

"We are healers," Teague said. He took a bite of a cucumber sandwich, and chewing around it he said, "We will do what we must for our patients, and the College must do as it pleases."

Lady Withington's voice was laced with fear. "I beg you, sir, save my son. You were able to save our nephew Simon, and I pray that you will have that same success with Leslie."

"Mother, I am sure these gentlemen will do everything in their power," Lady Benton said. Colin saw her eyes fixed on him rather than Teague, which disturbed him. After all, Teague was the physician while he was merely an assistant. Her gaze had something in it that made him uncomfortable.

Finally Lord Withington said, "Wilkins tells me that my son is still sleeping, and you must be tired. Wilkins, show these gentlemen to their rooms."

Lady Benton smiled. "Before you take a rest, Mr. Winslow, I would like to hear more of your treatment of my cousin Simon."

The invitation was more of a command, and after the others had left the room, Colin stood before Lady Benton awkwardly.

He'd had little experience with women, and this was the most beautiful woman he had ever seen. He knew that she was married to a nobleman, for she was "Lady" Benton. "Come, it's so beautiful outside. I love this time of the year. Let me show you my roses."

"Certainly, Lady Benton."

Colin followed her outside through an intricate isle of hedges until they came to a beautiful rose garden. He stopped and exclaimed, "Look at the colors! I've never seen such colors in flowers."

"My mother is a great lover of flowers, much more than I. I just enjoy them, but she loves them. Shall we sit?"

Colin waited until Lady Benton seated herself on the stone bench, then he seated himself beside her. It was a small bench, barely wide enough for the two of them. Colin was intensely aware of the pressure of her arm against his. She turned to face him and a smile crept across her lips. "I am surprised to see you are so young. No one told me this."

"Yes, my lady. I am nineteen."

"And yet Dr. Teague places such trust in you. I can see it in the way he spoke of you."

"I have been very fortunate, my lady, to study under Dr. Teague."

"Tell me about yourself."

"Myself? Why, there is not much to tell."

"Oh come now! A handsome young physician such as yourself must have a great deal to say."

Colin was awkwardly speechless for a moment, for there was a lingering smile on Lady Benton's lips, which was reflected in her eyes. At her insistence he told her a little of his life. When he was finished he noticed she was watching him in a peculiar way.

"Most of the doctors I've know have been older men. That's why I was surprised to meet a young handsome doctor such as yourself."

"My lady, I am not a physician."

Lady Benton only smiled. There was a sensuous turn to her mouth that fascinated Colin, and at the same time made him very nervous.

"Mr. Winslow, the physician has such an intimate relationship with his patients. I suppose you grow accustomed to such intimacy with your female patients." She laughed because she saw Colin's face redden. "Well, I did not think there was a man in England with a blush left in him! I like you for it, sir! I would guess that some of your female patients must have shown you signs of their favor."

Colin could not think of a single word to reply. He felt like an idiot sitting there. She saw his awkwardness. Suddenly she reached over and covered his hand with hers. "I like you, Mr. Winslow! It's refreshing to find a truly innocent man in our country. You must tell me more about yourself—I am truly fascinated."

Colin stuttered a little, then asked a question that had been on his mind. "Is your husband here, my lady?"

"Oh, no. I lost my husband more than a year ago. He was Aaron Caldwell, the Right Honorable Viscount Benton. He died in a riding accident."

'"I'm very sorry for your loss, my lady."

"Thank you, Mr. Winslow. It was a hard loss, but time does heal all wounds. One must go on with life." She smiled and said, "Now, tell me of some of your victories in your practice."

❧

When Colin entered his room he found Dr. Teague standing there waiting for him. "Do I have the wrong room, Dr. Teague?"

"No, this is your room. I wanted to get a report of your meeting with Lady Benton."

"Why, she merely wanted to know of the treatment for her brother."

Teague had piercing eyes, which he now fixed on Colin. He had a face like a bird, with a beak of a nose. Right now those eyes seemed to pin Colin on a board, as he himself had pinned butterflies and other insects.

"That is the first lie you have ever told me, Colin Winslow. I am sorry to see such dishonesty in you."

Colin dropped his head. "I—I don't know what else to say, Doctor."

"Well *I* do." Teague said abruptly. "I am not a man of God, but I remember a sermon I heard when I was younger. It stayed in my mind for some reason all these years. It is very simple. I don't know where it is in the English Bible, but it says, 'Let him that thinketh he standeth take heed lest he fall.'"

Colin straightened and moved his head slightly from side to side. "Yes, Dr. Teague, that's in the book of First Corinthians. But, sir, a woman like that would not be looking with favor at a poor physician, if that is what you are afraid of. She wouldn't be interested in any man without a title."

Teague laughed rather harshly. "So you think that all women are interested only in titles? You are wrong—dead wrong! Some of them are interested in what a man brings to the bed with him."

Colin was accustomed to Teague's rough speech, but this still shocked him. "You can't possibly mean she has any immoral interest in me?"

"You are the brightest boy I have ever seen—and the densest in some ways! You know all the cures that go back two hundred years, but you can't see when a woman has interest in you." He shook his head and said with something like disgust. "Listen to this, my boy—money, power, and women. These are the snares that destroy a man."

"Well, they will not destroy me, sir!"

Teague threw up his hands. "You did not hear a word I said!" he said with disgust. "'Let him that thinketh he standeth take heed lest he fall.' Just watch out for that woman. I've seen her kind before."

"Yes, sir," Colin replied neatly. After Teague left he shook his head. *Teague is not often wrong, but he has to be wrong about this.*

He looked about the room and studied the expensive furniture, the hangings on the walls, but his mind kept going back to when Lady Benton put her hands around his. He had seen something in her eyes that somehow drew him. He shrugged his shoulders in a motion of impatience and muttered, "Teague is wrong, he has to be!"

"I would like to see the record of what the physicians have done for your son, Lord Withington," Teague said.

"Of course. I insisted that they write them all down." He moved over across the room, opened the desk drawer, and pulled out a stack of papers. "Here it is, Dr. Teague."

Teague took the papers and Colin stood close beside him. The two men studied through the documents. Instead of replying to Teague, Lord Withington asked abruptly, "What do you think, Mr. Winslow?"

Colin was surprised, for he had expected that Dr. Teague would deal with the man. He said briefly, "I think you can guess my thoughts, my lord."

"Just tell me, what do you see, Mr. Winslow?" Lord Withington demanded.

"I am sorry, my lord, but what I see here is not the kind of medicine that Dr. Teague has taught me to practice."

"What do you mean?"

"Look at this, they bled the young man four times and one time only two days apart."

Lord Withington stared at Colin. "Isn't that common practice?"

"It is common practice and the old authorities all agree with it, but I see no value in it."

"Dr. Perry told me it was to bleed out the bad blood."

Colin could not help smiling. He did not know it, but he looked very young standing before the nobleman. "Bad blood, sir? No one has ever proved that there is such thing as bad blood. And if it did exist, how would anyone know that the blood bled out or taken by leeches was the bad blood and not good blood?"

Lord Withington stared at the two men, then his eyes fixed on Teague. "Do you agree with this?"

"I do, sir."

"And look at this, my lord," Colin said. "Purging! I have never *seen* such purging!"

"But I understood that was common also."

"It is common because physicians know of nothing else to do. Galen the old master said that bleeding and purging is good for men, so we do it, even if we do not understand why we do it."

"You amaze me, Mr. Winslow." Lord Withington laughed shortly and shot a direct glance at Colin. "Dr. Perry said you were a rebel."

"I think that is exactly what he is," Teague agreed slyly. "But you go to any physician and ask why purging is good and why bleeding is good for any disease, and they will give you long words and convoluted sentences. Which means in translation 'I do not know.'"

"And I am looking at the medications the physicians gave your son. Listen to this—horn of unicorn. There is no such animal as a unicorn, at least not known to man. What could they possible give him? Perhaps the horn of a billy goat?" Colin began to grow angry. "Here it says the grease of a heron and the fat of a vulture." His tone grew louder as anger filled his face. "And listen to this. They gave your son, so they say, a bezoar stone."

"What in the world is that? I asked but I could not understand the answer," Lord Withington said.

"It is supposedly the stone taken from the intestines of a Persian wild goat. And look, rooster testicles, crayfish eyes! On and on they tried all these remedies, not knowing what they were."

"I see you are angry, Mr. Winslow."

"I am a little, my lord."

"Well, what would your treatment be, sir?"

"That is for Dr. Teague to say."

"We would both say the same, my lord," Teague said flatly. "In the first place, no more bleeding and no more purging. Second, there will be no more of these harsh medicines that were poured down your poor son's throat. The thing I would prescribe, and I think my young colleague would agree, is a good diet, very mild at first, rest, and some very mild medication. That which has been tried and we know is effective. No more bezoar stones, whatever the blasted things may be!"

"Very well, gentlemen, we shall try. It shall be as you say."

❧

Leslie Farley prospered almost immediately with the treatment that two men set forth. He slept long hours, and without all the terrible purging and bleeding he gained strength. The diet was very mild at first, but then increased in richness. He grew stronger and the color returned to his cheeks. He was able to get out of bed after three days, and within a week he was well on his way to health. Satisfied, Teague said, "I must get back to my practice, I am afraid."

Lady Benton said, "I would be afraid for you to leave, Dr. Teague—unless you could leave your colleague here with us. I still fear for my brother."

Teague's eyebrows rose, and he said in a spare tone, "If you insist, Lady Benton."

Lady Benton did insist, and as Teague was leaving the last thing he said as he got into his carriage was "Be careful, boy!" He leaned out the window and grabbed Colin by the shoulder, pulled him close, and said fiercely, "That woman is a man-eater!"

"I think you are mistaken, Dr. Teague. The only time I have ever thought so."

Teague shook his head and released Colin, and said, "God keep you, boy, even though I don't believe in God. If there is a God, I pray he will keep you from the clutches of that woman. I repeat, she is a man-eater."

The driver spoke to the team of horses, and the coach left. Colin thought, *He is wrong about this. Dr. Teague is a wise man, but he knows nothing of women. He has never been married or even had a sweetheart as far as I know. He is mistaken about Lady Benton. He must be!*

WHEN *the* HEAVENS FALL

GILBERT MORRIS

Reading Group Guide

ABOUT THIS GUIDE

The following reading group guide is intended to help you find interesting and rewarding approaches to your reading of *When the Heavens Fall*. We hope this enhances your enjoyment and appreciation of the book.

INTRODUCTION

Set in Tudor-age England, *When the Heavens Fall* tells the epic tale of Brandon Winslow, a devious and troubled young man struggling to find his way and place in the world.

At the same time that Mary takes the throne as queen of England, the mischievous young Brandon Winslow decides to become a soldier, much to the dismay of his spiritually sound and noble parents, Stuart and Heather Winslow. It does not take long after enlisting for Brandon's womanizing, gambling, and drinking to get him into serious trouble.

Thought to be dead by his parents and the soldiers who knew him best, Brandon finds himself wandering futilely, struggling to survive among vagrants. He befriends a pair of Spanish gypsies and makes a small fortune moving between towns playing cards with rich gentlemen. Brandon soon hears of Queen Mary's zealous and bloody behavior in her determination to return England to Catholicism.

When rumor spreads that Mary is beginning to execute protestants on the basis of their religion, Brandon knows his family is in trouble. He is faced with a serious decision—to return home to protect his uncle, the protestant preacher Quentin Winslow, or simply to vanish into the vagabond life he has become accustomed to.

DISCUSSION QUESTIONS

1. The opening scene of the novel gives an example of Brandon Winslow's troublemaking ways. How do his parents manage the situation with James Elwald and his daughter Becky? Do you think Brandon is immoral or just naïve?
2. Describe the relationship between Stuart and Heather Winslow. Do you feel their relationship deserves the attention it receives toward the end of the book?
3. What does Heather mean when she repeats to Brandon, "I gave you to God the day you were born"?
4. Discuss the power of prayer in relation to each character. Consider the way the act of prayer brings clarity to those who need it in times of great challenge.
5. What role do Lupa and Rez play in the novel? Do you see them as moral or immoral characters? Does your opinion of them change as you learn more about them?
6. What does Brandon feel when he witnesses the burnings at Smithville? What does he learn from the experience? How did you feel as you read the descriptions, particularly of the smiling elderly woman?

7. Compare and contrast Catholicism and the "New Religion" (Protestantism) as portrayed by Morris in the novel.

8. Discuss the differences between Queen Mary and Queen Elizabeth. With whom do they surround themselves? What are their strengths and weaknesses? How do these characteristics influence the way people perceive them?

9. Why does Quentin refuse to leave the country?

10. What is the dilemma Brandon faces when Lord Fairfax approaches him? Do you think he made the correct decision in his situation? What would you have done?

11. Brandon refers to the Song of Solomon when he is courting Dolores/Eden. What does he feel is the importance of this book? What does Dolores/Eden derive from his description?

12. Is the approach Brandon takes in convincing Eden to return to England a permissible or forgivable strategy?

13. Starting on page 94, Quentin delivers a sermon to his congregation. What does he discuss? How does this relate to the characters in the novel?

14. What advice does Quentin give to Eden Fairfax when she comes to his service? How does she make use of this advice?

15. What changes in Brandon when he accepts Jesus? How does he struggle with this decision, and what ends up influencing him above all?

ENHANCING YOUR BOOK CLUB

1. Make a family tree of the Tudor dynasty in England. Compare and contrast the differences in ruling style and religion among the Tudors.
2. Critically evaluate the Song of Solomon, just as Brandon Winslow does when he is in Spain. If this is your first reading, what stands out for you? If you have read it before, do you find anything new or different?
3. Brandon indulges in many regional meals throughout *When the Heavens Fall.* Make a traditional British recipe—consult http://www.britainexpress.com/articles/Food/ for recipes and ideas!